Georgia Stories On My Mind

Jackie Rod

Touch Not the Cat Books
Haughton, Louisiana

First Edition, June 2018

Cover: Gina Dyer
Interior Design: Sarah Hamer
Introduction: Jackie Rod
Editors: Sarah Hamer and Mary Marvella

Table of Contents

Acknowledgments

Not all of us can do great things. But we can do small things with great love.

~ Mother Teresa

This is my wish for you, my readers. I hope you do everything with great love. You are the reason for these *Georgia Stories On My Mind*.

Loving others is easy when you have a loving heart. My world is filled with loving people, family and friends. I am blessed.

Human beings have been telling tales for thousands of years. We need to hear stories and we need to tell stories. Something magical happens when we tell each other true stories. When we share our lives we form warm relationships.

I believe something unique happens when writers release stories they have worked on for a long time. They do more than share their thoughts; they give part of themselves to the world.

There are so many who have encouraged me to go forward with this project. I want to thank Sarah Hamer, Mary Marvella, and Barbara Barth for pushing me and helping me polish my stories. My critique groups, The Fabulous Five, Rod's Rangers, and The Wordsmiths, have offered me excellent suggestions over the years. Dear helpers: Alesia, Brian, Cindy, Colleen, Martha, Melba, Nancy, and Patricia always made time to read my work. Thanks to every person who inspired me along the way.

Friends at the Atlanta Writers Club, Georgia Romance Writers, East Metro Atlanta Christian Writers, NOLA STARs, and Walton Writers have inspired me by their talent and encouraged me with their friendship.

I salute the teachers and youth with whom I worked.

Colleagues and students at Lakeside High, Oglethorpe University, Open Campus, and Georgia Perimeter College made my thirty-one years of teaching a walk in the park.

My friends at Covington First Methodist Church had faith in me—especially my fellow Singing Saints Choir. Thanks for reading my work.

Thanks to my family which has been super supportive from day one. My three children, Norman, Cindy, and David believed in me. Rocky, my son-in-law and fourth child, has cheered me on. My grandchildren: Connie, Kristin, Molly, Hannah, Melody, John, and Lucas are successful young adults and enthusiastic readers. My brother and his wife, Bill and Mary, are fans.

My prince and primary cheerleader, Leslie John, is a jewel for putting up with stacks of books all over the house. He is an organized neatnik, but he never complains about my shortcomings. When I get up at five o'clock in the morning and walk across the hall to my office, he patiently rolls over and exhales. He generously sponsors me as I attend writing conferences and workshops all over the country. He is an avid reader of great literature but still takes time to read my work. How cool is that? Best of all, he loves me. I am truly blessed.

Thanks to my readers who read and dream. I hope you enjoy this book, because you are the reason for these *Georgia Stories On My Mind*.

Introduction to Georgia

GEORGIA IS LOCATED in the southeastern United States. It does not have the Statue of Liberty or any famous steel arches, but the state has a varied terrain which covers mountains in the northwest, farmlands in the middle, coastal islands on the east and swamps in the South near the Florida border. You have to love a big state that has mountains, farmland, swamps and beaches. It is the largest state east of the Mississippi River.

Georgia is known as the Peach State. Franciscan monks introduced peaches to the coastal islands in the 16th century. Also, the state is the country's largest producer of pecans, peanuts, and Vidalia onions. The nuts in Georgia are the best. Believe me, I know a few.

Founded by James Edward Oglethorpe, Georgia began as a British penal colony in 1733. The province, named for King George II, stretched from South Carolina to Spanish Florida and west to Louisiana (New France).

The climate of Georgia has short mild winters and long hot summers. It has four seasons offering beautiful colors year round. The spring and fall are spectacular.

Georgia has bragging rights for many "first" events. It was the first colony to grant college degrees to women. Born a slave, Eliza Ann Grier became the first African-American woman to be granted a license to practice medicine in Georgia. Wesleyan College became the first institution in the world to award degrees to women. Georgia became the first colony to give women the right to own property. John Wesley founded the first Protestant Sunday school. Georgia was the first colony to cultivate grapes and one of the first states to prohibit alcohol. The cotton gin was invented near Savannah and soon enabled the South to produce two-thirds of the world's cotton. The first discovery of gold in the United States occurred in Dahlonega, Georgia.

My personal favorite first: Georgia was the first state to reduce the legal age to vote from 21 to 18.

Cities of interest:

Atlanta, the capital of Georgia, has been labeled *The Gateway to the South*. About six million people live in the metro area. It is the seventh most visited city in the United States. The Martin Luther King Center, the Carter Center & Presidential Library, and the High Museum of Art are located here.

The city is known for special events: Dragon Con, the Atlanta Dogwood Festival, Atlanta Film Festival and the Peachtree Road Race.

Atlanta is the home of Coca Cola, Home Depot, AT&T, Chick-fil-A, and UPS. The Varsity is the largest drive-in restaurant in the world.

Hartsfield-Jackson Airport is the busiest airport in the world, handling one hundred million passengers a year.

Atlanta is considered a center for higher education with thirty colleges and universities located here. It is the city where I grew up and went to school and college. It is the city where my children grew up and went to school and college.

Columbus is the second largest city in Georgia. Named one of the one hundred best communities in the U.S., the city prides itself on its quality of life with a diverse arts district and national military museums.

Augusta is the home of the Masters Golf Tournament. Membership at Augusta National is considered the most exclusive in the world. It hosts the first tournament each year. Augusta was the childhood home of President Woodrow Wilson.

Macon is located in the middle of the state. Wesleyan college, founded in 1836, was the first college in the U.S. to have sororities and the first in the world to award degrees to women. Macon's Music Hall of Fame boasts the names of hometown boys including Little Richard, Otis Redding, and the Allman Brothers.

Savannah is Georgia's largest port. It was the original capital of Georgia and known for its historic charm. It hosts the second largest St. Patrick's Day parade in the nation, and is home of the Girl Scouts of America.

Athens is home to the University of Georgia. *Rolling Stone* labeled it the No.1 College Music Scene in America. Athens native son Henry Grady, great journalist and orator, envisioned a "New South" after the Civil War.

Georgia's Coastal Islands:

Cumberland Island—known for wild horses and nature

Jekyll Island—Sea Turtle Center and home of Rockefeller-type millionaires

Sea Island—Presidents Coolidge to Clinton lived and played here

St. Simons Island—known for Epworth by the Sea—100-acre Conference Center, and the African Gullah-Geechee language, people and culture

Tybee Island—Historic lighthouse (1736) off the coast of Savannah and Ft. Pulaski of the Civil War Era

Famous Georgians:

Sports:

Ty Cobb—Narrows, GA

Jackie Robinson—Cairo, GA

Rosie Grier—Cuthbert, GA

Hulk Hogan—Augusta, GA

Georgia has produced many well-known athletes. My favorite is Jackie Robinson, who broke the color barrier for future baseball players.

Art:

Jim Harrison—painter—Leslie, GA

Jasper Johns, painter, sculptor, printmaker—Augusta, GA

Leila Ross Wilburn—architect—Macon, GA

Nellie Mae Row—Fayette, GA. Her work is found in Folk Art Museums in New York, Atlanta, Milwaukee, Santa Fe, and at the Smithsonian in Washington, D.C.

One of my favorite artists, Jim Harrison, started painting Coca Cola signs on the side of barns and country stores. Today he paints scenes from Georgia in the old days—days that are gone or fading fast.

Medicine:

Doc Holliday—Griffin, GA

Eliza Ann Grier—born a slave, first African-American woman to practice medicine in Georgia

Crawford W. Long—Danielsville, GA Crawford Long's use of ether as a general anesthetic moved medicine into the modern era.

Entertainment:

Julia Roberts—Smyrna, GA

Joanne Woodward—Thomasville, GA

Jeff Foxworthy—Atlanta, GA

Spike Lee—Atlanta, GA

Among the entertainers I've selected Joanne Woodward, because her parents lived in the Atlanta school district where I taught for thirty-one years. She and Paul Newman came to visit several times a year.

Music:

Ray Charles—Albany, GA

Gladys Knight—Oglethorpe, GA "The Empress of Soul"

Johnny Mercer—Savannah, GA

Otis Redding—Dawson, GA

Travis Tritt—Marietta, GA

Like most people, I love music, so it is difficult to decide on just one favorite. I will go with Ray Charles, because he put Georgia on the map.

Poetry:

David Bottoms—Canton, GA

Sidney Lanier—Macon, GA

My favorite Georgia poet is Sidney Lanier, a true Renaissance man. He graduated from Oglethorpe College, the same university where I graduated many years later.

Writing:

Pat Conroy—Atlanta, GA

Lewis Grizzard—Fort Benning, GA

Terry Kay—Royston, GA

Alice Walker—Eatonton, GA

Carson McCullers—Columbus, GA

Writing is the hardest category to judge, because there are so many great Georgia authors. To me, the most poignant first sentence in a book is from Carson McCullers's *The Heart Is a Lonely Hunter*.

Government:

Jimmy Carter—Plains, GA President of the United States

Clarence Thomas—Pin Point, GA Justice on the U.S. Supreme Court

Richard B Russell—Winder, GA “A senator’s senator”

The names of these three statesmen speak for themselves. Their devotion to their country is well known. Who can pick a favorite among such statesmen?

TEACHING PROVIDED ME with a passion for thirty-one years. I would not have chosen any other career for twice the money. My students brought me joy each day, and I learned more from them than they did from me. One of the greatest things I learned was to appreciate my own children.

Rules for teaching have changed over the years. I thought readers would enjoy taking a look at the teaching life back in the day—145 years ago.

1872 Rules for Teachers

Teachers each day will fill lamps, clean chimneys.

Each teacher will bring a bucket of water and a scuttle of coal for the day's session.

Make your pens carefully. You may whittle nibs to the individual taste of the pupils.

Men teachers may take one evening each week for courting purposes, or two evenings a week, if they go to church regularly.

After ten hours in school, the teachers may spend the remaining time reading the Bible or other good books.

Women teachers who marry or engage in unseemly conduct will be dismissed.

Every teacher should lay aside from each pay a goodly sum of his earnings for his benefit during his declining years, so that he will not become a burden on society.

Any teacher who smokes, uses liquor in any form, frequents pool or public halls, or gets shaved in a barber shop will give good reason to suspect his worth, intention, integrity and honesty.

The teacher who performs his labor faithfully, and without fault for five years, will be given an increase of twenty-five cents per week in his pay, providing the Board of Education approves.

You may ride in a buggy with a man, if the man is your father or your brother.

The Historical News—State of Georgia January, 2018

Dedication

This book is dedicated to my family, friends, and all readers who enjoy heartwarming stories.

I am grateful to my husband, Leslie John Rodriguez, for encouraging me to follow this dream.

Thanks to the dear people in my life for your spoken or written words that have flooded my world with an ocean of loving support. My wish is that during these moments of unguarded sharing we forge a bond—heart to heart.

Abandoned

In life there is hope. Hope sees the invisible, feels the intangible, and achieves the impossible.

~ Helen Keller

WORKAHOLIC MISTY DUPREE loved, loved, loved sleeping in on Saturday mornings. She worked late every night so she could treat herself on the weekends. By Friday night she was beyond weary.

The ringing cell phone startled her. She'd forgotten to mute it. "Sh—!" She groaned in disgust. Though tempted to roll over and ignore it, her conscience won. She reached for the offending device. "Hello."

"Good morning, Miss Dupree. This is Gladys Bloom from Rest Haven."

Her heart jumped. Nursing homes only call for two reasons—a problem or a death. "Yes?"

"I'm afraid we have bad news. Your grandmother passed away this morning."

Her breath stalled. Her lungs couldn't get enough air. A long silence followed. Finally she screamed, "No... no... no!"

"You okay, Miss Dupree?"

"I... I don't understand. Grandma seemed fine last weekend." Unable to lie still, Misty threw off the covers and stood. She paced up and down the room in her silk nightgown. She did her best thinking while pacing. *This can't be happening!* Pacing wasn't helping today.

"Miss Dupree? Are you there?" The woman's concerned voice stopped her.

She forced herself to answer. "Yes, I'm okay."

"I'm terribly sorry. Your grandmother developed pneumonia early this week and stopped breathing a couple hours ago. She had a DNR order, which means Rest Haven was not allowed to put her on a ventilator. We have you and her son listed as contacts. We've been unable to reach him. We need one of you to come in to make arrangements."

Guess I'm elected because they'll never find him. "Okay, thanks. I'll call you back." She tried to sound as though her heart wasn't broken.

Her eyes teared up. She repeated the words. "Grandma is gone, Grandma is gone, Grandma—is—g-gone." Her heart's staccato beat rose to match the grief in those words.

Abandoned yet again.

Memories drifted across her mind. Grandma in an apron pulling delicious food out of the oven. Daddy with his strong hands lifting her into a chair at the table. Family. On her tenth birthday her life changed forever. That day her daddy disappeared. Sixteen years he'd been gone. She still didn't know whether he was dead or alive.

Her pulse raced, and her head felt big enough to explode. Misty reached for an aspirin. She would not allow herself to crawl into that deep, dark hole. *Don't go there.* She turned and walked toward the shower. The near scalding water felt like heaven as it cascaded over her head down to her toes, taking her tears with it. Each morning this was her time of solitude, her time of escape.

An hour later she phoned Rest Haven and gave instructions for Grandma's body to be transported to her hometown, Evergreen, a sleepy little town in North Georgia. Then she called the church and arranged the funeral. Grandma would rest beside Grandpa in the family cemetery.

Misty packed a few things for an overnight stay, if necessary. She didn't plan to be in that town of narrow-minded people any longer than needed. She'd promised herself to rid her life of unkind folks when she left Evergreen. They'd gossiped about her mother for years. Besides, she was weary. Her brain had been stretched like a sling shot since she'd finished graduate school and begun her employment with a top architectural firm in Atlanta.

Four days later her shiny red Mustang cruised through her hometown of Evergreen. Little had changed in the ten years she'd been gone. Misty saw a man and his brown dog in the distance. *The dog looks like our family dog, Brownie. Has the same markings.* Mesmerized, she watched them until they turned the corner. *Wish I could see the man's face. Maybe next time.*

Her stomach churned. Dread hung over her, matching the rainless, black clouds overhead. The church ladies and the busybodies would be speculating about what she did for a living and why she wouldn't ride in the funeral limo. *There will be snide comments about why I ran away. Uncle Ben knows why, but he'll never tell.*

"God, give me the strength to manage this day with the dignity my caring grandma deserves," she prayed while she parked the car. "Amen."

Entering the church, Misty lifted her chin and tried to smile the way Grandma had taught her. Her palms sweated as she scoured the room for Ben.

Her maternal cousin, Ellen, came and sat beside her during the service. "Where's Ben?" Misty hissed and scanned the mourners.

"Not now," Ellen whispered. "Don't worry. He won't be here."

"Too bad. I'd like to stand up to him now that I'm older, wiser and stronger," she said, scowling. Inside, relief flooded through Misty's mind and body. She exhaled. "Thank God, he isn't here. I wouldn't want to make a spectacle at Grandma's funeral."

The eulogy was brief but lovely. Townspeople came and offered their condolences at the gravesite. They told her how much her grandmother had meant to the community. *These folks are nicer than I remembered.*

"You're not staying for the food and fellowship?" Ellen eyed Misty's slender waistline. "C'mon. You can afford the calories."

Misty shook her head. "Work." The cousins hugged. She returned to her car. After taking a deep breath and letting it out slowly she drove away. She breathed a sigh of relief when she passed the city limits sign. Her hands trembled, her head throbbed, and her heart shattered like broken glass.

The sign at the next exit noted food and gasoline. Her stomach growled, so she headed toward the local hamburger joint. She ordered, reached for her cell and called her boyfriend, Walt Griffin.

They'd met when Misty was a senior at Georgia State and Walt was getting an MBA. They liked the same food, music, movies, and sports. Several weeks into the relationship he told her he loved her. She felt something, but love required trust—

something she dared not afford herself. *I'm afraid to love.*

Walt's voice interrupted Misty's thoughts. "Hey, babe. How'd it go?"

She exhaled. "Okay, I think. I'm drained. The funeral is over and I'm headed home. Talk to you tomorrow." She stretched, trying to relieve the tension in her muscles.

"Love you," Walt said.

"Thanks. Me, too." Misty choked on the word *love* again. The people who professed to love her ended up leaving. First her dad, then Mom, and now Grandma. She shook her head and cleared the cobwebs. She had work waiting on her.

This was her second year on the job, and she had to prove her worth. Otherwise, she'd be searching the internet, pounding the sidewalk and interviewing again.

She and Walt found time to squeeze in their usual Friday night dinner date. He knew about a dry wine to pair with dinner and ordered for both of them.

"Nice choice," she admitted. The steaks and salad melted in her mouth. "Yum, I forget to eat when I'm involved in a big project."

They spent a couple hours together at her place before she feigned exhaustion. She yawned and stretched. "I hope you'll forgive me, but I'm truly bushed."

Walt headed for the door. "I understand. It's been a tough week for you."

"Thanks for empathizing. Delicious dinner. We'll talk tomorrow." She kissed him good night and then locked the door. Guilt crept up on her like a spider, but she needed space.

Misty hated to renege on her promise to Walt, but she needed to catch up on the work she'd missed while attending Grandma's funeral. She texted him and begged off on their next date.

OK. I'll pull back until you get caught up. He added a frowny face.

Saturday afternoon the doorbell rang. The postman held out a special-delivery letter. "Sign for this, please."

Misty's fingers trembled as she tore open the envelope. *It can't mean what I think it does! That makes no sense.* She read the words again.

Article II: *To my darling granddaughter, Misty Leigh Dupree, I bequeath my home-place, Riverside Road Farm.* She pushed the words back, trying to scrape them off the walls of her skull. She had not been back to the farm in ten years. No need since Uncle Ben put Grandma in a nursing home.

She sighed and muttered, "Another challenge." She'd finally reached a place in her life where she felt comfortable. She had Walt and her work. Now this. It seemed she always faced new challenges.

For a few seconds the past wrapped around her like a warm sweater—softened by distance and years. She pictured her grandparents' five-room farmhouse set on twenty acres in North Georgia. Part of the property was flat and the other half rocky and mountainous. Arm-in-arm at the doorstep stood Grandpa in overalls and a plaid flannel shirt and Grandma in a plain A-line cotton dress belted at the waist.

We moved in with them when Daddy lost his job. He helped Grandpa on the farm, but Mama didn't do much around the house. Her excuse, "Don't want to be in Grandma's way." Folks called her lazy and even worse names.

Misty fingered a picture of them on her nightstand. Grandpa died of a heart attack when Misty was eight years old. Grandma grieved in stoic silence for months.

Grandma was there on the most fateful day of my life. Of course, her grandma became her greatest source of strength.

The day before Misty's tenth birthday her dad promised her a wonderful surprise. "How about a hint?" she begged.

"No can do. That'd spoil all the fun." He chuckled.

"Oh, why do grown-ups always say that?"

He leaned over and kissed her on the forehead. "You need to be patient. You don't have long to wait."

He left that April morning with his dog, Brownie. "I'm off, Dimples. See you in a little while. Brownie and I have something special up our sleeve." He and the dog never returned. What happened to him? Panic followed when the shadows lengthened, night came, and no daddy to sit by her at dinner.

Grandma insisted Misty go to bed, but she couldn't sleep. Her beloved daddy had not come home. She needed his good-night kiss. *I sobbed until the wee hours of the morning. Who knows where Mom was? She popped in and out like a traveling salesman.*

Grandma had called the sheriff's office and two men came out. Several neighbors brought their hunting dogs and joined the deputies scouring the woods for two whole days. Nothing. Not a trace.

The sheriff and his deputies searched everywhere. They searched the immediate property, areas where Daddy hung out, and queried everyone. Misty's father was nowhere to be found. Grandma was overcome with grief, Mama not so much.

Grandma offered a reward. It didn't help. Nobody came forth with any new information.

My daddy just vanished at the most beautiful time of the year. Spring brought forth new life to the earth, but I felt dead inside.

Misty wiped her tears away when the doorbell rang. Walt sauntered in. He and Misty talked about the implications of the new inheritance. "Have any idea what you'll do with the property?"

"Not really. I've never given it any thought. Didn't expect to get the farm. Uncle Ben lived there last I heard."

"I'm sure Ben expected to inherit it, since he put your grandma in a nursing home."

"I guess," she said.

"You can't ignore the property. You'll have to make some kind of decision." Walt believed in treating every aspect of life in a businesslike manner.

Misty felt the pressure building. She knew Walt wanted her to get this out of the way and out of their lives. He liked things simple.

"God, I hate thinking about going to Evergreen again. Three

months after my daddy disappeared, my mother took up with a boyfriend. Clark Hamilton was a moocher. Dead beat. Rumors circulated that perhaps my mother had something to do with Daddy's disappearance."

"Did you think that at the time?" he asked.

"No, but..."

"But you were a kid," Walt finished the sentence.

"Yes." She squirmed.

"And..." He urged her to continue.

"Clark resented every penny spent on me. Mama took me shopping for school shoes. When we returned Clark went into a jealous rage. I heard him yelling at her. 'Why are you spending money on the kid when we need the money to get away from this dump?' The next day she packed her bags and left me with Grandma. I caught the last glance of them through dust as the car flew down the dirt driveway and headed west toward Alabama. At least my mother looked back."

Walt held his hand in the air. "Enough! What do we do now?" His tone sounded harsh.

On the surface she froze, but her blood pressure rose to match her resentment.

"What did you say? This is about me, not you. I know I must go back and settle the property issue." Misty huffed. "But I dread it."

"I just meant the sooner, the better. Get it off *your* plate," Walt insisted.

She struggled to remember Walt was the best thing that had ever happened to her. Usually patient to a fault, he'd endured her every mood with understanding. *Until now.* Anger became a slithering snake and struck her heart. *Wait a minute! I don't need another boss.*

"Well?" He waited for an answer I didn't have.

"I've changed my mind about a few things since my return from Evergreen."

"Like what?" he asked. He didn't look pleased.

"The people were pleasant to me. I went there hating the town for trashing my family but found most people kind and respectful."

Walt stared her down, his teeth clenched with his jaw jutting forward. He raised his voice and pointed his finger at her. "You know what you have to do. Call your boss, set a time frame, and go take care of this inheritance thing."

This was a new side of Walt she hadn't seen. He'd taken charge, rattling off orders without asking her opinion. Misty felt a little bewildered, a lot annoyed. "Who died and made you boss?"

He folded his arms and stared at her like she was a stranger. "Suit yourself. I'm out of here."

"That's probably best before I say something I shouldn't."

She called her boss, explained why she needed a few days off, and packed for the second time in days. She headed back to North Georgia.

The farther north Misty drove the more colorful the landscape became. Fall had always been her favorite season. She associated it with Indian-Summer lore that had led to her name. Her daddy had named her the name Misty, because he believed in the Indian Legend of the Mist. Often in her dreams she searched for Daddy and Brownie. It was always misty and foggy. The morning after such a dream, Misty recalled the legend. *Someone special finds answers to problems and finds peace after having these misty, foggy dreams.* Fog locked out many distractions of the world. She prayed to know the answers about her dad and find peace someday.

Driving into town, Misty rolled down the window and felt the wind waft through her long auburn hair. The air smelled fresh and inviting away from the big city. N*ot sure what I'll find here. Cousin Ellen is the only person I have in Evergreen to give me guidance. Growing up, she gave me advice about girl stuff—makeup, hygiene, boys.*

"No time to worry about anything," she muttered. "I'm here to see Grandma's attorney and sign some papers. The farm may be a burden I don't need."

She pulled into the parking lot at the grocery store. All she needed today was coffee and something for breakfast tomorrow. Her favorite herbal tea bags and her favorite protein bars were in her briefcase at all times. A busy woman couldn't be too prepared.

Pushing a cart through the store, she rounded a corner and almost ran into her cousin. "Whoa, I'm sorry. I darn near mowed you over, Ellen."

Ellen stopped short and laughed. "Do you drive a car like that buggy in Atlanta traffic? What brings you to town so soon after the funeral?"

"Business."

"Oh? I had no idea your work ever brought you this far. Is your company designing a new building in this small town?"

"No. I need to see Grandma's attorney."

"Yeah, that'd make sense. The property needs to be settled. You've got a lot to deal with."

"I'm sorry I can't talk about this now. I'm overwhelmed." Misty grabbed the coffee and bagels out of the buggy and walked away—leaving a few items in the grocery cart when she hurried to the checkout.

She stomped out to the car and took a deep breath. Calmer, she drove to Grandma's house. Her breath still came in bursts and her chest felt heavy, but she wasn't crying. *This isn't going to work. I don't need to be here. At least I'm ahead with the new project at work. I love design. Architecture must be the most interesting job in the world.*

"Oh darn, I'm half way to the house without a key. My brain is not working." Nothing to do but turn around and go by the attorney's office and get one.

Luckily, Mr. Patterson was in the office. He seemed grayer than he had at the funeral a few days ago. Maybe she hadn't paid much attention to anyone at the cemetery.

"Hi, Misty. Good to see you." He held out his hand and smiled.

"I'm sorry to barge in, but I got into town this afternoon and wanted to ride out to the farm. I don't have a key. Thought you might."

"As a matter of fact, I do." He moved toward a filing cabinet, reached in and retrieved a key.

"You're a life saver." She sighed. At least she had calmed down. "I'll come in tomorrow, and we can go over the paperwork."

"Absolutely. Do you have any plans in mind?" His brow furrowed a little.

"Not at all. I've got to do some soul searching over this one."

"Take your time. Your grandma would want you to be happy."

"Thanks, Mr. Patterson. And thanks for being there for Grandma."

Back at the farm, memories hit Misty in the middle of her chest. Pictures of her mama and daddy, grandma and grandpa sat on the mantel. *Grandma's ghost keeping order in her house.*

Misty choked on her tears and wanted to run—run from this place with such sweet and yet horrific memories. Good days, when Mama brushed her hair until it shined or Daddy took her fishing. Bad days, when Daddy disappeared and Mama left with another man.

Misty's nerves threatened to overwhelm her. She opened the front door, ready to bolt when Ellen's car pulled up in the driveway.

"A peace offering." Ellen waved a bottle of wine like a white flag. "I'm so sorry I upset you. Stupid me. But I brought the stuff you left in the buggy."

"No, no, no. It isn't your fault. I've carried this burden for years." Misty broke down and started sobbing. Ellen sprang from the car, slammed the door shut and put her arms around her cousin, just as she did when they were children. They sat on the porch and talked for hours, sipping the wine Ellen brought, and finally finding common ground.

"I never understood why you left. Your grandma was so sad."

Misty explained, "Uncle Ben returned to town to live with Grandma. I was sixteen, remember? He made overtures, came on to me. Creepy. Thank goodness I was tall for my age and could hold my own and fend him off. I tried never to be alone with him."

Ellen gasped. "Oh, my God. He tried the same thing with me. I went out to the farm to show your grandma I had learned to drive. She wasn't at home. Ben grabbed at me, but I outran him, jumped into the car and burned rubber."

"Good for you. I wasn't that lucky. One day a neighbor took my grandmother to the doctor. I came home from school and Uncle Creep took advantage of the seclusion. He pinned me to the wall and ran his hand up under my dress until his fingers maneuvered into my panties." Misty's throat went dry. *I squirmed to get away, but his body pressed harder and harder against me until he groaned. That scene remained etched on the back of my eyelids for years. It invaded many dreams, causing full-blown nightmares.*

"Lord, no wonder you ran away." Ellen got out of her chair, moved over to Misty and patted her on the shoulder. "I sort of thought he had tried his monkey business with you."

"Now you know." Her hands felt clammy.

"Could be the reason he left town months ago, in such a hurry nobody saw him. He could've been running from an irate father holding a shotgun."

They both laughed a nervous laugh. "What a letch."

"What would you do if he showed up here at the house?" Ellen asked.

"I'd ask him what in the hell he was doing here? And then I'd tell him to get off my property."

"But what if he didn't go?" Ellen pushed the point.

"I'd spray him with my pepper spray and threaten to have him arrested if he ever came here again."

"Yes! I'd step toward the door and stand by you and shout, 'And if she doesn't, I will, you low down bastard.' Then I would point to the highway."

"Ben would back away, hustle out to his car, and zoom down the driveway toward the main road." Misty slapped her hands against each other in a gesture. "Good riddance."

Ellen's cell rang in the middle of their pretend game. "Sorry," she said to someone. "I'll be there in a jiffy."

She turned to Misty. "I need to run an errand. Do you feel okay?"

"Sure, I'm safe." She patted her pocket. "I have my pepper spray."

"Great. I'll check with you tomorrow, hon." She grabbed Misty's cell phone and added her own number to Misty's contacts. "Call me so I'll have your number."

"Thanks for coming by and thanks for the food. You made my day." She grinned her little girl grin for her cousin.

After Ellen had gone Misty wandered around the backyard. She remembered a favorite rose bush her grandma had said wasn't a rose but a rare hibiscus. She called it a Confederate rose.

In the distance she noticed a dog about the size of Brownie, but she knew Daddy's dog would have died years ago. She started walking toward him, calling, "Come here, boy. Brownie, is that you? Did you have a puppy that looks like you? Here boy." She continued to walk in that direction, but the closer she got the more the dog faded in the distance.

She stopped and looked at nothingness. "Daddy?" Goose bumps covered her skin as an eerie feeling zipped through her body. *Am I hallucinating? Perhaps I'm overly tired.*

Misty went back into the house and put away the groceries Ellen brought. Using her grandma's old kettle, she heated water and made a cup of tea. She pulled a recent *Architecture for Tomorrow* magazine from her briefcase and read, sipping the soothing beverage.

The next morning, after tossing and turning on the sofa she had covered with blankets and sheets from a cedar chest, she showered and dressed. Heading out to Mr. Patterson's office, she passed the mantel filled with family photos. Grandma and Grandpa embracing at their wedding. And a picture of Daddy holding baby Misty. *Their spirits are here.*

On the drive into town a flock of geese headed south for the winter crossed the sky in perfect formation. The leader honked orders to the remainder of the V formation. She slowed to admire the magnificence and precision of the birds. *I wish I had my life that organized.* "I'm sure Walt would organize it for me if I'd let him." She chuckled.

Approaching the square, she pulled into a parking space in front of Square Perks. Her stomach grumbled, since she hadn't bothered to eat breakfast. "Coffee time." She locked the car and breezed into the café. After ordering a latte to go she looked toward the back of the room and spotted Ellen approaching.

"Morning, cousin." Ellen grinned like a kid who knew a secret.

"What's up?"

"I have someone I want you—-" Ellen motioned toward her booth.

Misty groaned. "Oh, please, not this early in the morning. Besides, I have an appointment."

"It'll only take a minute. I promise."

Ellen reached for her hand and led her toward the back. As they approached, a tall man slid from the booth and stood. Turning, he held out his hand.

"Misty, I'd like you to meet—-" Ellen began.

"Kevin Dennison?" Misty gasped. Automatically she felt the biggest smile flash across her face since she'd returned to Evergreen. "Is this some sort of joke, Ellen?"

"Misty DuPree! Looks like the joke's on us, Princess. Where have you been most of my life?" He touched her shoulder. His hand felt warm through her clothing, and she surrendered to the comfort of his touch for a brief moment.

"Working in Atlanta." She straightened her back. Kevin was a flash from the past. They'd had a brief puppy love experience back in the day.

"What brings you back to North Georgia?"

"Business." She looked at her watch. "And speaking of business, if you'll excuse me, I have a meeting. Great seeing you, Kevin."

"I hope to see you again while you're in town." He gazed into her eyes but said nothing else.

She coughed to break the eye contact. "Thanks, that would be nice." She turned and walked toward the entrance. *Yes, nice. But I don't need any more complications in my life.*

Mr. Patterson waited in his office. He went over the details of Misty's grandma's will. The property consisted of twenty acres of land, the main house and a smaller building.

"Why didn't Grandma leave the farm to her son, Ben? Surely she discussed it with you."

"Not really. Something about some trouble he's been in lately. Seems she was disappointed in him. I don't think he'd ever been any good. There's a rumor going round town that he's in jail somewhere near Memphis."

"I can believe that, but I never expected to own the farm." Misty fidgeted and looked down at the floor.

"Have any idea what you might do with it?"

"Not a clue," she blurted out. "Why does everyone ask me that?"

"Everyone is curious, maybe thinking about what they could do with such an inheritance. You'll figure it out when the time comes." He smiled and told her where to sign. "It's official."

"Thanks for your help. I appreciate all you did for Grandma after Grandpa died."

"She was a charming little lady."

They shook hands and Misty walked out into the fresh air and took a deep breath. Her world had changed. She wasn't sure how or how much, but she felt the change.

A truck sat parked on the opposite curb. It reminded her of Daddy's old truck. A brown dog stared at her from the truck bed. By instinct she started across the street. She glanced down at the uneven brick pavement, worried she'd catch her high heels. When she looked up the dog was no longer there. Goose bumps spread across her arms, and she swallowed hard. *The dog could have jumped from the truck and gone in search of its master.*

She snapped to attention. She had to get busy working on her to-do list. A week didn't leave her a lot of time to get things sorted out before she had to be back in the office.

The dripping faucet in the bathroom would only get worse. Time to call a plumber? Perhaps time to call an inspector and check the roof, wiring, etc.

She dropped by the hardware store for extra light bulbs and a new coffee pot to replace the one she'd tossed into the yard last night after seeing mold growing in the unemptied grounds. They must have been there since Uncle Ben ducked out. "Good morning, Mr. Smith."

"Well, hello, Misty. I heard you were back in town."

"Yes, I'm only here for a week, trying to take care of a few things at the farm."

"How can we help you today?"

"I need light bulbs, a coffee pot, a heavy-duty flashlight, strong trash bags, and the name of a good plumber."

"My nephew is the best in town. I'll give you his card."

"Thanks, you're a big help." She looked around the store while he packaged her purchase.

"Coming right up." He handed her the bundle. "I put a coffee maker in there for you. It's on sale and comes with a supply of gourmet coffee packets that ought to last you a couple of weeks."

"Great."

He swiped her credit card and smiled. "Good to see you." His broad smile had not changed since she was a child.

"Thanks again." She headed to her car.

Half a block away, Kevin appeared on the sidewalk and waved. She waved back but kept walking. Kevin belonged to her past. She didn't have time to get chummy with the town folks. Her mission was to check on the farm and make an assessment. Sell or rent? *Be done with it, like Walt said, but in my own time, not his.*

She started inventorying everything in the house. What to keep, what to sell, what to lease with the house should she go that route. It proved a harder job than she'd imagined. Ben had left the house in a filthy mess. She checked dates on the contents of the pantry. Some dated back to before he put her grandma away, the jerk! Then she pulled stuff off shelves and out of cabinets. That filled four trash bags. She had never imagined so many bug-infested packages or rusted cans in one place. She lugged the bags out to the back porch. The fridge posed a different problem. White and green mold decorated some of the food. Acrid smells hit and her stomach threatened to spew. Everything must go. Two more trash bags proved too heavy to move. She double bagged them and dragged them across the kitchen out back. *Six trash bags filled and I'm bushed.*

The extra bedroom closet came next. Misty started placing things in bags to give to charity. She pulled and tugged until her back screamed, "Whoa."

One side of the closet was filled with lovely quilts made by Grandma and her sister, Penny. Fabulous quilts: a Dutch Girl design, a Wedding Ring pattern, and a Star Burst. She took one from the stack, placed it over the bed, and crawled up on it. She smelled a trace of mothballs, which Grandma had used to protect the beauty of her long hours of work. With one roll she relaxed into a downward spiral of pure comfort, the comfort of coming home. It almost felt like coming home where she belonged.

The next day the plumber came early as he'd promised on the phone. He looked familiar but had not been in her class at school.

"Thanks for coming out on such short notice. This wasn't an emergency."

"You caught me between jobs. My uncle asked me to work you in as soon as possible." He shrugged.

"My lucky day."

"I should check out the tub faucet and your kitchen sink while I'm here. Make sure everything's working well."

"That's mighty neighborly of you. Thanks for taking the extra time."

"You coming back here to live?" he asked in a reserved manner.

"Odd question. Probably not. I'm not sure yet." She fidgeted, picking at her nails.

He sounded disappointed. "My cousin will be sorry to hear that. He had a hard time getting over you leaving town."

"Your cousin?"

"Yeah, Kevin Dennison."

"You're Kevin's cousin?" Her stomach flipped. "No wonder you look familiar."

"It's a small world." He grinned. "Some folks notice the resemblance."

Misty cleared her throat, offered him a bottle of water, and showed him the plumbing areas he wanted to examine. While he worked she stripped both beds and filled the old washing machine.

When he completed his work he packed up the tools and headed for the door.

"One last favor, could you turn two mattresses for me?" Someone had sold all but those two, and she had no idea which one Ben the letch had used.

When he finished turning them he started out again.

"Thanks again for the fast service." She handed him a check and felt relieved.

"I'll tell Kevin I checked the plumbing. It looks like a few other things need to be done. I'll be glad to recommend local craftsmen anytime."

"Sounds good."

She stood on the front porch and waved while she watched him drive away. *Nice guy. He looks a lot like Kevin—has a slight trace of Cherokee heritage.* In two minutes her thoughts whizzed back a decade.

A week before Misty ran away from Evergreen, she and Kevin had gone to a movie. After the show they'd shared a banana split in the ice cream shop. They ate slowly and gazed into each other's eyes. She sensed something different that night, a special tenderness between them.

Kevin had borrowed his dad's car for the evening, and they drove at a crawl the seven miles to the farm, holding hands but uttering not a word until they were halfway there. Kevin pulled over and stopped.

"You know the rules," she reminded him.

"Yes, I know the rules. But I know I love you." He turned off the engine and moved toward her. Then he slid his hand inside her collar, rubbed her neck and inched her head toward him.

"We haven't finished school. We need to wait."

"I'm a senior, and you're a junior. We aren't kids anymore." He leaned in, cupped her chin, and kissed her.

She felt her lips curve into a smile under his, and soon they both laughed breaking the tension.

"It was a good try," he joked.

"A fantastic try and I'm dizzy. But… I'm afraid we'll go too far."

"You're right. I'll try to behave." He chuckled. "I'll try."

"I want to… someday." She squeezed his hand and nuzzled his cheek.

A crack of lightning crossed the sky and jolted Misty back to the present. She shook her head. "What am I doing? Where did that memory come from?" Thunder rolled and roared. Wind brought sheets of hard rain across the porch. She dashed into the house. Next trip she'd tackle the out-building. *Who knows what's stored out there?* Over the years the added lean-to had been used for a sewing room, a workshop, a guest bedroom and other things.

In the bottom of a drawer she found a notebook that belonged to her grandma. In it Grandma had noted the best thing and the worst thing that had occurred each year for forty years. In 1998 the saddest entry was the day Misty's daddy had disappeared. Simply vanished. A wave of gut-wrenching nostalgia hit her. *I crawled into the safety of Grandma's lap and bawled and bawled and bawled my eyes out. I was sure my daddy loved me. He'd never leave me. Some evil person must've kidnapped him or worse.*

Her cell rang. Ellen's voice sounded chipper today. "Hi. Want some help with inside chores? This rain squashed my outdoor plans."

"Oh, I don't know. Most of this process is rummaging through family history, trying to make sense about what to save and what to ditch."

"Okay." Ellen said in a no-nonsense tone. "I'll give you two more hours. Then I'm bringing chicken salad sandwiches. You'll need a break. Family mess can get to you."

"That sounds great. You're right. Can you bring me some laundry detergent and some paper towels? See you in a bit. Thanks." The phone clicked.

Anything that could be purchased or replaced at a later date became fair game. Pictures, letters, handmade items had sentimental value and should be cherished.

A mist replaced the rain and the sun tried to peek out. She looked out a back window. The brown dog appeared, but he never came close to the house. *I wonder where he belongs or if he's a stray looking for food.*

When she heard Ellen honk the horn, she went to unlock the front door. "You brought good weather."

"Not soon enough for me."

"You don't like the rain?"

"Not unless I'm sleeping with a handsome man under a tin roof." She smiled.

"Honestly, Ellen, you haven't changed a bit. Still a flirt."

"I'll take that as a compliment. Speaking of compliments, Kevin said you looked prettier now than when you left. I think he's still stuck on you."

"You're making that up."

"No, I'm not. He mourned over you as if you were dead. He wore a hang-dog look for a year."

"Kevin and I had a good thing, but you understand why I couldn't stay. I didn't have the heart to tell Grandma about Ben. She'd already lost one of her two sons. There was nothing else for me to do but run away."

"You must have been desperate."

"Of course, I was scared to death. I had nowhere to go, no money, no skills, no way to make a living." She looked down, fiddling with her hands.

"You poor kid." Ellen reached over and patted her hands. "Let's have our chicken salad sandwiches."

"I made some tea. You like vanilla chai?"

"One of my favorites. How'd you know?"

"We're cousins. It's in the genes. We're a lot alike. I even thought you might end up with Kevin." Misty smiled.

Ellen giggled. "Not in the cards. We're just friends. He's a detective, you know."

"I had no way of knowing."

"Matter of fact, the first year on the job he tried to find your dad. He treated it like a cold-case, started from scratch."

Misty flinched at the mention of her dad. Her hand trembled as she poured the tea from a pitcher she found in the back of a cabinet. They sat at the kitchen table, sharing like they were sixteen again. "What did he find out?"

"He went to nearby towns and spoke to people who had done business with your dad. He searched the obituaries in newspapers in the neighboring towns and counties. Six months later he hadn't uncovered a clue."

"Daddy had vanished without a trace." Misty sighed.

"It seemed so, but Kevin thinks we should try again. Now that you're back, he wants to look for new evidence."

Misty held up her hand to stop Ellen. "Whoa! First of all, I'm not really back. Secondly, do you think we have a chance of finding anything new? Deep down, I know I've never given up hope of finding Daddy."

"Well, it's worth a try. Kevin investigated a cold-case last year, and they uncovered evidence that led to the real killer of a man over in Dahlonega. Some poor man had been in prison six years for a crime he didn't commit."

"Okay, I'll think about it."

"How about me coming out tomorrow to help you? I can do the grunt work while you sort and take care of the personal items."

"That's a deal."

They hugged and Misty closed the door. Her mind started churning about the possibilities of finding her father. Perhaps Kevin could help find a resolution.

She remade the bed in the spare bedroom with clean sheets and pillow cases then snuggled under her favorite quilt.

Fitful dreams interrupted her sleep. She tossed and turned most of the night. Best scenario, Daddy had another family and happily played with Brownie and two little boys in the yard. *They would be my half-brothers.* Worse scenario, Daddy had been murdered. She woke up in a cold sweat. "Yes, I'll ask Kevin to look for Daddy," she muttered to an empty room.

Ellen arrived early the next morning. They made coffee with her new coffee maker, which Misty really needed.

"I never knew where you went when you left Evergreen," Ellen began. "It worried me to death for ages."

"When Grandma went to sleep that night after Ben jumped me, I sneaked out of the house carrying my little suitcase full of clothes and a few pictures. I walked two miles to the main road and hitched a ride into town."

"But you had no money." Ellen gasped.

"I'd saved a little money from chores and kept it in a jewelry box. I took a bus and rode for almost two hours. The bus made three stops before the driver told me to get off in Roswell."

"You must have been scared out of your gourd."

"It was dark and cold. Tired and hungry, I went into a diner and asked the owner to let me wash dishes for something to eat. The owner's wife asked if I'd run away from home. I told her I had an aunt who lived near Roswell."

"That took guts." Ellen grimaced. "But the woman knew you were a runaway.

"They felt sorry for me, let me sleep on the couch in the office that night. They said I reminded them of their daughter who had died of leukemia at age fifteen."

"Aw." Ellen sighed.

"The next day they got in touch with Grandma's sister, my

great Aunt Penny, who came and picked me up. She called Grandma and told her Ben and I had a fight. Later Aunt Penny got permission and I lived with her during my senior year. She was good to me, but I felt so lonely without my grandma."

"How did it work out?" Ellen seemed genuinely interested about those years.

"It worked out. Through every crying, lonely night I kept telling myself everything would be better when I finished high school. And attending a good school system allowed me to get into college."

Ellen looked at the time. "We'd better get cracking."

Their organized effort got the project off to a good start. The house began to take shape. Finally, Misty could make sense of what to keep and what to toss.

"Did you think more about Kevin's offer?" Ellen asked.

"I had a dream last night and made up my mind to go forward with the investigation. I realized I've never given up hope."

"Great. Let's meet him for lunch tomorrow."

"Thanks for all your help today. It seemed like old times."

They hugged. Ellen loaded her car with things she wanted or could sell and drove away.

Misty put on her walking shoes, jogged down the driveway and completed a mile on Riverside Road. Weariness crept up on the return home. She walked the remainder of the way.

Coming up the driveway, she caught a glimpse of the brown dog near the rocky area of the property. She whistled for him. "Come here, boy," she yelled. Then she clapped her hands together, and he looked up. He took a few steps toward her, and she called again. "Good boy." He stopped, turned his head to the left but came no closer. *I'll try again tomorrow.*

The next morning the dog was not there. She showered, dressed and drove into town for lunch with Ellen and Kevin.

The food at Sassy's Southern was delicious, but the menu took a back seat today. They'd come to discuss a plan to solve the mystery of her dad's disappearance.

"I suggest we canvass motels, diners, gas stations, post offices and police stations within a fifty mile radius." Kevin pulled out a map, stuck a compass in the middle and made a circle around Evergreen.

"Sounds good, but how can I help? I've got to get back to the office in a couple of days."

"Maybe you can come on weekends and follow up on any leads Kevin uncovers," Ellen suggested.

"The main thing is to get started," he replied.

Misty looked at Kevin. "Agreed. When you find a hint of something worth looking into, I'll take a weekend and question people in the outlying areas."

Kevin pushed his chair away from the table and gave each of the girls a hug around the shoulders. "Hate to run, but I have an appointment." He looked at Misty and asked, "Is it okay if I call you sometime?"

She handed him one of her business cards. "We're partners. This trio has a mission." She laughed.

"Hear, hear," Ellen said.

Two days later Misty headed back to Atlanta. Her desk held a new set of blueprints staring her in the face. She sighed. "We have not even finished the building to compete with the Bank of America Plaza yet." She'd thought she was ahead. It would take her two weeks to catch up after the one week she'd been gone.

Walt played the wounded boyfriend, acting resentful and downright snarky. He'd sent texts, but they didn't talk much. The usual nice fuzzy feeling started wearing thin.

I'm too busy, too tired and too stressed. Walt needs to get with the program or get lost.

~~~

Kevin began his search beyond Misting Falls near the North Georgia border. He drove up early in the morning to spend the entire day questioning folks. He ate breakfast at a small local café. While he waited for his order he introduced himself to the owner.

"I'm investigating the disappearance of a man named Daniel
~~~

Dupree. He lived down in Falls County and vanished about sixteen years ago. I've got a few pictures of him." Kevin reached into his briefcase and brought out a large padded envelope.

"Sorry, fella. Don't think I ever saw him. Maybe some of the older customers might know him. You're welcome to pass the pictures around." He walked back to the cash register.

Local folks in the diner looked at the pictures, but one by one they shook their heads, signaling no recognition.

Kevin smiled and said, "Thanks, anyway. I'll keep trying." He gave the owner a handshake and went back to his car.

The gas station on the corner down the street had two mechanics working the bay. He filled his tank and went inside. A boy took his money for a bottle of water and a pack of gum. "Is the owner around?"

Pointing toward the bay, the boy said, "My dad's breaking in a new mechanic."

Kevin approached the older of the two men and produced his identification. "Hi. I'm doing a little detective work for a family investigating an old case. I'd appreciate it if you could look at a few pictures."

The man wiped the grease off his hands with a cloth and waited for Kevin to produce the photos. "No, I don't know this man, but I've seen the woman with him. She came through here several years ago with a younger guy. They were here a time or two. A long time between visits."

"Are you sure?"

"Think so. Never saw such curly red hair on a woman before. A bushel basket full of hair."

"Thanks, pal."

He phoned Misty with the news. Pacing the floor, he worried as he unraveled the details. "Don't get your hopes up yet. But at least it's something."

"Do you think my mother knew Clark before my daddy vanished?"

"We have no idea at this point. I'll see what I can find out about his background during that time period."

"Thanks, Kevin. You're a godsend." Her sigh drifted through the phone like honey dripping from the comb.

I wish I could reassure her things would be okay. "I'll be in touch."

He searched the legal records of Clark Hamilton. He'd had couple of petty run-ins with the law, but the man had no convictions. He was not a felon, but Kevin needed to find him. Perhaps he'd been involved in Daniel Dupree's disappearance. Perhaps not.

~~~

Back in Atlanta, Misty sat on her bed eating pizza and working. The phone rang, startling her.

"Hello?" she asked with a mouthful of food. "Kevin?"

"Hi. Did I catch you in the middle of something?"

"Nothing that can't wait." She finished chewing. The suspense was killing her. "Did you find anything?"

"Nothing good." Kevin continued, "Clark Hamilton is clean on this. He was nowhere near this area when your dad vanished. He dumped your mom several years ago and moved on."

"I've wondered about my mother for years." Misty groaned. "But why should I try to find her? She obviously never tried to find me. Guess we can close the book on that trail."

"I'm not giving up on finding your dad. We will turn the corner and start down a new road," Kevin assured her.

"Thanks, let me know if I can help." Misty hit the off button, put her face in her hands and sobbed. *What in the hell am I doing?* The days dragged on. She went into a blue funk and the tenseness in her muscles begged for a massage.

Walt had no patience with this new adventure to find Misty's missing father. "This is a wild goose chase if you ask me. After all these years the trail is cold."

"I didn't ask you."

Misty remained determined no matter what Walt thought. In fact, his opinion didn't mean much to her anymore. They had drifted apart over the past month or so.
~~~

A week later Kevin called again. "Hi, sweetheart."

"I think I like that." She smiled at her reflection in the dresser mirror. "Nice of you to call while I'm at home. The office is always crazy."

"I don't want to get your hopes up, but..."

"Yes?" She squirmed, curiosity grabbing her.

"There's this guy, an indigent, who comes into a convenience store about thirty miles away. He always orders the same thing—black coffee and a Slim Jim. Been doing it for years."

"And?" Misty shoulders tightened.

Kevin paused a beat. "He said he's seen a man who resembles your dad. Even has a dog that looks like Brownie, I think."

Misty's heart jumped and she hopped off the bed. "Really? Should I come up this weekend?"

"Maybe. Let me follow the trail and I'll get back to you as soon as I know something."

She made the decision to drive up to Evergreen that weekend, regardless of what Kevin said. If the lead didn't pan out, the house needed more cleaning anyway.

Early Saturday morning Misty met Ellen and Kevin at the restaurant. By the looks on their faces, they didn't even have to tell her. Nothing had come of the lead.

Her cell vibrated. She glanced at the caller ID. "Hi, Walt." She rolled her eyes, looking at the ceiling.

"Hey, Misty. I can't believe you took off work again. Your boss must be tired of this. Seems foolish to push your luck with a good job."

"Yes, I came back hoping we'd found a good lead about my dad. My boss seemed okay with it. He understands my concern about Daddy."

"What? When are you going to grow up and stop chasing a dream?"

His tone ticked her off, but she calmed herself before responding. "I'm with Ellen and Kevin. We can talk later."

"We can talk now. Just sell the damn house as is. People will understand it's a mess. You can make some money and be done with it."

Misty's resolve broke. "This isn't working, Walt. I need to do this my way. In fact, I need a break from your nagging."

He shouted, "Then have it! I won't be around to help you pick up the pieces."

The call disconnected. It was the best thing Walt could have done for her. *What did I see in him in the first place?*

Misty turned to Ellen and Kevin. "I'm sorry. Let's get back to business."

"The man, a drunk, now claims he has seen Elvis and Jimi Hendrix." Kevin shook his head.

The false claim aggravated her. "I'd like to strangle that drunk for giving me hope. Empty hope."

Kevin reached across the table and rested his hands on Misty's. "I'm sorry," he said. "Usually, we let the entire scenario play out before notifying the family so this doesn't happen. Otherwise, the families build up their hopes."

A single tear dropped from Misty's cheek, and she squeezed her thumb around Kevin's fingers. Disappointment seeped through her like stagnant pond water. She had already gotten too involved in the search.

For the next two days the three of them stuck together inside the perimeter he'd drawn. Splitting up would have covered more ground, but neither Misty nor Ellen had Kevin's training or expertise. Likewise, he did not have Misty's knowledge of her father. Of course her daddy could have changed greatly over the past sixteen years, but her memories stayed vivid.

They'd often shared father and daughter talks while he grabbed a smoke behind the lean-to out back. She envisioned him wearing a faded denim cap and a white trail coming from his cigarette. She sat mesmerized by his tales of the legend. "When you dream of fog and mist, the outcome is a clearer solution to your problem."

She shook her head and snapped back to reality. Kevin would keep them focused. They needed to push forward. Any day could bring them a new clue, send them down a new trail.

Following a series of dead ends, they caught a break when they stumbled onto a different lead. The news reported the discovery of ragged clothing and a dog collar that could be related to a shooting near the edge of Evergreen. Nobody knew the timeline, but the news report established the items had been there for a while.

"A *while?*" Misty asked Kevin over the phone. "Like *sixteen years* a while?"

She could tell Kevin doubted but didn't want to disappoint her with his answer. "Maybe." His voice seemed strained.

Misty understood he wanted to deliver some good news, wanted to be her hero. "Be honest with me," she said, holding back tears. "The real estate agent says I can have cash in hand for the farm and house, now that I've gotten it cleaned up a bit. Say I sell it. Is there a reason for me to come back to Evergreen? Are we chasing a ghost?"

He cleared his throat. "I wish I knew."

Silence. "When should I come?"

"Right away."

She was under fire at work already for missing so much time. Her colleagues had little patience these days. She would play sick if she had to. This was way more important. "I'll be there."

The next day the river flooded and decomposed bodies appeared. The excavation took place on a brisk morning. When Misty pulled up to the police blockade she sent a text message to Kevin that said, *Here*.

Minutes later he ushered her through. Together, they stood several feet away as the bodies were dragged out of the river. She buried her face in Kevin's jacket until she couldn't wait anymore.

"Now can I look?" she asked in a muffled voice.

"Not yet," he said into her hair. "Ellen will meet us afterward. She said she doesn't have the gag reflex to watch this."

It sounded like something Ellen would say. "When will the DNA results be back?"

"Optimistically? Four to six weeks."

More time? Yet another disappointment. Misty slumped in Kevin's arms, but he supported her weight. This time, at least, she wasn't alone. She could always count on him.

After a minute, he murmured, "Okay. Now you can look."

Misty let go and forced herself to look. Her stomach roiled with nausea at the sight of the gruesome remains dragged out of the river. What she saw was unrecognizable except for one detail—a blue denim hat.

She gasped. "Oh my God. That's my dad." She grabbed Kevin's arm. "How could the hat still be there? Wouldn't the current have washed it away?"

"Not necessarily. And, don't get your hopes up. I've seen a lot of those hats."

Misty shook her head. It had to be a sign. The body belonged to her father, she convinced herself. All that remained was waiting for the official word.

After a month of vacillating between hope and despair, the DNA report finally came back and the boss allowed Misty to blow off an office party, so she could go home to Evergreen and get the results in person. Her heart pounded the entire time she drove to Kevin's house, the one where he'd grown up. Looking at it felt odd. He'd made improvements, but it felt warm and welcoming.

He'd made a fire by the time she arrived. "Cozy," she commented.

"Ready?" he asked her. He had the DNA report in hand, a large, unmarked white envelope.

She shook her head. "I don't know, Kevin. What if it's not him?"

He put his arm around her shoulder. "Then we keep looking."

"We've chased a ton of leads. What if I'm tired of looking?" She sighed.

Kevin handed her a cup of hot chocolate. "Let's sit."

The re-covered loveseat faced the fireplace. Once they sat, Misty nuzzled against Kevin's shoulder and placed her hand on the envelope he held.

"Do you know what's in it?" she asked him.

He nodded but gave her no inclination whether or not the man and the dog were Daniel Dupree and Brownie. "I had to. It's my job."

Misty opened the envelope. Its contents sent her into a fit of wild tears. She opened the fireplace guards, tossed the papers onto the logs, and then she returned to the loveseat. The DNA did not match her dad's.

After a while Misty stood and faced Kevin, her manner resolute. "Enough is enough. I'll go through the house and sell everything I don't want—before it goes on the market."

"Don't be rash," he begged.

"I need to go back to the city and walk away from the hurt forever. I have hung on to this dream way too long."

"I'm sorry I've let you down, failed you." He hung his head.

She reached for his hand. "Don't be. I found you again."

He squeezed her hand but did not speak.

Misty declared, "This is something I must do alone. You understand."

"I'm trying." He swallowed hard and his Adam's apple bobbed up and down.

"We're all trying." She walked toward the door and he followed. He started to speak. She put her fingers on his lips and whispered, "Not another word."

The following day Misty took one last walk through the fields behind her grandma's house. *Dad and I had our special place where we picnicked and watched the birds. This is the place where I will tell him goodbye.*

Not far from their meadow she saw the chestnut brown dog in the distance. He barked and looked over his shoulder to see if she was following him. "Okay, fella. Today I'm going to see what you're up to." He led her off the beaten path.

After a long, long walk, she decided to go back toward the house. "Sorry fella, I think we've gone too far. I don't want to get lost and stranded out here."

When she turned to go, the dog barked and barked, urging her to follow. "Okay, just a little farther," she huffed. Soon they came to what appeared to be an old abandoned mine she'd never seen before. The brown dog kept leading her toward a fissure then disappeared into a hole she never would've seen if the dog had not shown her. He barked from inside the tunnel, and Misty couldn't coax him out. It was getting dark, but she hated to leave without at least trying to get him out.

The light on her cell phone allowed her to see a short distance into the tunnel. The barking echoed through the cave but stopped when she came to a rock fall.

There, to her great shock, as if it was begging for help, she saw a skeletal hand reaching out from under the rocks. "No!" Her screams reverberated around the cave walls and returned like a boomerang. She jumped back and hit an old wooden support beam that groaned above her head. The dog barked, and she realized the roof might cave in at any time.

A tiny, shiny spot caught her eye. She stepped a little closer to the bones, fighting nausea. "What's that, Brownie? Looks like a ring on the finger." She snatched it up, cringing as the broken bones fell away. Her breath hitched. "No...," she whispered. "It's Daddy's ring."

The roof groaned again. Her pulse raced like a runaway roller coaster speeding downhill. The dog barked. She swung the light around. A dog's skeleton lay on the ground close to her dad's. "Brownie, is that you?"

No reply. As if now that she'd found them he could rest.

Misty slid the ring onto her finger and clenched her fist tightly so it couldn't fall off. A dash of color attracted her attention. She leaned over and brushed away the dust to find a small package with a card attached to the bow. She shined her phone light on the card. In barely legible letters, she read "Happy Birthday, Misty. Love you, Daddy."

Tears ran down her face and she choked on the dust and her memories. He'd kept his promise. Something had happened to him before he could get there, but he was coming home for her birthday.

She wiped her face. "I love you, too, Daddy."

Another groan from the ceiling—this time it morphed into a loud crack as beams broke. Dirt and rock showered down around her. With a last glance at the bones, she scrambled and fell, but she managed to crawl out with her father's gift in her pocket.

Behind her, the roar stopped, and everything became still.

The cave had collapsed and closed the mine entrance with boulders half the size of a car. Her mouth caked with dust choked her. She looked back at her father's grave.

She heard a sound, rolled over and listened.

"Misty! Misty, are you okay?" Kevin ran toward her.

She sat up. "How... how did you know where to find me?" She sputtered and wiped the grit from her mouth.

He sat her down on a rock. "I followed a dog that kept barking at me and then running off."

"Brownie's ghost," she whispered.

"What happened here?"

"I found him." Misty stuttered and sobbed through her story. Then she held out her hand and showed Kevin the ring and the package. "Now I know. Daddy didn't abandon me."

"And I will never abandon you." Kevin placed his hands on each side of her face.

They looked at one another and kissed—a long awaited kiss.

The fog rolled in bringing the peace mentioned in the legend. Misty had found her answers.

Notes from the Heart

They are renewed by love when the heart of each holds infinite sources of life for the heart of the other.

~ Pyodor Dostoevsky

STORED ON THE top shelf of her closet, there *it* sat, holding secrets from over two decades ago. Bethany Ward envisioned the beautiful Valentine heart through the sealed shipping box. Filled with small photos and notes, *it* beckoned to her from the closet shelf where she had placed it yesterday. Thomas Boyd, her steady boyfriend in high school, had given her the heart full of chocolates. She couldn't throw it away, even after she had eaten the candy and dumped Thomas months later. Not even after she'd married Brad and had two children. Not even when she had divorced him and moved back to her hometown, Oak Hill, Georgia.

Earlier Bethany had unpacked most of the kitchen items, books, and personal mementos. Relieved that she had made some progress, she concentrated on the remainder of the house.

Tackling her bedroom, she lifted one last item to the closet shelf. She had to move the special small box to make room. When she touched it her heart hitched, and her fingertips tingled. Bethany hadn't opened this box in years, but she'd saved it and continued to take the heart with her whenever she moved. A rush of nostalgia hit her, and questions flooded her mind.

Where was Thomas now? How old would he be? *Two years older than I am, of course. Funny how we don't think about others aging when we do. In my memories he's still a young man.* What would he look like now in his early forties? Did he still have that easy-to-love smile and those ultra-white teeth? She sighed. So many questions! Would she ever have those answers? Did she even want those answers?

Bethany hadn't thought of him in ages, and none of her friends ever mentioned him on Facebook. She reached for the box with the Valentine heart, held it for a moment, then put it back in the closet without opening it. One note, frozen in her memory, began to thaw her heart.

Dimples, I know I will love you forever and ever. You are my life. -T

Tears welled in her eyes but didn't spill over. "I must be hallucinating," Bethany mumbled. "Thomas, the ever idealistic sentimental dreamer." *What's happening to me and why are these thoughts plaguing me after so many years?* Perhaps a sixth sense was trying to tell her something. Perhaps Thomas needed her. Perhaps he was thinking of her.

The phone rang. Her hands trembled when she reached for it. She breathed a sigh of relief when the caller ID read Cindy. "Hi, sweetheart. How's my favorite daughter?"

"Fine, Mom. Thought I'd come over tomorrow and help you unpack and get things stored away."

Bethany took a deep breath and let it out slowly. "Thanks for the generous offer, but I think I've got it under control."

"Are you sure? I'm only an hour away."

"Yes, I'm sure, but let's get together for lunch this weekend."

"Deal. Promise you'll call if you need me." Cindy's voice sounded hopeful.

"I promise." But she knew she wouldn't call her daughter or anyone else for a few days.

When the phone clicked Bethany sighed, glad she didn't need to chit-chat with anyone today, especially her daughter. She had decisions to make and plenty to do, but most of the chores she wanted to do by herself. Where should she hang the oval white wicker mirror? In a guest room or in one of the bathrooms that has plenty of wall space?

Her stomach growled, demanding to be fed. Bethany realized hours had gotten away from her and she hadn't eaten. She made a cup of chai vanilla tea, rustled up a tuna salad, and grabbed a box of Triscuits. "My Lord, I'm famished," she groaned.

After Bethany finished eating she sat staring into space. The heart niggled at her brain. It wouldn't go away. *I wonder if my half of the sterling friendship ring is still in there.* She jumped up, washed the dishes, and turned on the TV. She'd try anything to get her mind off the past and back to the present.

The chime of Dad's old clock told her it was bedtime. Thomas had repaired it once. He loved old clocks. Her mind seemed stuck on Thomas. Like the broken hands of the clock were stuck in time.

Physically and emotionally weary, she headed to bed. She tossed and turned for an hour with her mind whirling around the recent events of her life. *I don't know if I fell out of love with Brad, or if I ever truly loved him.* At this point it didn't matter much, what was done was done. Time to write a new chapter in her life.

The next morning Bethany awoke fuzzy headed. She ran her fingers through her thick hair and yawned. When her fingers caught in a tangle, she pulled a handful forward and examined the auburn strands. "Need to wash my hair."

She opened her eyes wider. Her new room looked brighter and more feminine with the peach bedspread and shams. It felt good to make decisions without having to please a man. When she was married she'd even had to drive the make and model car that Brad chose. No more. A yoke had been lifted off her.

The house felt cold. She reached into the closet, took a robe from a hanger and pulled it on. She always felt chilled when she was weary. Heading down the hall, she made a mental list of things she needed to do today.

"Coffee. I need coffee." She headed to the kitchen, made coffee, stood and watched it brew. The fragrance of hazelnut tickled her nose and perked her up.

She drank the hot liquid while she finished her *to-do* list on a notepad. When she looked up, bare walls stared back at her, so pictures needed to be put up. She gobbled down a piece of toast with PB&J. No time for a real breakfast.

Bethany searched the drawers for hardware to hang pictures. No luck. "Damn," she grumbled, staring at the framed art propped up against the walls. She dressed, grabbed her coat, and headed to the store.

Within thirty minutes she was walking up and down the aisle of Andy's Hardware, searching for wall hangers. When a woman bumped into her, she turned and faced Ruth Stevens pushing a small buggy.

"Oh, my gosh, Bethany Davis. Is... is it really you?" she asked. Surprise registered on her round face.

"Yes, it's me, but the name is Ward, remember?" She smiled

to cover the worry that Ruth still blamed her for ditching Thomas. "You look great! Love the red."

"Of course it's Ward. Sorry." Ruth grinned sheepishly. "You look great, too. This is a surprise. Are you in town for long?" Anticipation brightened her green eyes.

"Hope so, just bought a house over on Ivy Road." Bethany grinned.

"You... you're moving back to Oak Hill?"

"Looks that way." Bethany straightened her back, standing tall.

"Surprised, but I'll take it."

"Don't be shocked. I'm a new woman now and spreading my wings. Besides, I will be nearer Savannah for the huge Savannah Book Festival every February."

Ruth moved closer and hugged her with one arm. "I've always hoped you'd come home someday. I dreamed we'd be best friends again until we got to be old ladies, having lunch together and sitting in the park."

Bethany felt a broad smile creep across her face. "Did you? For real?"

"Oh, yes. You know your friends loved you, but who could stop a stubborn teen, hell- bent on leaving, thinking she was in love?"

"Or one crazy in lust." Bethany laughed. "Feels good to be back, even if I haven't seen any of our old friends yet."

Ruth's cell pinged with a text message, she looked down at the screen. "Oops, gotta run pick up my daughter. Give me your number and we'll get together." Ruth grabbed a pen from her purse and started scribbling, then decided to enter the number into her phone.

"912-..." Bethany rattled off her newly memorized number.

Ruth hugged her again, tighter this time. "See you soon." She smiled, turned and walked toward the checkout line.

Bethany's throat tightened. *The hug felt genuine, a good beginning*. Humming, she finished her shopping, went through the checkout line, and headed home.

~~~

Bethany pulled into her new driveway and sat a moment. The house had a charm about it. Great potential. The one story brick bungalow sat on a rise of manicured lawn with solar lights framing the curved walkway leading to front double doors. Three bedrooms allowed for an office, a guest room for Cindy, and a master bedroom. She'd have plenty of space to write once she got settled.

Two paintings hung in place within two hours, a long rectangular oil painting over the sofa and another in the dining area. The Impressionist oil in the dining room had been a wedding gift from her father. It cost more than her solid mahogany furniture. Dad had referred to it as an investment. "I might need it if I don't get my next book advance soon," she mumbled.

She stood and admired her handiwork, proud of her capabilities. Married to a man with too many hobbies, she'd learned basic skills around the house. Brad had no time for a house or his family. Why had he wanted children? He ignored them, never saw his daughter's piano recitals and never took his son to a ball game. *Too late now. His loss.* She fought to keep the resentment at bay.

Midafternoon she brewed a cup of tea and sat reading but found it hard to concentrate. Her mind drifted to the notes in the Valentine heart. Finishing the last sip of tea, she rose and walked down the hall, opened the closet door and stared at the unopened box. Half annoyed, she fisted her hands and frowned. "Okay, you've got my attention," she snapped, then she grabbed a chair, stepped up and brought the box down. She ripped the tape and opened the box. The heart peeked out of the top at her. *Do I dare open it?* A shiver crawled up her spine. No, not yet. It's too soon to face any additional emotions right now.

Her cell buzzed and brought her back to the present. "Hello."

"Mrs. Ward, this is Jean Johnson with the welcoming committee of the Women's Club. If you'll give us a time, we'd love to come by and meet you," she said in a singsong voice.

"That's so nice of you, but I'm familiar with the town. I grew
~~~

up here." She didn't want to be bothered with visitors until her wounds healed and she settled in.

"Oh, I didn't realize that. But we'd still like for you to have our basket of goodies and welcome you back home."

"How about tomorrow, midmorning?" Bethany wanted to be friendly but not get involved with too many townsfolk right away. She'd recently signed a contract for a new book and was excited about getting started.

"We'll be there. One of the ladies is making brownies, hope you have a sweet tooth."

"I can never turn down chocolate. I'll have the tea pot handy." Bethany laughed.

That afternoon she unboxed more books and culled a few to discard. Bethany busied herself arranging the bookshelves, finding the right spot for her favorite authors, and placing the older leather-bound classics at eye level for a better vantage point. A card peeked out of one, and Bethany pulled it free from the edge. It was a Valentine to her mother from her father, signed and dated on Mom's twentieth birthday. *Funny, I never knew Dad to be a romantic.* How did the card get there? Was this a book Mom had given her long ago?

Evening approached and she turned on the TV and listened to the news for an hour. *So many sad stories. Depressing.* She reached for the remote and clicked for a menu of movies. Nothing she was in the mood for at the moment. "Never mind." She clicked the off button.

Weary, she ran the garden tub full of water and dumped in bubble bath. She inhaled the decadent scent of jasmine as she lowered herself into the silky feeling of the luxurious additive. The long soak relieved her tight muscles. It had been a while since she'd pampered herself.

She pulled on pajamas and a robe, and reached for a new Lisa Wingate book. *If I could ever learn to write like this, I'd feel like a success.* Her author friends had warned her that writing was not easy. Soon she would have time for more writing workshops.

Checking the doors to make sure they were locked gave her a feeling of security in her new yet old environment. Then she prepared for bed. Sleep would not come. Memories flooded her mind. Brad had been the new boy in town, a charming firebrand. Her flesh had embraced the present with no thought of the past or future. I *never wanted to hurt Thomas, but the excitement of our relationship had worn off.* Thomas never had a chance against Brad.

An hour later, she finally dropped off to sleep.

Night winds howled, cold weather drifted down from Canada until it finally hit the Southeast, and Bethany woke up cold. She hopped out of bed, adjusted the thermostat, and jumped back under the covers until the house became warm enough for humans.

The aroma of coffee drifted down the hall. Coffee always smelled better than it tasted. She scurried to the kitchen and poured her cup half full of coffee and half milk. “Hmm, better,” she moaned and made a mental note to buy a quart of milk in the future, no need for a half gallon anymore.

Fully awake, she finished dressing just before the doorbell chimed. The ladies from the Oak Hill Women’s Club arrived. She opened the door and held out her hand. “Welcome, ladies. I’m Bethany. Please come in.” She plastered on a smile and motioned toward the living room.

“I’m Jean and this is Viola,” said the younger woman.

The older lady stared at Bethany and interrupted. “Oh, honey I know you. You went to school with my nephew, Thomas.”

Bethany’s eyes opened wider. Her insides did a half somersault. “Yes, Thomas and I were good friends.” She cleared her throat.

Oops! That slipped out. Did I sound excited? Trying to compose herself, she lowered her eyes, reached over and busily examined the basket of goodies to cover her uneasiness. “You ladies have gone to too much trouble. The basket is very beautiful.”

“It has a few things to help you out for a couple of days, so you won’t have to run to the store every hour. Moving is always chaotic.”

“These brownies look delicious. Why don’t I make some hot

tea and we can share them?"

"Hot tea would be a treat," Jean agreed and Thomas's aunt nodded.

The hour passed quickly as the ladies caught her up on a few local townspeople. Bethany stared into space as she recalled some of them from her childhood. Mr. Bob, owner of the general store, had passed on, but his wife still ruled the meat counter like a military general.

"How about our local poet laureate?" Bethany asked.

"Sadly, we lost him two years ago," Jean answered and dropped her chin a little.

"I'm so sorry to hear that, he was almost as good as Sidney Lanier." Bethany's heart melted and she thought of all the good writers Georgia had produced. She had a soft spot for local writers. *Wonder how many more we've lost?*

Jean stood. "Well, we've kept you too long. I'm sure you have plenty to do besides listen to two old ladies chatter the day away."

Bethany smiled. "Thanks for coming."

The car slowly backed out of the driveway. Bethany exhaled, closed the door and straightened the kitchen. "I wanted peace. I hope I haven't made a mistake returning to such a small town," she muttered. "Everybody knows everybody's business. By mid-afternoon everybody in town will know of my return." She sighed, holding back the anxiety.

Looking out a large back window, she envisioned the flowers she wanted to plant under the hanging moss-covered trees in the spring. The house needed a true cottage look, *Better Homes and Gardens* style. She looked at the yard again. Daddy would know exactly what she needed to plant, just like he did at her first house. He'd grown up on a farm and had a green thumb. Those were happy years before Bethany began to yearn for more independence. After the children came along, she'd been too busy to think about her own needs.

When her cell buzzed, she checked the caller ID. Ruth's name and number.

"Hey, girl. How's it going?" Ruth chirped happily.

"So-so, I guess. It'll take a while for me to feel at home, but I like the house."

"You'll be back in the saddle in no time. And the sooner you start reconnecting to the town, the better. What about lunch tomorrow?"

"Oh, I don't know. I have so much to do." She took a deep breath. "Wish I had Daddy to help me with the yard. Too bad he and Mom retired and moved to Florida."

"Don't worry about the yard. There's nothing that can't wait. I'll see you at Sadie's Diner on the Square, twelve sharp."

Reluctantly Bethany agreed. "Sure. That'll be nice. Thanks for pushing me."

Bethany awoke to a day that looked promising. The short blast of cold had moved on. Moderate weather in the winter was a blessing. She stared at the closet. *What will I wear?* It had been months since she'd gone shopping. The younger crowd wouldn't mind her dress jeans and a pretty sweater. But the older ladies in the town probably wore pants and blazers. She veered on the side of comfort and chose the jeans.

The charming diner had booths and tables facing the Square. With a good view, Bethany settled in to wait for her friend. Oak Hill had grown and improved in the past twenty years. But the charm of the town remained intact. Bethany glanced out the window at the clock tower on the other side of the Square. She recalled the night Thomas had pulled her into the shadows and kissed her for the first time.

She blinked and saw Ruth approaching the eatery, dressed to impress. She wore a pencil skirt, a silk blouse and a cashmere sports jacket. She opened the door, waved and strolled toward the table.

"You look stunning, as usual," Bethany greeted her with a smile.

"Thanks, I have an afternoon appointment, business attire, you know."

They ordered and chatted like two bees buzzing. The old

friends reconnected so easily.

"Do you have time for dessert?" Bethany asked, nodding toward Big Scoops Ice Cream Parlor.

"Not today. But next time." Ruth shrugged.

"You're on!" They both laughed, knowing how much they loved sweets.

Ruth reached into her purse, fished out her keys and looked up. "I need a favor, if you're up for it. Keystone College over near Savannah is hosting a Valentine's Day dance, and I'm in charge of personnel for the night. I need another volunteer to chaperone and someone to talk to for a couple of hours." She fingered the keys, waiting for an answer.

"Whoa, hold on. Don't know if I'm ready for that much involvement yet." Bethany felt a clutch in her stomach and frowned.

"Please, pretty please. It'll be fun. I promise." Ruth put on her big-eyed, pouting-lips face.

"Okay. As usual, it's easier to join you than to argue with you." Resigned, she exhaled and rolled her eyes, imagining Ruth as a bulldozer just like she'd always been.

Ruth's grin spread across her face until brighter-than-bright teeth sparkled like a cosmetic dental ad. Forty-one looked good on her.

They finished their lunch and promised to call each other soon. Ruth dashed away for her business appointment, while Bethany ambled by the shoe store. *Window shopping had been a hobby for Thomas and me back in the day*. "Stop it!" She chided herself.

The wind had picked up. The rustle of the large brown oak leaves waiting to be pushed off by new ones sang to her. Bethany pulled her sweater tighter and hugged her arms around her waist. Time to go home and get her nest the way she wanted it.

She rushed inside, closed the door and hung her jacket on the coat rack. Shivering, she grabbed a throw and settled in a comfy chair. Lunch with Ruth had brought her thoughts back to their days as best friends in school. Bethany had never needed a lot of friends, because she had Ruth and Thomas. He walked her to class and walked her home every afternoon. Somehow he still found time to write her love notes each day.

Those notes teased, "Come read me, again." She heard them all the way down the hall. She clenched her fists, stomped toward the closet, stood and stared. Admitting she'd lost the battle, she lifted the box with the Valentine heart from the shelf and set it on her bed. "Okay, okay, but I'll only read one note," she promised herself.

Tentatively, Bethany touched the spray of embossed roses on the top of the heart, letting her fingers linger there. Her insides quivered. Thomas had spent half his weekly check from his part-time job. Good chocolates were expensive. She recalled the proud expression on his face as he handed her the gift.

"Hope you like it," he'd said, standing a little taller.

"You make me feel like a princess. Candy and a movie." She had blushed.

On the way home from the movies they'd stopped under a large tree hanging over the sidewalk. The dripping moss blocked the street light. Thomas took her in his arms and slowly kissed her. When she'd trembled, he lifted her chin and kissed her again. She hadn't wanted him to stop and felt disappointed when he had released her and they resumed their walk home.

The rumble of the furnace turning on brought Bethany back to the present. She looked down at her trembling hands. She opened the treasured heart and lifted a note from the bundle. As she unfolded the note and stared at Thomas's handwriting, her heart thrummed like a tennis racket with new strings.

Dimples, you make my world sparkle with your glow. I love you with all my heart.—T

Tears welled up in her eyes and flooded over the rims like a dam had burst. She sobbed uncontrollably, shaking like a tender leaf in a windstorm. Moments passed before she regained her composure.

After several tries, Bethany managed to fold the note. She

replaced it in the heart and returned the box to the shelf in the closet. "Well, I won't do that again, any time soon," she murmured.

The rest of the day Bethany worked nonstop. No job was too large or too small for her to tackle. She was determined to keep busy. When she fell into bed that night she passed out from exhaustion.

~~~

Ruth called bright and early Saturday to remind her of the Valentine dance that night.

"What have I gotten myself into?" she asked, still half asleep.

"Oh, hush. Put on your best dress and you'll be fine."

"Yes, mommie dearest." Her sarcasm rang false this early in the morning.

"As I recall, conservative classic was your cup of tea anyway."

"Check," Bethany answered.

Bethany took two outfits from the closet. She held one up to herself and looked in the mirror. *Ah, I'll wear the navy, below-the-knee, number.*

After she showered she started to pull on the dress. It seemed a little snug for dancing—just in case someone asked her. Making a frowny face in the mirror, she replaced the navy one and selected a slinky purple that ended above the knees.

When Bethany arrived at the dance hours later, she almost laughed out loud. The kids were dressed in a potpourri fashion, from dress jeans to formal gowns. Several girls had purple, pink or blond streaks in their hair. The guys sported every haircut known to man—crew cuts, moussed, spiked twigs, long wavy locks and braids. Unbelievable.

Spotting Ruth across the decorated gym, Bethany waved and made her way through the crowd. She recalled her first dance. She had worn a flowered chiffon gown handed down from her sister. Thomas had borrowed a sports jacket from a friend. They'd looked better than they danced. He stepped on her toes twice. Her fault. She had absolutely no rhythm.
~~~

"You look great." Ruth stared at her, surprise reflecting in those big eyes.

"I tried, only took me an hour or so." They both laughed.

"I know what you mean. Every year it takes longer to paint my face on right."

They mingled a while as Ruth introduced her to a few parents and faculty members. Then they walked over to the refreshment table, poured themselves cups of punch and found two chairs.

"How's the cottage coming along?"

"Slowly but surely," Bethany answered. "I have too much stuff. Should have thrown half of it away, but I'm too sentimental."

"We're all hoarders by nature. Can't take it with us, but we keep on gathering stuff like we're going to last forever."

"I think you're right." They both laughed again. Bethany felt so comfortable with Ruth, as if she'd never gone away. Like true friends, they caught up on old times in a heartbeat. She'd been foolish to stay away so long and deprive herself of the warmth of friends. Deep down in her soul, Bethany knew she had feared the return to her hometown.

Two young men, one with curly red hair and one with a shaved head, came by and spoke to Ruth. "Need any help, Mrs. Brown?"

"I think we're okay for now. But I'd like for you to meet my best friend, Bethany Ward."

"Glad to know you," they said, one after the other.

"Bethany, meet Sam and Dam."

"Did you say Dam?" Bethany blinked in disbelief.

"Yeah, our mom named Sam before he was born. She wasn't expecting twins. When I popped out, my dad yelled, "Damn!"

"Officially they are Samson and Damon," Ruth explained.

"But everyone calls us Sam and Dam." The twins chuckled. They shook Bethany's hand and then sauntered back toward the crowd.

A parent chaperone came by and asked Ruth to dance. Watching her friend glide across the floor brought tears to

Bethany's eyes, but she fought to keep them from spilling over. *Ruth is still so beautiful, time has been good to her.*

A faculty member came over and introduced herself to Bethany. "I moved to Oak Hill four years ago and can't imagine living anywhere else. I hope you'll like our town."

"I'm sure I will, once I get settled," she answered, not wanting to explain to a stranger that she'd lived here before.

Ruth returned, panting. "I'm out of practice and out of breath." She smiled and thanked her dance partner.

"My pleasure." He bowed and walked away.

"Just like Ms. Susan's dance class!" Ruth said and they giggled together.

"This is delightful. I'm glad I came." The evening filled Bethany with nostalgia. *I might fall in love with this area of coastal Georgia again—being with old friends and living in Oak Hill.*

Across the room a tall figure entered the decorated gym. The familiar gait made Bethany's heart race. She didn't want to stare, but she knew the man. She turned to Ruth. "Is that Thomas Boyd?" she asked, squinting.

"Yes, it's Thomas," Ruth answered without meeting her eyes.

"Why didn't you tell me? Warn me, say something?"

Ruth shrugged. "I didn't want to upset you."

"Why would I be upset? Thomas and I loved each other once and ended as friends."

"Friends? Are you kidding? He was devastated when you married and moved away." She huffed and crossed her arms.

"I think you're exaggerating, Ruth."

"How would you know? You've been gone for over twenty years," she snapped, with color rising from her neck toward her face.

"Sorry. My life took a different path. Sadly, the road had a lot of potholes and puddles—better known as obstacles."

"But you never looked back!" Ruth spat out the accusatory words.

Bethany winced. "I came home occasionally," she argued, trying to defend her choice.

"Oh, yes, you dashed in for a holiday and left town before anyone could see you."

"Do we need to have this conversation tonight and ruin a lovely evening?" Bethany asked.

Ruth took a deep breath and replied calmly, "Of course not."

"I'm sorry I hurt so many friends. Truly I am." Bethany rolled her shoulders to loosen the muscles tightened like a boa constrictor ready to crush its prey.

"And I'm sorry I overreacted. I'm thrilled to have you back again." Ruth smiled and wrinkled her nose in the old affectionate manner.

"And I'm happy to be back." She returned the sign of forgiveness, reached over and patted Ruth's hand.

Thomas Boyd mingled through the crowd and approached them. His hair had grayed slightly, salt and pepper at the temples, but his blue eyes sparkled like always. He stared at Bethany for a long time but didn't speak.

"Is... is it really you?" he stammered, as though he couldn't believe it. He wiped the surprised look off his face and recovered. "It is you!"

Bethany squirmed but managed to speak, despite a lump in her throat the size of a golf ball. "Hi, Thomas. Good to see you."

"Tom is a Psychology professor here at Keystone." Ruth broke the tension.

"Congratulations. I've always believed in you Georgia Tech grads," Bethany said remembering when he left for college. "But I thought you'd become an engineer. You were so good at math."

"I still love math, but I believe my true calling is Psychology," he said.

"I can see how you'd be well suited at both ends of the spectrum." She nodded.

Thomas cleared his throat. "What brings you to town, Dimples?" His eyes never left hers, as if he were searching her soul. Those eyes held a lifetime of mystery and intrigue.

"Bought a cottage. Going to write."

A slow smile spread across Thomas's face. He sighed. "You've come home," he whispered. "You owe me a dance." His voice held all the charm she remembered but with more confidence.

It felt like there was no one else in the room. He reached out, took Bethany's hand and led her onto the dance floor as the band played one of their favorite songs. She was back in Thomas's arms, enveloped in his warmth, gliding across the room. Their bodies fit together like peanuts in a shell. Both had learned to dance over the years.

Neither of them spoke, words unnecessary. Each lost in the moment. The intoxicating music oozed through her veins like liquid fire. She recognized the fragrance of Old Spice. He'd worn that scent over twenty years ago. When the song ended she slightly pulled away and faced him. His jaw tensed as if he was holding himself back. A reality check for both of them. *We don't need to assume anything too soon.*

"Thanks for the dance," he said firmly and smiled his Thomas smile.

"Thanks for the memories," she added with a wistful, half smile.

They returned to Ruth, said their goodbyes and he walked away.

Bethany knew Ruth tried to lighten the mood when she mouthed, "The divorcee and the widower. Stay tuned for coming attractions."

"Did you say widower?"

"Yes, he lost his wife two years ago. Cancer."

"How sad for him. I'm having mixed feelings right now. What can I say?"

"After watching you on the dance floor I don't think you need to say anything." Ruth tilted her head, rolled her eyes and smiled.

"Let's get out of here. We have a date to go shoe shopping tomorrow. I need a break from housework."

As soon as Bethany got inside the house she closed and locked the door. She headed straight to the closet. "Hello, friend," she whispered to the Valentine heart. She retrieved a note and began reading.

Dimples, you are my reason for living and I'll love you forever... —T

"Oh my gosh. I think I dropped the ball on this one. No, I let a good man get away." She hugged the note to her breast and sighed before she returned it to the box. Thomas wouldn't have left her lonely on the weekends as Brad had, to pursue his hobbies.

The following day she and Ruth stood outside the shoe store window, admiring spike heels and sexy sandals. They loved shoes.

"I'd kill myself if I tried to wear those six inch beauties," Bethany said.

"We should go to the outlet mall, to Shoes-A-Million. It's only thirty minutes away, and they have a fantastic selection. You're too young to dress matronly, my dear." Ruth flipped her hair, pulling a Hollywood pose.

"Comfortable doesn't have to be plain." Bethany winced as the word "plain" rolled off her tongue.

"Damn right. You're a free spirit on the market again. How about double dating with Jim and me next Saturday night?"

"Double dating?" Bethany snorted. She hadn't heard that expression in more years than she'd like to remember. "With whom would you suggest?" She struck a pinup-like pose.

"Morning, ladies." A familiar voice startled her.

"Well, speak of the devil and he appears," Ruth blurted out and chuckled.

"You were discussing me?" Thomas asked.

"Not really. It's just that Ruth doesn't know how to be subtle, she's as transparent as a crystal ball."

"Let me in on the secret, ladies."

"I asked Bethany to double date with Jim and me this

weekend, but she laughed in my face."

"If you're looking for a volunteer, I'm your man." He grinned.

Bethany's spine tingled and she blushed. She couldn't look at him for a moment but finally managed a smile.

"Ruth gave me your number. I'll be in touch." He started walking away but turned and added, "I like the black patent ones on the right."

Bethany turned to Ruth. "Now look what you've gotten me into."

"Don't pretend you're not pleased." A mischievous grin swept across her lips.

"Let's look at shoes." Bethany grabbed Ruth's arm and started tugging her inside the store.

"Okay. Ask them to bring out the black patent ones first." Ruth chuckled.

"Now you're being silly and jumping to conclusions."

"Am I? We'll see."

They went by another shop and browsed while time slipped away.

When Bethany got home her feet ached from standing and walking. She slipped into something casual, poured a glass of Moscato and opened the Valentine heart. She savored the wine and the next note.

Dimples, you are my soul mate. No matter where you are, the wind that brushes your face will touch me and I will feel you.—T

When Thomas called her the next day, they did a lot of catching up. A year after his wife died, he had briefly dated a woman he called Charlene. It hadn't worked out.

"I'm sorry to hear about your wife. It probably took you a long time to recover from the loss. Maybe that's why the Charlene person didn't work out. You weren't ready yet."

"It could have been a factor, but Charlene and I were just never suited for each other," he said with no emotion.

Bethany rubbed the back of her neck, needing to change the subject. "My daughter graduated from Georgia State last year and works one hour from here. That's one of the reasons for my return to Oak Hill. She's been a great source of strength during the divorce. I honestly don't know what I would've done without her."

"You're blessed. My wife and I never had children. She couldn't, and it wasn't important to me," he told Bethany without a trace of sadness in his voice.

"Well, my son is in the military and stationed in Germany. He may stay in Europe and never come home. Still resents his father."

"Guys often resent their dads. I wouldn't worry about it."

"Not a lot I can do about it at this point. I should have left years ago. We all would have been better off. Thanks for your support, Thomas."

"Everyone calls me Tom." He cleared his throat. "See you about seven tomorrow night?"

"Sounds grand, Tom." Butterflies took wing inside her. *I won't get much sleep tonight.*

The next evening, waiting for Tom to arrive, Bethany fiddled with her hair and changed her jewelry three times. This was a time of yin and yang. The next minute she scolded herself for even thinking about a relationship this soon after her divorce.

The minute Tom walked into the house and grinned, she felt like a teen again. He held her coat and lightly squeezed her arms. A familiar comfort raced through the fabric into her pores and mellowed her insides.

All the way to the restaurant she and Tom chatted like the old friends they were, as though she hadn't left him for another man. Bethany smiled as Tom held the restaurant door open, and she saw Ruth and Jim scanning their menus.

"Hi, guys, good to see you." Jim stood while Tom held Bethany's chair.

"We're starving," Ruth announced.

"I've been good all day, so I could have dessert." Bethany

looked at Tom.

He laughed. "Some things never change."

Bethany leaned toward Ruth. "Love your heart pendant."

"Jim gave it to me after the Valentine dance. It's a Jane Seymour design."

Time stood still for the foursome, friends together again. But the hours on the clock flew by and they promised to get together again soon.

Bethany and Tom held hands as they waved goodbye to their buds. They still had so much in common. He was her best friend.

Overhead the full moon shone, occasionally softened by wisps of clouds. The mild weather and the twinkling street lights made Bethany wish they could walk home like in the old days, but Tom had driven his car. He parked in her driveway, escorted her to the door, kissed her softly and said good night.

He turned and waved. "Thanks for making my day complete." He didn't drive away until she went inside and closed the door.

Leaning against the door, she sighed. *Okay, he's affectionate, but I'm not young anymore. Does he find me sexy?* Bethany felt puzzled and drained. She pulled her gown on and read for half an hour before she gave in and fell asleep. Handsome eighteen-year-old Thomas invaded her dreams, and she was young again.

The next morning Bethany made a major decision. She decided to see how Tom felt about her after all these years. *Do I dare make the first move?*

The phone rang. Thomas's number. She grinned. "Well, good morning."

"Good morning, Sunshine," he boomed.

"You're up bright and early."

"Had to call and tell you how much I enjoyed last night. I feel more alive today than I have in months."

"Me, too. A lot like old times." Her pulse raced like a teenager's.

"Mind if I come by for coffee?" he asked.

"I'd like that." Her breathing became irregular.

"I'll pick up croissants, still your favorite?"

"You devil, you remembered," she teased, almost giddy.

In five minutes she had done a complete makeover. No woman ever had faster feet or hands making herself look beautiful. By the time Tom arrived she looked refreshed and ready to take on the world.

She opened the door. He entered, leaned over and kissed her. She ran her tongue along his top lip. He responded, holding her in his arms, but he went no farther.

Clearing her throat, Bethany took the bag from one hand and held his other hand, leading him into the kitchen.

"Coffee's hot," she announced.

"Along with other things." He laughed and looked at her for a long time. "It can't be this easy."

"My thoughts exactly," she responded.

A long silence. They looked at each other, smiled and started laughing so hard she almost peed her panties.

When he left Bethany danced from one room to the next. A fairy had conjured up this situation. It couldn't be real. *I must call Cindy, and tell her I'm dating an old childhood friend. She might freak out thinking about her forty-ish mom dating again.*

Tonight she had a date with an old friend waiting in her bedroom closet. This had become her new ritual, perhaps an obsession. Thomas's words had the power to inspire her and draw her closer to him. One note each night to mull over her feelings then and now.

Dimples, the joy I find in you is nothing short of bliss.–T

Every spare moment found them together for the next week. Each day he briefly dropped by for coffee, lunch, or whatever his schedule allowed. When he departed she busied herself with mundane chores around the house. Her anticipation of the evening with Tom crept into her thoughts throughout the day. The nights belonged to sessions with the Valentine heart.

Dawn broke and Bethany sprang out of bed, showered and waited. The phone did not ring. She looked at the clock a hundred times. Midday came and no call. Something was wrong. *Should I call Tom?* "No" the voice inside answered. He doesn't owe me. She decided to wait.

At three o'clock the phone rang.

"Hello, stranger." She tried to sound pleasant.

"Hello, yourself." His smooth voice penetrated her heart.

"What's up?"

"Trouble. You remember Charlene, the girl I mentioned dating last year?"

"Yeah, I remember." Her throat tightened.

"Well, she's in Oak Hill, had some bad luck, needs my help." He ran the words together.

"Slow down. Take a deep breath." She tried to remain calm.

"Easy for you to say. I don't know how long this will take."

Bethany fidgeted. Imaginary worms crawled all over her. She couldn't breathe.

"Are you still there?" he asked.

"Yes, I'm still here," she whispered.

"I'll get back to you when I can," he promised.

"Take all the time you need. I'm not going anywhere." Her happy mood disappeared as fast as ice cubes on a sidewalk in July. Anger and resentment entered her happy place.

"Love you," he said and hung up before she could reply.

She slammed the phone down on the table, took a deep breath and started banging her fists on the table. He was a free agent, but jealousy crawled over her.

The next day Bethany called Ruth and invited her to lunch. She needed to get out of the house and talk to someone. They met at a café out toward Tybee Island. The girls lost no time before the subject of Tom came up.

"Once you hooked up with Tom, I wondered when I'd see you," Ruth said.

"We've been pretty busy catching up and getting to know each other again."

"So, tell all, tell all. Is he as wonderful as ever? How many times have you been out?" Ruth squirmed, anticipating some juicy gossip.

"Slow down, girl. Yes, he's more than thoughtful. Good for my ego. We've seen each other every day for a week, whenever he's had time to get away."

"Oh, my gosh! You're in love again." Ruth threw her hands in the air. "I knew it, I knew it."

"Hold on a minute. It's been a fabulous week, but an old girlfriend just got back in town."

"Who? What old girlfriend?" Ruth's forehead wrinkled.

"I have no idea. Someone named Charlene. He dated her a year ago, but it didn't work out."

"Hell no, Charlene didn't work out. She was a two-timing gold digger with raging hormones."

"I only know they went their separate ways." Bethany clinched her teeth.

"When she found out Tom had no intentions of remarrying and spending all his money on her, she left town with some jailbait," Ruth spat out the words in her usual caustic manner.

"Tom will deal with it in his own way." Bethany half smiled, but the tension inside was like a tug-of-war between monster trucks.

"No, he won't. He's too tender-hearted for his own good. People take advantage. Makes me so mad I could spit!"

"Listen to yourself, Ruth. You're overreacting again."

"I don't think so. Tom's like a brother to me." She sputtered and stared at Bethany.

"That explains why you jumped down my throat about my leaving him years ago. Looking at it from your perspective, I acted like a real bitch."

"Pretty much sums it up." Ruth shrugged and laughed.

"Tom's a big boy. He can take care of himself." Sounded good as she said it, but Bethany wasn't completely convinced by her own words.

The girls said their goodbyes, promising to pass on any news of Tom's situation.

When Bethany got home she found a comfy chair to fold up in, physically and mentally. She did not dress or leave the house for two days. The phone did not ring. She felt isolated from the world as she sat at her computer and tried to write. Nothing came. Writer's block.

Tension had the muscles between her shoulder blades in knots. She aimlessly wandered around the house. Nothing helped. The blue funk engulfed her.

Finally the phone rang. "Just checking in. You okay?" Tom's voice covered her like a medicinal balm.

"I guess," she lied. "How's it going with you?" Bethany struggled to sound cheerful.

"Charlene's still a pain, but she needs me right now."

"I'm sure it'll work out," she lied again and squirmed. She didn't dare ask the question on her mind.

"I'll call you tomorrow. Love you." He hung up.

Not terribly reassuring under these circumstances. Bethany laughed until she cried. The tears became an unending flood.

Looking in the mirror at red swollen eyes, she decided to snap out of it. *What the heck am I doing? Tom has made me no promises.* But she reached for his new note, the one he had handed her last week. The first note he'd written since her return home.

Dimples, I'm so thankful for the road that brought you back to Oak Hill and the bridge that returned your heart to mine. –T

She realized the truth of the note. Her heart had traveled back to Tom. She had truly fallen in love with him. She had loved him when they were teens, now she was "in love" with him—for the first time.

Ruth called. "Any news?"

"Nothing for two days, but he called this morning."

"And?"

"Seems Charlene needs him." Her throat tightened just saying the words.

"I'll bet. That little witch is shaking her booty, trying to lure him in again."

"If that's what he wants, there's nothing I can do about it. Besides, I treated him badly before. Maybe he doesn't trust me."

"The hell you say! We'll confront that sack of garbage and put her in her place." Ruth huffed.

"Give it a rest, Ruth," she said.

"You're making a mistake, girl. I've dealt with her type before. You need to fight for your man."

"I have a headache, call me tomorrow."

The phone remained silent the following day. Bethany was relieved and sad at the same time, suspended in space and time, going nowhere. Her heart hurt, her body ached and her mind raced with a thousand unanswered questions.

Evening came, but she could not face the Valentine heart or look at another note. Perhaps the last few days had been an illusion. Weary from doing nothing, she dragged off to bed where she tossed and tumbled for hours.

Bethany dreamed that night, dreamed of time reversal and role reversal, of what might have been. She had married Thomas, and they were blissfully happy. Their skin held some sort of magic for each other. She rolled and felt his fingers glide all over her. Their desire had not abated since they'd first made love. Their passion was grounded in slow caresses rather than the hasty raw need of the first time they'd made love.

A jarring noise awakened Bethany from her dream. Still in a fog, she reached for the phone. "'Lo," she managed without opening her eyes.

"Good morning, sleepy head," the voice boomed in her ear.

"Tom? What's up?"

"I'm up and it's time for breakfast with my best girl."

"You're mighty upbeat for a guy who's been AWOL for a

week," she scolded.

"Be fair. It's only been five days," he countered.

"Sure seemed like a week to me." Her tone lightened. "How's your runaway friend?"

"Charlene left town," he assured her.

"For now, you mean. Who knows when she'll pop up again?" she said sarcastically.

"Do I note a hint of jealousy, ma'am?"

"Anger, disappointment, jealousy, whatever you want to label it."

"This is my lucky day." He laughed so loudly it pierced her ear through the phone.

"Get dressed, we're having breakfast."

Tom appeared in a sweater and dress jeans. His handsome chiseled features made Bethany shiver from sensations racing through her body. She fought the impulse to jump into his arms and never let go.

He grinned that little boy grin. "I brought the fixings for breakfast. We'll cook together."

They worked in the kitchen as if they had been cooking together for ages. A platter of bacon, eggs, cranberry-bread toast and fruit. They leisurely sipped coffee and talked.

"Well?" she asked.

"Well, what?" Thomas shrugged and frowned.

"When are you going to tell me what happened with you and Charlene?"

"There is no me and Charlene!" he retorted.

"She came running to you, didn't she?" Bethany heard the harsh tone in her voice. "So what's that all about?"

"Charlene had nowhere to turn. She's kinda like a long-stem rose with a manner full of thorns ready to draw blood at any minute. She had used up her friendship points with everyone else."

"I see." She folded her arms and leveled him with a stare.

"No, you don't see at all. Her lover had beaten her up pretty badly. She had no money and no place to go."

"So she came run..."

He held up his hand like a stop sign. "Yes, she came to the only man who had treated her decently and asked nothing in return," he spat out.

The silence was deafening. Bethany rose from her chair, walked around the table and placed her hand on Tom's shoulder. He covered her hand with his. Neither said a word.

"Let's not ever fuss." He caressed her hand and stood facing her. "Let's build a fire."

"Great idea. You get started while I clean the kitchen."

They sat cuddling on the couch in front of the fire. Moments melted away, contentment poured over her like warm chocolate sauce over ice cream.

After a while, Tom stood, went to his coat and retrieved a large envelope. He walked over to Bethany and dumped the contents into her lap.

"Oh, my gosh! These are my notes to you a hundred years ago. I can't believe you kept them."

"Believe me, I kept every one of them." He beamed with pride.

"You wrote me every day, so I only kept my favorites," she said sheepishly.

"Yeah, I know. You penned a few, I wrote a lot." He smiled and traced her cheek with his right hand.

"Wait! Wait." She got up and raced down the hall, returning with the Valentine heart. Flipping it upside down, she dumped her letters with half a friendship ring next to his notes. The notes were united at long last.

He spied the ring, lifted his keys out of his pocket and grinned. "Think I have a match for your ring."

Bethany squealed like a kid on a roller coaster. "Our rings are reunited after all these years."

They sat on the couch, taking turns reading the notes. Tom read his to her, and Bethany read hers to him. It was as if the notes told them all over again how much they meant to each other.

When they had finished reading the old letters, Tom handed Bethany a new note.

Dimples, we may never know the tender yearnings of our first love, but I never knew what it meant to be truly loved until you loved me again.–T

Tears rolled down her cheeks. Her throat closed, she couldn't speak. Joy flooded over her. *I've come home.*

Tom put his arms around her and eased her off the couch onto the rug in front of the hearth. A few of the love letters tumbled down around them. They laughed, hugged and rolled around like playful kittens creating the inspiration for their future love notes to each other.

Depression Apples

The game of life is a lot like football. You have to tackle your problems, block your fears, and score points when you get the opportunity.

~ Lewis Grizzard

ANNALEESE ROBERTS GRIPPED the steering wheel of her new white 1962 Corvette as it zoomed up the long curving driveway to the well-lit Northside Country Club near Atlanta. The chance for the life she'd always dreamed of waited inside.

Slamming on the brakes, she brought the car to an abrupt halt a few inches from the Jaguar right in front of her. She took a deep breath and turned the engine off. "I can do this," she muttered. "I can make this happen."

She grabbed her purse, opened the door, and swung her legs out, glad to see the valet took note. Even if she wasn't a member of the posh club, she made sure she looked the part.

Smiling at him, she tossed him her keys. "Thanks."

Dashing up the front steps in killer spike-heels, she nodded at the attendant who opened the door for her. The foyer screamed of money, status and power. She popped into the Ladies Room and paused in front of an ornately framed mirror to compose herself, refresh her lipstick, and fluff her long blonde hair.

Music drifted from the ballroom and she recognized *Georgia On My Mind.*

"Georgia, Georgia..." She hummed, closing her eyes and swaying as the band played. This old favorite made new again by Ray Charles two years ago always made her a little homesick.

Many years ago her grandfather sang to her grandmother while they danced together in the tiny kitchen of their house. Sweet memories of how much they'd loved each other through good times or hard times whispered from the past. She wanted a love like theirs. And they had encouraged her to follow her dreams.

Tonight she'd follow those dreams, because this might be the man who would love her the way she deserved. A new path lay open in front of her, even though she'd only met this man a brief time ago. Her heart raced like a school girl's. *I must not blow this!*

Gathering her courage, Annaleese took a deep breath and stood tall. She descended the marble stairs leading into the sunken ballroom, loving the slight hush that came over the crowd and the heads turning in her direction. She concentrated on making her body move like liquid silver, but inside her stomach tied itself into knots. *No one here knows me,* she reminded herself. *They don't know where I came from.*

Lifting her chin slightly, she hid her discomfort and surveyed the entire room with a slow, sweeping motion of her head.

The plush environment reeked of distinction as it wrapped itself around her. She studied the lush surroundings, drinking them in. The lavish ballroom furnishings of antique mahogany pieces, parquet flooring and brilliant Waterford crystal chandeliers would have looked at home in a palace. Elegant. *Seems that nothing's too good for these grand Southern gentlemen from aristocratic families and "old money."*

Several businessmen she had met extended welcoming smiles, letting her breathe a little easier. Her position as a minority in the legal profession was tenuous. Female lawyers were still quite rare in 1962. As the "new kid on the block," Annaleese had been treated graciously during her orientation on the job. A few of her new law associates were members of this Club, but most were merely invited guests as was she. One of them had told her the exclusive club did not allow single women to become members.

The women here tonight wore similar attire to hers. She felt the sensuous, black silk dress clinging to her body and knew it was the right choice for tonight's party. More importantly, she was wearing her Givenchy black stiletto heels that emphasized her height with grace. A girl had to wear the right shoes.

Scanning the room, she searched for Justin Jackson, her main objective. Looking like King Arthur, he sat with a group of friends at a round table. His wavy black hair moved as he swung around in her direction. *It should be a crime for anyone to be that handsome. He reminds me of someone.* She shrugged off the odd feeling.

Annaleese wiggled a long-fingered wave at him. He smiled and motioned her toward his table. To her delight, he rose from his chair and excused himself from his companions, hastening in her direction with an eager expression on his aristocratic, handsome face.

"Hello, Justin." Annaleese kept her voice low and sultry, knowing how it affected men, hoping it would affect Justin the same way. A mutual colleague had introduced her to the successful businessman at a corporate breakfast a few weeks earlier, and Justin had been giving her a lot of attention ever since. "Thank you for the invitation to join you tonight."

Justin took her hand and leaned in closer. "I was a little surprised by your bold entrance, my dear. One does not usually draw so much attention by simply entering this room, but then you are not just anyone." His grin widened.

Her mind triggered the hope of her dream beginning to come true. She granted him a genuine smile of joy.

"Come, I want you to meet some friends." He took her hand briefly and guided her back to the table. "Everyone, this is Annaleese Roberts, the attorney I've told you about. I'm trying to persuade her to do some legal work for our firm."

All eyes settled on her, and there was a slight hush. For a brief second, Annaleese felt the old anxiety. Then, one by one, the friends began to introduce themselves, welcoming her as if she belonged here. Justin's smile of approval reassured her.

Justin pulled out the chair beside him and settled her in it. He snapped his fingers for a server to take her order.

"Hi, it's good to be here," she addressed everyone at the table. "This is such a beautiful club, and I'm looking forward to getting to know all of you."

Everyone else seemed to be drinking wine, so she ordered a glass of chardonnay and her normal Waldorf salad with lots of the apples she loved. She sipped the wine and listened to the couples around the table talking about work and politics. Obviously they were all old friends. The conversation sparkled as they tried to outdo each other.

Struggling to quash a feeling of timidity, Annaleese forced herself to interact with the group and comment on the discussions. The man sitting next to her leaned close. "You're too darned pretty to be an attorney. How does your firm feel about women in your position?"

Jerk. Annaleese pasted a smile over the words she wanted to say. "They've been courteous and fair to me," she replied firmly. "I think they admire someone who can get the job done."

Justin swooped down before the man could say anything else and held out his hand in an elegant pose. "Shall we dance?"

Standing, she excused herself from the table and quickly moved into Justin's waiting arms. Their bodies cruised onto the dance floor in a single fluid motion, as if they had been dancing together all of their lives.

"You certainly have on your dancing shoes tonight," he said. "And by the way, I love those shoes, but how do you manage to walk in them?"

"Practice." She chuckled. "Thanks, I have a passion for shoes. When I was growing up shoes were a prized commodity."

Twenty-seven-year-old Annaleese had come a long way since the days of being the little girl who dreamed of becoming a lawyer and living in a large city. She felt like a fuzzy caterpillar evolving into a fantastic butterfly, skimming across the dance floor in the arms that possibly held her future. She closed her eyes and gave herself up to the music as memories of her youth and the Depression washed over her.

~~~

Seven-year-old Annaleese adored her big sister, her best friend, confidant and defender. They were complete opposites in coloring. Lauren had dark hair and brown eyes like their mother, while Annaleese was fair like their father. The bond between the sisters held strong, despite different personalities and tastes. Annaleese's independence bordered on defiance at times, while Lauren had a laid-back attitude of cooperation.

Two weeks before Lauren's twelfth birthday, Annaleese asked her what she'd like as a present.

"I need some new school shoes," Lauren responded with a grimace. "My old ones are too tight and hurt my feet."

"You should tell Granny Bella. She always buys us something nice for our birthdays with her widow's pension check."

"I'll do that right now." Lauren rushed down the hall with
~~~

Annaleese trailing behind.

The girls loved their grandmother's room with its rose-patterned wallpaper and sweet smell of lavender sachet. Granny had just finished wrapping a package the shape and size of a shoe box.

"Oh, Granny Bella, that looks beautiful, and I love the big pink bow," Lauren said. Her voice softened. "Is that for me?"

"Well, I wanted to get your gift wrapped before I got busy and forgot to do it. I'm getting a little forgetful. Now you two scoot out of here and don't go snooping around!" She put on a pretend frowny-face for the girls.

"Yes, ma'am." They beamed and dashed out the door.

"Just think, I'll have new shoes to wear to school and won't have to go barefoot until cold weather like the poor kids in the neighborhood," Lauren said.

Lauren mentioned new school shoes several times as two weeks dragged by. Finally the big day arrived. Lauren opened the present from Mom and Dad as though the butcher paper wrapping with drawings of flowers was priceless art. She held the skirt and blouse against her body and preened like a princess. Annaleese wondered when her mom found time to make the clothes without being seen.

"Thanks, I love the color," Lauren said appreciatively to her parents, giving them both big hugs.

Next she opened Annaleese's thoughtful token of a handkerchief with her initials. Tears began to form as she embraced her little sister. "Thanks, baby girl."

"Granny helped me embroider the initials." Annaleese stood tall and felt proud.

Then Lauren opened her grandmother's long anticipated gift. In the shoe-sized box sat a tin lunch box painted with pink and white flowers.

"I wish I could have given you a pair of new shoes, but I just didn't have enough money this year."

A look of disbelief came over Lauren's face as tears brightened her eyes. She breathed deeply, composed herself quickly and fought back the tears.

"I love the gift, Granny Bella. And thank you anyway for wanting to buy me new shoes. I understand it has been a hard year for everyone."

Lauren quietly gathered her gifts and gave each person a big hug. "Thanks again and I love you all," she said softly as she left the room.

Back in their room, Lauren cried until her chest started heaving, and she was gasping for breath. She and Annaleese both sniffled and hugged each other until exhaustion claimed them and they fell asleep.

The following morning, the girls still clung to each other. "You're very, very sad and disappointed aren't you, Lauren?" Annaleese threw a pillow across the room in disgust. "Things are not very fair, are they?"

"No, things are not always fair, but I guess shoes aren't the most important thing in the world."

"Shoes are important, 'cause you needed those shoes. We may not always get what we want, but everyone should have the things they need. You needed those shoes."

Annaleese reached for Lauren's hand, lowered her head and prayed, "Lord, someday I want to be able to buy all of the things my family needs. You understand I don't want to be rich, but I'm tired of being poor. Everybody ought to have shoes!"

~~~

Justin stepped on Annaleese's shoe, jolting her back to the present. He gave her a sheepish grin as he apologized. "I can't remember when I've been so clumsy. Perhaps I'm simply dazzled by your presence. It may take some time before I'm no longer overwhelmed by the wonder of you," he teased.

In return, she squeezed his arm and smiled. "Perhaps we should sit the next one out."

"Great idea." Justin guided her to a table by a window looking out on the lake. The moon worked its magic, revealing a breeze rippling across the water, ruffling the leaves on the dogwood trees at the edge of the lake. Annaleese could almost feel the soft
~~~

wind caress her neck.

"What a breath-taking view." She sighed, peace and contentment momentarily filling her insides.

"You really love this place, don't you?" he asked.

"Yes, it's so new and special to me. Before my grandfather died he opened a window that gave me a glimpse of a bigger world than the one into which I was born. I remember watching him whittle small animals out of wooden spools. Listening to his stories fascinated me, especially about his favorite trip to the World's Fair in New York City."

"That must have been cozy for you two," Justin commented. "My grandfather was too busy to spend a lot of time with me."

"Yes, we were best buddies."

"I envy you." Justin smiled.

"Grandpa would say, 'Oh, the buildings are so tall they nearly reached the sky. The city is very energetic, the people love to sing and dance and eat. There is no other city in the world quite like New York.' He sparked my dreams of big cities and traveling. It sounded so wonderful. I knew I wanted to go there someday."

"And you will. I'll take you." Justin reached out and touched her hand. "As a matter of fact, I have a business trip to the Big Apple in a month or so. Why don't you come with me? You can learn a little more about our firm on the trip. It will help you make a decision about joining the company."

Annaleese couldn't believe her ears. "That sounds wonderful—too good to be true." She felt an adrenaline rush and fanned her face.

"I can show you the town, and you can do some shopping."

"Oh, I'd love to go! I know you must think I'm a hayseed, a country bumpkin, because you've always been exposed to such a broad lifestyle."

"You're no hayseed, but perhaps you're right about our experiences having been quite different."

"Absolutely, you're used to this country club, big-city life, so perhaps it has lost its charm for you."

"Well, what seemed commonplace to me a few months ago

has taken on a renewed enchantment now that you're here," he admitted. "So, you'll go with me?"

"I'll think about it. Thank you for asking me."

The music tempo picked up. The band started belting out Chubby Checker's number, and everybody on the dance floor started gyrating to *The Twist*.

"Come on, let's dance," Annaleese urged Justin. "I love this song."

"Not sure how limber I am dressed like this." He laughed, rolling his eyes. "Here goes." Holding his arms out, he rolled his hips to the music. "Now it's your turn."

A few gyrations later Annaleese joined in, surprising herself at how close to the floor she could twist. The music changed to a slower dance before Annaleese had time to break a heel or throw her back out. "Probably for the best. I might have trouble in these shoes." She laughed.

Justin grabbed her hand. "Let me impress you with my fancy steps," he bragged, giving her an outward twirl and bringing her back into his arms. Then he whispered, "We were meant to dance together." Some of his mannerisms seemed so familiar to her, but this wasn't the time to think about that now. She wanted to enjoy the moment.

There was no place she'd rather be than in his arms, but she knew it was getting late. "I have a busy day tomorrow. So perhaps we should say good night for now." She hoped she had whetted his appetite.

"Yes, that's a big part of being a working girl. But don't rush off before you promise to have lunch with me next week," he pleaded, flashing her a sunbeam smile.

She chuckled. "I'd love to."

Justin escorted her to the door, asked the valet to bring her car around, and secured a date to meet for lunch on Monday. He gave her a brief hug, and she felt a familiarity she could not quite place. She hadn't entirely recovered when the valet appeared with her car. Justin pressed money into the young man's hand. Escorting her to the driver's side, Justin helped her into the low-slung car. Annaleese saw him in the rearview mirror, waving to her as she drove away. Her pulse raced to match the speed of her Corvette.

~~~

When Annaleese arrived at work on Monday, stacks of folders littered her desk. All this work had to be handled before she could think of anything else, but thoughts of lunch with Justin kept interfering with her project as noon approached.

Later strolling down Peachtree Street toward the restaurant, she still wasn't sure how she felt about rushing into this relationship with Justin. She'd rushed into a marriage when she was a teen and was divorced by the time she turned twenty. *Don't want that again.*

She arrived at the restaurant and stepped into the lobby, but he was not there. Her breath quickened, and a moment of anxiety crawled over her. Had he changed his mind? A few minutes later he appeared, sending all doubts out the window.

"Hi there." He grinned and touched her shoulder. "I hope I haven't kept you waiting."

"No, not at all. I just got here." She smiled at him. "Good to see you."

"Well, I hope you're hungry. The food's great."

"Yes, I've heard it's delicious." She would eat anything to be here with Justin.

The hostess escorted them to a table. While they waited to order he again broached the subject of the possibility of her doing legal work for his company. He scooted his chair around the table to sit closer to her while they looked over his proposal. The smell of his tangy aftershave drifted toward her, filling her senses with pleasure. His body heat drew her as he leaned closer to explain the details of the contract.

At first she was reluctant to commit to a business arrangement that could interfere with any personal future they might have together. But he kept pressing her for an answer.

"I guess I'm a little apprehensive," she admitted. "I'd rather have you for a friend than as a boss." Her body tensed waiting for his response.
~~~

"Don't worry about that, we will be friends. If the work agreement doesn't pan out, I can always hire another lawyer. Good friends can't be bought." He gently patted her hand. Again, a slightly familiar gesture.

"Okay, I accept your offer on those conditions." She sighed, relieved to have the decision behind her.

"Now that's settled, let's order." He motioned for the waiter. "Ready?"

"I'll have a Rueben and a dish of stewed cinnamon apples, please." Annaleese ordered from habit.

"Apples again? At the Club I noticed you had a Waldorf salad with walnuts and apples." Justin smiled. "Sounds pretty healthy."

"Yes, I've always liked apples, but I like other things, too. I love my family, shoes, and pithy quotes. I need respect, success, and security. There's more to me than just apples, you know." She grinned.

"I assure you, I think of much more than apples when I look at you." He chuckled.

"That's good to know. Should I take that as a compliment?" she dared ask, not wanting to sound too forward.

"Yes, indeed."

The charged atmosphere sent tingles down her spine. They chatted during lunch. When they left the restaurant Justin took her hand and leaned close. "I want to see you again. Perhaps this weekend?"

"I'd like that. I'd like that a lot," she answered softly.

The next day seemed to go by slowly. Little doubts niggled at her when Justin didn't call. Although work kept her busy, she looked forward to spending more time with him.

Relief flooded through her when he called on Wednesday morning and asked, "Is Saturday a good time for lunch and perhaps a trip to the zoo? I think you'll like it. The Atlanta Zoo is one of the oldest in the country."

"Of course, that sounds like a perfect plan for the day."

Saturday turned out to be a nice day for their outing, but

Annaleese grew famished before they finished seeing all of the exhibits.

"What do you like best?" Justin asked toward the end of their tour.

"Oh, the silver-back gorilla," she replied without hesitation. "Willie B is beautiful, big and powerful."

"He was named for the mayor." Justin filled in the info on their tour.

"Look! See how intelligent he acts. First he flirts with me and walks backward. Then he just stares right at me, like he can read my mind," Annaleese bragged.

"I wonder if he can tell I'm hungry?" Justin laughed.

"I think that makes two of us," Annaleese chimed in. "We should have had lunch earlier like we had planned."

"Well, what are we waiting for? Is the Rose Tea Room okay with you?"

After devouring a plate of vegetables, Annaleese ordered apple cobbler for dessert.

Justin turned. "Apples again?" He leaned back. "I don't know about you, but I'm stuffed."

"Yes, and I'm ready for a nap," Annaleese admitted.

"Home it is."

"Thanks for a great day." Annaleese offered a sweet smile, wishing she could invite him up to her apartment. But she knew that Mrs. Marshall down the hall would be shocked if she did.

"I'll call you tomorrow." He kissed her hand then headed down the walk. Watching his car pull out of the driveway, Annaleese licked her lips and tasted the residue of the cinnamon apples and the bittersweet memories of her childhood flooded back.

~~~

The old '32 Ford rambled into town carrying the family to pick up government food supplies. Five-year-old Annaleese had become weary and fallen asleep in the backseat while her older sister, Lauren, read. Sensing the car stop at their destination, she
~~~

awakened, yawning and stretching. When she looked out the back window her eyes opened wider.

"Look, so many people," she said. It was still early, but the parking area already looked full. People stood waiting in long lines.

Annaleese and Lauren jumped out of the car and ran to greet a neighbor.

"Hi, Mr. Davis. We came to get some food the government agents are giving away today. Did the kids come with you?"

He smiled and nodded, but Annaleese's father motioned for them to join him in the line. The townspeople seemed cheerful while they waited their turn. As the line grew shorter and they got nearer the agent, a somber quiet replaced the chatter. Annaleese noticed her father's expression change.

"Why is Daddy so sad? It makes me sad, too," she whispered to Lauren.

"He does look uncomfortable, like he's choking," Lauren responded.

Annaleese watched her father step to the window. With an apologetic smile, he raised his eyes and met the eyes of the supervisor in charge. Then he looked at the ground in shame.

"Look, buddy, you need not be embarrassed. That's why we're here. Glad to help."

Her father tipped his hat and mumbled, "Thanks, fella, you're a life saver."

They returned to the car. Daddy took Mother's hand tenderly and whispered softly, "I'm sorry I can't properly provide for you and the girls or give you what you need. I'm so sorry, so..." Then his voice broke.

She cradled his face with her hands, gazed into his eyes and replied, "It's not your fault. Other folks are here for the same reason we are. The country has been in an economic depression for almost ten years, and everybody has been adversely affected. But we're family, so we'll be okay. And, Mister, you're all I need for the rest of my life."

Annaleese hugged her parents and then her sister. "I'm glad

we came, 'cause I love these dried apples! Let's call them Depression Apples."

Everyone laughed. With grateful hearts, they loaded the car and headed for home.

~~~

The phone rang and ended her daydream. Before she could answer, the ringing stopped. "Probably a wrong number," she said to an empty room, then began her chores.

It had been three days since she'd heard from Justin, the longest three days of her life. One minute she told herself she didn't care, but the next minute she was holding her breath—waiting for the hours to pass. In the back of her mind a nagging concern awakened. Nathan, her ex-husband, had blown hot and cold on her, clingy and lovey-dovey one minute and mean as a snake in the next. She'd divorced him for it. She wouldn't take it from anyone else, either.

Even a talk with her mother hadn't helped. She'd been pleased with Annaleese's new job. But, when Annaleese had told her the name of the company, she'd acted strange and hung up almost immediately, before Annaleese could even tell her about Justin and their budding friendship.

The jangle of her phone made Annaleese jump. She blinked the cobwebs away.

"Hello, there." Justin's voice immediately calmed any concerns she had.

"Hi, yourself, stranger." She let out a long breath.

He apologized for not calling. "I made an emergency trip to Savannah to see my maternal grandmother and take care of some company business. She has been quite ill and wanted to share a few things with me just in case anything happened to her."

"I was a little worried about you, but I hope your grandmother is better."

"Yes, she's much better, thank you, but I'm so glad I went. We have always been close. And while we're talking, may I see you tomorrow? I've really missed you."
~~~

"Of course, all of my tomorrows are free at the moment." She chuckled.

"I'll keep that in mind. Is that a promise?" His voice made it sound like a pass, but she was glad to know he cared.

For the next two weeks she and Justin were inseparable when they were not working. They found little hideaways to meet for more privacy. It seemed like one of those whirlwind affairs she'd read about. The speed of their bonding took her breath away at times. But in the back her mind there was always the nagging concern over meeting his family. Would they like her?

The few times they saw someone they knew, they passed it off as work, since Annaleese had accepted a job with his company.

Annaleese didn't know why she wanted to keep their relationship such a secret. She knew that eventually she had to become more sociable with his colleagues and friends, but it was as if they were the only two in the world. She liked it that way.

Justin called and invited her out to the country club the next Saturday night for dinner. "I need to be there early, but I can send someone to pick you up," he said, with his thoughts obviously elsewhere.

"Don't bother. I have some errands to run, so I'll just meet you there."

"Great! Everyone has been asking about you. They want you to come out more often."

Bouncing from foot to foot, she did a happy dance as she hung up.

While she was getting ready Saturday afternoon, her phone rang. "Hello."

"So, I understand you and Justin are becoming quite the item." Lauren's voice was full of laughter.

Annaleese's breath froze. She'd told Lauren, of course, because she didn't keep secrets from her sister. "Where did you hear that?"

"One of the secretaries at your office told me. She said that her boyfriend knows Justin and told him. It's all over that you two were seeing each other. Why? Are you ashamed of him?"

"Of course not! But I can't believe Justin is talking about it! I haven't even met his parents."

"They'll love you, sis."

"Not if they find out about me being so poor before Justin has a chance to explain it to them. They'll think I'm a gold digger!"

"Are you ashamed of us?"

Annaleese sat down on her bed and wiped at a tear. "No. Not in the least. In fact, I'm very, very proud to be where I am. But I don't want people to gossip. About me, about my family, about Justin and me."

"Sounds like you and Justin need to have a talk then."

Annaleese fumed about it all the way out to the club. How could he? What should she do?

She swept through the front door in a flash and stood at the top of the stairs looking for him. Several people looked up. There was a brief hush when Justin noticed her and motioned her toward a secluded corner of the room.

He gave her a brief hug. "What are you doing here so soon? I thought you were coming a little later." His furrowed brow revealed his bewilderment. "Is there a problem?"

"Are you telling people about us? After we discussed the fact we needed to talk to your parents before we announced anything?" Justin pulled out a chair and motioned for her to sit. "I thought we'd agreed... I only told a few friends. It's not like we haven't been seen, Annaleese."

"Let's hope it isn't too late to keep things somewhat under wraps. We don't need any catty gossip linking us together before your parents know we're dating."

"Why does it matter?"

Annaleese placed her hand on his wrist and squeezed. Touching him made her heart beat faster, matching the tempo of the adrenaline rush. *Here stands the man who represents everything I've ever needed in life. I don't want anything to jeopardize this relationship. But he has to understand.* "We don't want to become a public item at this point. Your parents will be offended if they are the last to know."

Justin looked stunned for a moment but quickly collected himself. He leaned closer so they could speak more freely. "Please don't be angry." He squirmed. "I only confided in a few close friends."

"Well, we certainly don't want things spinning out of control." She frowned. "As far as your friends are concerned, we're just casually dating. We should probably keep them guessing for now, at least until I've had a chance to meet your parents. They may not approve of me at all, businesswise or socially."

"It doesn't matter what they think." He took her hand to calm and reassure her, his thumb circling over her smooth skin. Anna's reaction to his touch was immediate, as a warm current flowed through her body. She breathed deeply and exhaled slowly in order to keep herself grounded in the moment.

"But Justin, it's important that we don't get ahead of ourselves," she pleaded, knowing she sounded like a broken record. "We haven't known each other that long, and we're from very different worlds."

He lifted his eyebrows. "So, what's the problem? Don't you remember Romeo and Juliet?" he teased, trying to coax her into a better mood.

Her posture rigid, she shot a glare in his direction and growled. "Don't joke. Romeo and Juliet didn't live in Atlanta in the twentieth century. You've grown up in a world of privilege, and your perspective is not the same as mine."

"That's one of the things I love about you, your independent spirit. Your mindset and accomplishments are your very own. On the other hand, I'm sure my opportunities and achievements were greatly influenced by my family's name and connections. Most people are victims of their birth, for good or ill."

"Can't you see that I don't want folks to think I'm interested in you for your money?" Annaleese protested, throwing her arms and hands open in desperation.

He threw his head back and laughed a hearty laugh. "Anyone who knows me knows I'm not one to get sucker-punched. You're certainly not the first woman I've ever dated. You're simply the only one I've ever wanted to keep."

Joy flooded over her with a feeling of weightlessness. She placed her hand over her mouth, fighting back the tears. "Obviously that wasn't always the case with me. I started dating early and married quite young."

"Yes, you really did marry young. Eighteen. But you weren't married very long. Why didn't it work out?"

"We wanted different things, which I didn't realize until after we were married. Then he hit me. And I had to leave."

"I'm sorry. I'm glad you were strong enough to do so. That's just one of the reasons..."

"There you two are! Making out in the corner." One of Justin's friends slapped him on the back. "What's going on? When Annaleese first came sweeping in here we thought we were about to witness a quarrel, but now you two look mighty cozy."

Justin laughed, moving in front of Annaleese to shield her. "Tom, you people are just plain nosy. Well, knock it off. You're supposed to be my friends."

"Okay, okay." Tom held up his hands and backed away. "Didn't mean to intrude."

"When there's something concrete to tell we'll let you know. Until then don't speculate."

As the man walked away Justin hugged Annaleese tightly. "I'm sorry. I'll honor your wishes to keep our private life 'private' and try not to be so impatient."

"Thank you." She fought the desire to snuggle close to his six-foot frame as he took her hand and walked with her out onto the patio. "I feel so safe and comfortable with you, a rare feeling for me."

"You'll always be safe with me."

"Can we meet your parents soon? I want to get it over with. After all, they may not approve of me and you'll walk away."

"Don't be a silly goose, they will love you. What's not to love?" He shrugged.

Annaleese felt a lump in her throat, a familiar feeling caused by years of needing to prove herself worthy. Her past was not the rosiest scenario for a blue blood family to accept. "I just don't want there to be a problem. Please, can we do this?"

"You're probably right. Mom and Dad aren't really very big on surprises. Come to think of it, nobody in our family has a sense of humor. Okay, that's settled. It's time for you to meet my parents. I'll call them tonight and pick you up tomorrow morning around ten o'clock."

~~~

The next day Annaleese paid particular attention as she dressed to meet Justin's mother and father. She chose something nice but conservative.

"I have to make a good impression on them if I want them to like me," she told Lauren who had come to visit. "I'm sure these people want their son to date and eventually marry someone in their immediate social circle and will always see me as an outsider."

"Don't be so hard on yourself," Lauren said as she gave her a hug and placed Granny Bella's pearls around her neck. "Justin seems very fond of you. In fact, he probably even loves you already. You're excited and overwhelmed by your entire new lifestyle. Slow down. I don't think you should rush into this or any other relationship. Take your time and let all of it soak in before you begin adding anything permanent into the mix."

The doorbell rang just as she finished giving herself a last glance of approval in the mirror.

"Wish me luck," she said to Lauren as she left the apartment.

She rushed downstairs to answer the door. Justin stepped inside, swooped her up into his arms, and kissed her as he had never done before.

"You make me so happy," she exclaimed as he loosened his grip.

"That makes two of us." He grinned. "But we have an appointment with destiny on the other side of town."

He took her by the elbow and guided her out the door. "Get your pretty self in that car, woman. Times-a-wasting."

When Justin guided his Lincoln through the ancient magnolia trees lining the family driveway her stomach flipped. Maybe she
~~~

should forget this meeting. She felt as though she could soon face an inquisition. When she rubbed her stomach he laughed.

"The lions have already been fed." He patted her knee. "They'll love you."

That joke put her fears away for now.

An older gray-haired gentleman with a mouth full of white teeth greeted Annaleese and Justin at the door.

"Good morning, Bronson. Annaleese, Bronson here taught me how to tie my shoes. Don't know what we'd do without him."

"Miss. So nice to meet you." Bronson took their things and escorted them into the formal drawing room where Justin's parents waited. As they entered the drawing room, Justin walked toward his parents to embrace his mother and shake his father's hand.

"Hello, Mother. Hi, Dad. I have someone I'd like you to meet. This is my friend, Annaleese Roberts. She's doing some legal work for our company, and we're getting to know each other." He threw her a quick smile of reassurance.

Annaleese admired the way Justin finessed their relationship in front of his mom and dad.

Justin continued, "I'm showing her the high spots of Atlanta, and she's teaching me how to keep my mind on business."

"Well, that's certainly advice you can benefit from." Mr. Jackson's posture was perfect as he stood erect and looked Annaleese over, from head to toe. Then he stepped forward and extended his hand. Annaleese felt stiffness in the handshake. Was it because of a physical problem? Or because of her?

After shaking her hand, he motioned toward a middle-aged porcelain doll of a woman, perfectly clothed and coiffed. The faint hint of wrinkles did not mar her flawless ivory skin.

"This is Justin's mother, Savannah."

"Welcome, my dear." Her voice had the lushness of velvet. "Justin tells us that you're a Georgia girl from my old hometown."

"No, ma'am, I grew up in a very small area just south of there. Braeburn is a rural farm town, nowhere near the ocean. I'm afraid it's about as country as you can get, not sophisticated like Savannah."

"Now, now, I'm sure it's charming," she assured Annaleese. "Let's have something to drink, shall we? What would you like, my dear—lemonade, a mint Julep, or a pink lady?"

"Lemonade will be fine, thank you." *I hope I don't strangle on it and make a fool of myself.*

Mrs. Jackson crossed the room and pulled a long tapestry cord on the wall to summon a servant. "Daniel, please bring some lemonade and tea cakes for the ladies, and mix some martinis for the gentlemen."

They sat and made small talk while they had refreshments. First they exchanged a little family history. Annaleese explained how her grandfather had influenced her life. "My grandfather encouraged me to travel when I grew up. He carried a souvenir World's Fair medal in his pocket all his life. He left it to me, and I keep it with me all the time."

Next, they reminisced over their alma maters. Justin's father was glad she had chosen to attend Emory Law School just as he had done a generation ago.

"Emory was a dream come true for me. I'm the first person in my family to finish graduate school," Annaleese said.

"Justin was the first to break the family tradition. He went to Georgia Tech, because he wanted to be a CPA," Mr. Jackson added. "And that's worked out well for our company."

When the conversation began to lag they discussed current events. Everyone seemed overly polite. Tension and discomfort filled the room like fog in the early morning.

Justin rose and expressed his regrets at having to leave so soon.

"We hate to rush off, but I'm playing tennis with my partner this afternoon and we're meeting some friends for dinner at the club this evening."

"Yes, we're picking up my sister, Lauren," Annaleese added. "Justin invited her to come along with us tonight, and she's so anxious to meet him."

"How nice," Mrs. Jackson said. "Lauren is such a beautiful name."

"Yes, I think so, too. My mother is quite particular about names. She never liked hers."

They stepped to the door. Annaleese offered his mother a brief hug and shook his father's hand. "Thank you for having me, and I hope to see you again."

"It was our pleasure," both parents said. Annaleese had her doubts.

As soon as they were in the car Justin inquired, "Well, what do you think? They're not very warm to outsiders, I'm afraid. Oh, they are super polite but always guarded." He reached over and placed his hand on her knee to reassure her. In return, she put her hand over his and left it there to absorb his encouragement.

"You're right, they were overly hospitable. Obviously they're on guard against me until they know more about me. But I think it went well. Thank you for taking me."

He dropped her off at the apartment, waved and drove away, promising to be back in a couple of hours to take her and Lauren to dinner.

Lauren wanted to know everything about the house, the help, and especially about his mother and father. "Was the father tall and good-looking like Justin? Was the mother beautiful? Were they warm and pleasant or rigid snobs?"

"Whoa, lady, slow down! Yes, Justin's father was handsome, and the mother was absolutely exquisite. She looks like a porcelain doll. Yet there is a sadness about her."

"I wonder what that's all about. If I had her life I certainly don't think I'd be sad."

The girls had a leisurely afternoon before they dressed for the club. Annaleese wore ice blue, which complimented her blonde hair and navy-blue eyes. Lauren wore a burgundy dress that brought out her dark hair and dark eyes.

"Both of you look ravishing," Justin remarked when he arrived. "All of my friends will envy me. Most men are lucky to have one beautiful woman. I have two."

They all laughed, and then Annaleese said, “You’re not bad yourself.” His hair had a special sheen, and he wore a sharp charcoal Brooks Brothers suit.

Justin held the car door for Annaleese and then Lauren. They chatted all the way to the dance.

When they arrived for the gathering everyone welcomed them. Annaleese felt a little more at ease each time she encountered these new friends.

Justin took turns dancing with Annaleese and Lauren. Of course he danced more with the “baby” than her older sister. Once when they were drifting across the floor he told her, “Lauren is an excellent dancer. Where did she learn so much?”

“She volunteered with my mother to entertain the service men at the USO the last year of World War II. Several of the young men were crazy about her, but she was too young to date them. One Saturday while dancing with a sailor, she discovered he was our third cousin. He asked Mother and Lauren to show him around town, and they grew very fond of each other. Lauren never talked about him much, because she felt our parents would disapprove of her puppy love for him.”

“That’s a little sad,” Justin said.

“He planned a career in the military. Soon after that Lauren told us he had shipped out. We heard later that his ship was lost at sea.”

“That’s even sadder.” Justin sighed.

“Sometimes I think that’s why she has never married. She won’t talk about it.”

“That makes sense. I wondered why a pretty girl like her was still single,” Justin said.

For a moment Annaleese felt a little jealous of his interest in Lauren. They seemed to really connect in a special way. But she was having such a good time, why spoil it?

Besides it wasn’t the first time she’d had these thoughts where Lauren was concerned. It was even tougher having a pretty, older sister when she was a teenager. A lot of the boys she dated were intrigued with Lauren’s shapely figure.

There was no place Annaleese would rather be right now than in Justin's arms as they enjoyed a fairy-tale evening together. When the music slowed they waltzed.

He motioned her toward a table and suggested, "How about some punch?"

"Sounds good to me," she said as he walked toward the refreshment center.

They weren't neglecting Lauren, because several guys had asked her to dance. To be honest, Annaleese was a little relieved to have Justin all to herself for a while.

She wondered why she felt a gnawing discomfort when she watched Lauren and Justin together. They seemed so at ease with each other. It was as if they had known each other all of their lives. Meanwhile Annaleese was working at really getting to know Justin.

She wanted to know everything about him. *He must have been a handsome child.* She watched Justin return with refreshments, loving his slight swagger.

"Perhaps I will ask your mother to tell me all about you as you were growing up, when I see her the next time." She smiled when he handed her a glass of punch.

"I'm afraid I am not a very interesting subject. Won a few trophies like most kids."

"Let me be the judge of that."

"Speaking of Mom, she wants to get together with you soon."

"Sounds good to me." She smiled to hide her fear of being interrogated by his mother.

The evening had unfolded into a delightful experience for Annaleese, since she was becoming more at ease in this setting. Deep down, she almost looked forward to seeing Justin's mother again. Mr. Jackson was still a different story. It would take a while to get to know him... if ever.

Lauren and her new friend finished their dance and headed toward their table. "Sis, Justin, this is William." He nodded and said, "Hi. Nice to meet you."

"I don't mean to be a party pooper," Lauren said, "but I have a busy day tomorrow and need to say goodnight. Don't let me ruin your evening. I can see myself home."

Annaleese felt a sudden twang of disappointment but realized that it was getting late. "You're right, we really should go, too."

Lauren turned to the nice-looking man standing next to her. "Good night, William. Thank you for the dance and a lovely evening." Lauren held out her hand to shake, but William took her hand and kissed the back of it.

"I'll call you tomorrow," he said. "Until next time, my lady." He teasingly gestured with his hands and smiled.

Then he turned toward Justin. They shook hands. "Good to see you, Will," Justin said. "I'm glad we ran into you and hope to see you again."

On the way home they passed a military recruiting poster and the two sisters began reminiscing about their childhood during World War II.

"Remember when we were listening to the radio one Sunday and the announcer interrupted the program to tell everyone that the Japanese had bombed Pearl Harbor?" Annaleese asked. "I had no idea what that meant."

"That's why President Roosevelt declared war on Japan the following day," Lauren added.

"Soon people started buying Victory Bonds to help pay for the war." Justin joined the conversation. He loved history, too.

"Yes, we bought stamps each week at school and put them in a book to be converted into a war bond when the book was complete," Annaleese said.

Justin snapped his fingers, grinned and changed the subject. "Back to the present, ladies. What are you two doing next week? Perhaps we could take in a movie?"

Annaleese knew why Lauren hesitated to answer. It wasn't her call. The silence was thick enough to cut with a knife. Annaleese felt a smothering darkness close in on her. She failed to understand this togetherness pattern that Justin had fallen into with Lauren. Why did he feel the need to include her in a movie date? Did he think she was lonely or would be upset? Was he afraid he'd hurt her feelings? *After all, I am the one he's dating.*

"We'll let you know." Annaleese forced a smile.

"And thanks again for a lovely evening." Lauren got out of the car and dashed inside the house, leaving Annaleese and Justin to themselves.

He reached across and touched her face. "Are you okay? You seem unusually quiet." Then he leaned over and kissed her softly on the lips before she had a chance to answer. Just as quickly as the somber mood had come, it disappeared. She let out a sigh of contentment.

The next morning Mrs. Jackson called and invited Annaleese to lunch one day that week. Terror struck Annaleese the moment she got off the phone. What could this mean? Would Mrs. Jackson ask her to get out of Justin's life? The restless nights didn't help.

Wednesday rolled around and she found herself standing at the Jackson's front door. When she rang the bell Bronson informed her that Madam was waiting on the veranda.

"Welcome, my dear." Mrs. Jackson rose from her chair and shook Annaleese's hand. "I thought we'd enjoy eating and talking out here."

The gardens looked as impeccable as Justin's mother. "Oh, it's lovely, Mrs. Jackson." Annaleese tried to remain calm while squirming inside.

"Please call me Savannah. I know it's your lunch hour, so I will try to use our time wisely."

The food arrived and included Waldorf salad with lots of apples and nuts. "A little bird told me that you were fond of apples," Savannah Jackson said.

"It looks delicious." Annaleese smiled and explained, "Dried apples were available during the Depression and my mom soaked them for a dozen dishes—apple pie, apple sauce, apple cobbler, stewed apples, apple jelly, etc."

"You remember those days with fondness, don't you?" Savannah asked.

"Yes, those were hard times, but we survived with a loving

family."

While they ate Savannah carried the conversation. "I wanted to welcome you into our home, our life, and get to know you. Justin seems quite smitten with you, and I want him to be happy."

"What about Mr. Jackson?" Annaleese asked.

"Justin's father is not a warm fuzzy person, but he loves his son. Also, we've seen what tragedy can occur when a rich family tries to bar a poor family from their life. Mr. Jackson lost his brother in such a debacle. We never want to see that happen again."

A sixth sense told Annaleese that Savannah didn't like to be asked uncomfortable questions. She refrained from blurting out everything her curiosity begged to ask, to know.

Then she glanced at the clock. "I'm sorry I must run, but this was such a lovely gesture on your part." She smiled and pushed away from the table.

Savannah stood while Annaleese grabbed her bag. "I hope you will come again. It gets lonely around here sometimes."

"Thank you. I'd love to visit."

The ladies shared a quick hug, and the luncheon ended.

On the way back to the office Annaleese kept repeating the noontime encounter, the conversation and the family history in her head. *This has been an odd week.*

She took a quick minute to call home before she settled in to finish the day's work. But it was another strange phone call, especially when she told her mom she'd been to see Justin's mother.

"What's she like? Was she nice to you?"

"Oh, yes. We had a lovely talk. I think she likes me."

There was a long pause. Finally, Annaleese said, "Mom? Are you all right?"

"I'm fine. Can I call you back later?"

When Annaleese hung up, she shook her head. She needed to drop by and see what was wrong, but she couldn't today. Maybe

Lauren would have some insight.

But Lauren was even more involved than Annaleese. That evening Will called Lauren again. He hadn't missed a day since the dance. When she got off the phone she drowned Annaleese with the details of the conversation and all their plans for the remainder of week. "Will is just the nicest man I've ever met," Lauren gushed. "I think I've been looking for him all of my life. We have planned almost every hour of the coming weeks."

Annaleese had never seen Lauren so eager to become involved with anyone, especially a man. She adored her big sister and was thrilled she'd found someone she liked. It has been a long time coming. *I pray it's the real thing. She deserves to be happy.*

~~~

When the weekend rolled around Annaleese decided to run over and visit her mother. Who better to share the new developments in her life?

After an hour drive and a hug from her mother, they settled down to have a cup of coffee. Annaleese shared how her feelings for Justin had grown and that her visit with his mother had been pleasant.

"Mom, I think I'm falling in love with him. He is everything I've ever wanted. He reminds me of someone I know, his dark hair and mannerisms."

"I'm sure he looks like his father."

"Yes, but that's not it." Annaleese squirmed. Then she looked at her mother. "It sounds crazy, but Justin's mannerisms are a lot like Lauren's. You know, the way they both twist their left cheeks into a dimple when they are thinking or contemplating—trying to make a decision."

Her mother's face went ashen. "Really?"

"When they were dancing the other night, they looked enough alike to be cousins. Jeez, it brought goose bumps to my arms."

"Let me warm up our coffee." Her mother returned and looked into Annaleese's eyes. "I knew the day would come when you'd have to know..."

Annaleese interrupted, lifting her eyebrows. "Know what,
~~~

Mom?"

"Lauren is adopted." She looked down at the floor unable to continue.

"What? Adopted?" Annaleese gasped, the news boggling her mind. "How?"

"My cousin Dee died giving birth to Lauren. We adopted her and have never had the heart to tell her." Her mother slumped in the chair and started weeping.

"Mom, why are you crying?"

"Justin Jackson's uncle Joseph is Lauren's father."

Annaleese stared at her, trying to understand. "Justin? And Lauren?"

"He loved my cousin, but his family would not allow him to marry her. He was broken-hearted, but he died not knowing Lauren's mother was pregnant."

"Oh, my God. This is a nightmare!"

"No. It's life. When a rich family threatens to disown their son if he marries a poor girl, it is a done deal."

"That's so unfair." Annaleese frowned.

"That has been a common refrain of yours since you were little. 'This is unfair, that's unfair.' What's more unfair than anything is Lauren never had a chance to know her real mother or father."

"So you never told Lauren she was adopted?"

"No, her father committed suicide three months after he was forced to give up Lauren's mother. Dee heard about it a month later. It's a wonder she didn't have a miscarriage."

"This story gets crazier by the minute." Annaleese's head felt fuzzy and her stomach got queasy. "The whole thing was so unfair to the lovers, but it's especially unfair to Lauren."

"Absolutely! But it's time to get over what's fair and what isn't. Think about the reality of today's situation."

"Oh my gosh! Lauren's father is Justin's uncle."

"Exactly." Her mother groaned.

"This means Lauren is biologically as close to Justin as she is to me. No wonder they have the same mannerisms. No wonder they like the same things. No wonder they get along so well."

"Do you see why we've kept it secret? Lauren was so sweet when she was a baby and we wanted children, so it was easy to not tell her. Then you came along and made our family complete." Her mother fiddled with her hands. "Maybe we should tell her."

"Mom! We can never tell Lauren unless it becomes absolutely necessary. It would be cruel to dump this on her after all these years. Cruel for her to hear that her mother and father died without knowing her."

"That's why we never told her. She has always been our precious child."

"Does anyone else know?"

Color rose to her mother's face, flushed. "Not a living soul."

Annaleese stood up and fisted her hands. "We will take each day at a time and go on with our lives as usual."

"Yes, we will. Just as I've always done," her mother declared.

A flush crept over Annaleese. She was silent for a moment then looked at her mother and asked, "I'm not adopted, am I?"

"What?" her mom snapped. "Heaven sakes, no! I carried you nine months and ten days. Believe me, I looked like a whale." She held out her hand toward Annaleese.

"Love you, Mom. You're a strong woman and I'm proud of you."

"Ditto, my sweet girl. You and Lauren are my life. I love my sweet girls."

When Annaleese got ready to head back home, she hugged her mother an extra-long time. "I'm the luckiest girl in the world."

Sunday evening when she got home she called Justin. "Did you miss me?" She anxiously waited for his answer.

"Yes and no. I've been playing chaperone to Lauren and Will. I think they're sweet on each other," Justin said.

"Well, he acted like he was smitten with her from the get-go at the dance. Lauren is another story."

"You wouldn't say that if you had seen them together. She told me it was the best weekend she'd ever had, and I'm not lying."

"I hope that's true. Lauren has never loved any man. She's vulnerable. She deserves someone who will cherish her."

"I think she's found that someone. They are really tight. Watching them made me miss you even more. I was like a third wheel. When they held hands I felt out of place. I needed your touch."

"I missed holding your hand, too. But we'll make up for it. And you did a good deed for Lauren and Will while I was gone."

"Well, all I can tell you is for a quiet twosome they sure ran me ragged this weekend."

"Are you too tired to come over?" she asked.

"Lady, I will never, never be that tired." Justin laughed and Annaleese joined him.

A few minutes later Justin appeared at the door with a tiny gift.

"What have we here? A welcome home present?" she asked, curiosity crawling into her brain. She opened the package and her eyes widened as she lifted the lid from the small box.

A heart-pounding joy rushed through her, curling even her toes. An engagement ring with a huge diamond sparkled from a bed of dried apples, taking her breath away.

Justin went down on one knee. "Will you marry me?" he asked, a huge grin on his face. "I want you to be my wife."

"Yes, of course I will!" She reached for him and pulled him to his feet. "I love the ring. I love the apples. And I love you."

"Love you, too." He kissed her, a wonderful, sweet, warm kiss, then smiled down at her. "Welcome to my life."

Annaleese looked at Justin as if for the first time. She realized they were on equal footing. Her past, his past could merge into their present and together they would build a future.

Thanksgiving Road Home

No family is perfect. We fuss and fight. We often stop talking. But in the end, family is family. Love will always be there.

~ Unknown author

ASHLEY STONE STOOD motionless, afraid to move, as if she could disturb the love scene taking place in the city park two floors below her office window. The young man below smoothed his girlfriend's wind-blown hair. Watching, Ashley imagined his warm caress on her flushed cheek.

Then he took the girl's hand and slipped a ring on her finger. Ashley stopped herself from offering her hand to her imaginary lover. The couple kissed for a long time while the girl stood on her tiptoes. The scene echoed perfection.

With a deep sigh Ashley took a long breath and let it out again. Her soul sang. She could hardly contain the joy inside her. Before Brandon went out of town on business he had hinted about the next step in their lives together, an engagement, just like the one she'd just witnessed. Goose bumps ran across Ashley's skin. She wrapped her arms around her waist and continued to stare.

Leaves dashed across the lawn. The cool nights in Asheville had started the fall season. Wind whipped the girl's long dark tresses again. Her handsome guy tenderly lifted strands from her face. Ashley swallowed hard. The intimacy took her breath and she turned away. A little voice whispered in her mind. *Brandon, this is the moment, the perfect time. Why have I waited so long to let you know?*

Perfection played an important role in Ashley's life. Her personality demanded it. Her twin sister, Amy, had dubbed her "Little Miss Perfect." Planning and execution had been her hallmark. Ashley hated the nickname but had to admit excellence was her goal.

But now seemed the perfect time for Brandon to pop the question.

At first she'd wanted to wait until her career was more established before she married. Now she needed to make a leap of faith and move on with her personal life. Brandon had been so patient with her time frame. He had not pressured her for a decision.

Ashley turned and stared at the gorgeous floral bouquet that arrived this morning. She took a deep breath and inhaled the heavenly scent of roses. Though Brandon had been out of town on business, he hadn't forgotten to send her flowers. Every month he sent her favorites, baby carnations and mauve-colored roses, on their anniversary for the day they met. Ashley breathed in the fresh fragrance of the bouquet, again reminding her of his love.

She picked up her cell and sent him a text. *The flowers are lovely. Miss you. Hurry home.* The workload on her desk required attention, but she needed to savor this moment. A sigh of relief raced through her. "Brandon's coming home today."

Kristin, her paralegal, tapped on her door and interrupted her thoughts. "Need anything? Coffee?"

"I think I'm good right now, but thanks for the offer. It's great to know you have my back." Ashley smiled at the friend she had recommended to the company.

"Anytime." Kristin nodded and closed the door.

Ashley decided to take a moment to call her twin sister. "Hi, Amy, we thought we'd come down for Mom and Dad's anniversary. Will you be there?"

"Yeah, probably. You know how Mom is about finding any excuse for a party."

They chuckled. Ashley cleared her throat and said, "I may have some good news."

"Really?"

"I think Brandon is going to propose." She giggled like a school girl. Her stomach fluttered.

After a long minute of silence Amy finally muttered, "Hmm. That's nice."

"Can't you be happy for me?" Ashley's joy deflated like a balloon.

"Yeah, sure."

"Is it so hard for you to wish me well?" Her sister's continued refusal to wish her happiness made her heart ache.

"You don't need my consent."

"But I would like your blessing." *Why should I care? I just do.*

"Blessing. There. Are ya happy?" Amy's voice held no enthusiasm.

Ashley willed herself to ignore her sister's forced comment. *That's just Amy. Not going to let her ruin my day.* "Must run. See you at the party. Hugs."

Why can't she be happy for me? Amy never wants me to have anything she doesn't have. Ashley remembered when she'd planned to run for class president their senior year. Amy announced she had decided to run, also. Not wanting any issues between them, Ashley had withdrawn her name. Amy lost the election to another girl but at least not to her. Amy's self-imposed competition with Ashley was nerve-wracking, time-consuming, and disappointing. Couldn't they just get over it?

"Back to work," she scolded herself for wasting time on negative thoughts. Over the next couple of hours her computer got a callisthenic workout, but her body didn't. By the end of the day her neck felt stiff, her back hurt and she needed a massage.

Ashley stopped by the market and picked up two steak filets, salad greens and a bottle of sparkling mineral water. Brandon didn't drink, but she had a little Moscato in the house in case she wanted a small glass of wine.

Her heart skipped a beat. Brandon would be home tonight. They fit into each other's routines like a shoehorn into a slipper. He'd be tired, so they could retire early. She hadn't slept well while he was out of town. Never did. Often she'd roll over and reach for him, only to feel an empty spot. Cuddling his pillow to breathe in his scent wasn't enough.

At home she freshened up and got busy in the kitchen. She chilled the mineral water, chopped fresh cilantro into the salad and added cherry tomatoes. The steaks were ready for the grill. The only thing missing was Brandon. Hoping he would walk in the door any minute, she popped the steaks on the grill.

Minutes later the door opened and Brandon shouted, "I'm home." When he put his luggage down Ashley dashed into his arms.

"Whoa, this is what I call a true welcome." He tilted his head and laughed. "You must have missed me."

"Don't joke. I've been out of my mind this week. The office is driving me crazy, and I can't sleep when you're out of town."

He held his arms out wider. "Step into my cape and let me be your Superman."

She hugged him tighter, clinging for a few minutes. "All better now," she whispered.

"Good girl. What is that I smell?" He sniffed the air.

"Oops." She dashed to grab the steaks. "Dinner, of course. Are you ready to eat?"

They sat down at the table set with her great-grandmother's Depression glass dishes. The pink, green and amber colors created a festive atmosphere.

"Everything looks fantastic, and the food smells scrumptious, to use your words."

"I've missed you," she gushed.

"Your welcome told me." He grinned like a little boy with a new toy.

"We are blessed... our life together..." Her voice choked.

"Sh..." He reached across the table and took her hand. "You're my everything."

His words sent shivers all over her body. "We're soul mates." She looked into his eyes. *Perfect setting for a perfect proposal.*

With his other hand he brought forth a velvet box and flipped the lid open, revealing a halo diamond ring. The box and contents flew into the air, across the table and landed in Ashley's salad. The diamond peeked out from a bed of mixed greens and balsamic dressing.

"Oh my gosh!" Ashley grabbed her napkin and wiped dressing off the sparkling ring.

"Oops! My bad." Brandon slapped his hand over his mouth, suppressing a deep laugh. "Thank goodness it will wash off." He smiled at her. "Not quite perfect, sweet girl. Was it good enough?"

Her heart melted and she smiled back. "Yes. Good enough."

"So, what are we waiting for? Ashley Stone, will you marry

me?"

She blinked, took a deep breath and yelled. "Yes, yes, yes—a thousand times yes." She pushed her chair back, but he had already bounded around the table to embrace her. Sniffing his tangy aftershave, Ashley inhaled his essence.

"You've made me the happiest man on the planet." He scooped her up and they danced around the room, blending into each other.

She snuggled her head in the crook of his neck, took a deep breath and heaved a sigh of contentment. "The perfect ending to a proposal."

"I tried," he said. They both laughed.

A few minutes later Ashley pulled back. "Let's call Mom and Dad. Since we're going down next weekend for their anniversary, why don't we tell them about our engagement now? Maybe we can announce it at their party."

"Sounds like a plan," he agreed.

Ashley dialed home. They stood together with the phone on speaker.

"Hello." Elizabeth Stone's voice sounded a little sleepy.

"Hi, Mom. I hope it's not too late to call."

"Honey, is that you?"

"Yes, ma'am. Brandon and I cleared our calendars and can come down for your anniversary."

"Really? How wonderful."

"Brandon popped the question tonight, so I wanted you and Dad to be the first to know."

She could hear her Mom shuffling around. "Jack, come quick! It's Ashley."

"Hi, honey bear," he roared through the phone. "How's my girl?"

"Brandon and I are engaged, Dad," she blurted.

"You couldn't do any better, baby girl. I like Brandon. He'll make you a good husband."

"Oh, I'm so excited. Gives me a good excuse to decorate and

have a party," her mother chimed in. "It will be special for both of us."

"See you soon. Love you both." Ashley hung up, smiling from ear to ear. *Life can't get any better than this.* Then she thought of Amy and her sour reaction to Ashley's hints from earlier today. Would she find it special, too?

~~~

A few days later Ashley and Brandon were all packed. They planned to be in Stoneridge three days but packed for four, just in case.

"Shall I take my car, or do you want to drive?" Ashley asked.

"Why don't we take your Lexus, since it's more comfortable."

"Sounds good. I had Black Beauty serviced last week."

"I never understood why you gave your car a name."

"Like everything else in life, cars perform better when they're loved. Get it?"

Brandon laughed. "Gotcha."

All the way to her folks' house the weather cooperated with a perfect fall day. The drive down was beautiful. A few colored leaves tipped the trees in Asheville, but the farther south they traveled the more everything still blossomed. Bright colors peeked out here and there in wooded areas.

"It's amazing how the landscape changes in a few hours of driving. Encore Azaleas are still blooming in Middle Georgia," Ashley commented.

"They're almost as beautiful as you." Brandon smiled at her and she sighed. Love. Ashley floated on a cloud of contentment one minute and giggled with excitement the next. When Brandon put on their favorite music they hummed along.

With an occasional glance her way, he reached for her hand and brought it across the console and kissed her fingers. She knew he wanted her, wanted to run his hands through her hair and wanted to touch her. She put her hand on his knee, reveling in the moment.

~~~

Ten feet inside the city limits a rose-colored stone on the side of the road had large etched letters "Welcome to Stoneridge, Georgia."

"Hmm. Stoneridge. Does the name have anything to do with your name?" Brandon asked.

"My great, great, great grandfather founded the town of Stoneridge. He was an orphan and rode with the Pony Express. Unfortunately, the Express only lasted a year and a half. Then he moved east when the business adventure ended. The farm has produced great horses for over a century. Amy and I could ride before we learned how to read."

She enjoyed showing Brandon the town where she grew up. Stoneridge was a picture-postcard town. Ashley loved the town square with magnolia trees, park benches and year-round festivals.

"Look, there's the courthouse. It's the handsome building with the large clock tower facing the square. Southern towns are noted for their magnificent courthouses."

"Bet you loved the ice cream parlor." He pointed across the square and grinned, knowing how much she loved sweets.

"They make the best banana splits ever created, but we'd better move on before I'm tempted to spoil my dinner. We'll explore the town more when we return for Thanksgiving. The house is a few miles out of town."

Driving up the sandy lane lined with hundred-year-old oaks, Ashley scanned the big house with a critical eye. The grand, rambling place needed repair, which she knew her dad and mom couldn't do on their own. Maybe she and Brandon could take a couple of days off at Christmas and rehang the two shutters that hung askew and put a coat of white paint on the peeling columns across the front porch.

"My dad and his older brother bought the other siblings' shares. They were barely able to hang on to the original property. They're the only two who live in Stoneridge. All four of my dad's sisters married and moved away."

"Nice piece of land," Brandon said as he parked the car.

"Yes," she agreed, "it really is fine farmland."

Brandon grabbed the luggage. He and Ashley walked in cadence to the front steps onto the porch. She winked at him.

“Here goes nothing,” he said, holding his head high and pulling his body erect like a soldier on his way to see his commanding officer.

The family welcomed them with open arms. Ashley’s mom hugged Brandon first then turned toward her daughter, who had been swooped up by her barrel-chested dad.

“Boy, what a day,” he roared in his usual manner. “My little girl is about to be a married woman.”

“Jack, you’ll squeeze the life out of her before she has a chance to get married,” Elizabeth Stone teased. “Come on in, let’s get you settled. Amy’s already here.”

“Thanks, I’ll get our bags.” Brandon rolled the luggage into the house.

The décor screamed “party” with flowers everywhere. Matching arrangements on the mantle held Mylar balloons which read “Happy 30th Anniversary” and “Congrats on Your Engagement.”

Amy appeared at the top of the stairs. “I thought I heard voices.” She hurried down, a smile pasted on her face. “Hi, you two.” She hugged Ashley and held out her hand to Brandon. “It’s a pleasure to finally meet you.”

“Nice to know the other twin.” He smiled. “Wow, you are identical! How do people tell you apart?”

“That’s easy. We have different personalities.” Amy smiled and winked at him. “She’s the picky one.”

“Well, she picked me, so I can’t complain too much, can I?” Brandon grabbed Ashley’s hand and brought it to his lips. “I’m the lucky one.”

Amy’s smile slipped. That look Ashley hated darkened her eyes. “Yeah. I guess.”

~~~

That evening business friends of Ashley’s father arrived. He introduced the Bibbs and Turners to Ashley and Brandon.
~~~

Ashley's mother smiled and greeted them. "I'm so glad you could come celebrate with us." She had prepared a delicious dinner of baked chicken, potatoes au gratin, green beans and salad.

The doorbell rang and Ashley's best friend stood there with her new husband. "Hi, everyone. Sorry we're a little late. The traffic coming through Macon was heavy."

Ashley ran and hugged Leigh and then her husband, Lee. "Gosh, Mom didn't tell me you were coming, but I'm delighted she kept it a secret."

Brandon came and shook hands with the new arrivals. "Good to see you again. Your wedding was awesome."

Jack Stone clapped his hands. "I think everyone is here, so let the party begin." He made sure everyone in the room had a glass of champagne then raised his in a toast. "To my amazing bride of thirty years. I love you, honey." Then he turned to Ashley and Brandon. "And to the next generation of our family. Congratulations, you two. We wish you all the happiness in the world."

Ashley's heart brimmed over with joy. How could it be any more perfect than this? Even Brandon, who rarely drank, sipped champagne with everyone else as he hugged her close. He even toasted her mom and dad's anniversary with another swallow before finally allowing the crowd to convince him to tell how Ashley had finally said yes.

As everyone laughed and sat down to eat, he looked at her and mouthed, "I love you."

"I love you, too," she mouthed back. And she meant it with all her heart.

After dinner and the cutting of the cake everyone mingled, celebrating the two couples. Brandon leaned close to Ashley and she smelled the glass of wine he'd had with dinner on his breath. He stepped away to talk to her dad. Ashley watched him go, worry etched on her face.

"What's wrong?" Her mom stopped on the way to the kitchen. "Is everything all right?"

"Brandon never drinks," Ashley whispered to her mom. "But

he's had..."

"Don't worry. He's probably a little nervous about meeting all the family."

They glanced across the room where Brandon, looking great in his sports jacket and her favorite tie, admired her dad's golf trophies. Amy brought him another glass of champagne and rested her hand on his arm, chatting away.

"And I'm worried that Amy is flirting with him."

"I don't think you have much to be worried about. He's crazy about you."

"Hmm." *Wonder what she's up to now. Brandon probably hasn't even noticed her hand on his arm. Back to her old tricks?* Ashley stepped away from her mother and strolled over to stand by Brandon.

He put his arm around her and whispered, "I'm the happiest man in the world."

"Me, too," she said. "You probably shouldn't drink anymore tonight, sweetheart."

"You're right. Amy just brought me another glass. My head is pounding."

Her dad walked over to Ashley and put his hand on her arm. "You need to say goodnight to our guests, my dear. The Bibbs and Turners are leaving soon."

"Be right there." She turned to Brandon. "Why don't you go upstairs and lie down? I won't be long." She squeezed his shoulder.

"Good idea." He headed upstairs.

~~~

After the guests left Ashley and her mother cleared the dining table and went to work cleaning the kitchen.

"It's like old times, having you help in the kitchen," her mom said. "Amy wandered off, as usual."

"The party was great, Mom. You outdid yourself."

"Well, it isn't everyday a mother gets to announce her daughter's engagement."
~~~

Amy strolled into the room, disheveled—her hair all mussed and a top button undone.

"About time you came to help. Most of the work is finished. Great timing, one of your talents," Mom said.

"Sorry, I was tied up."

Ashley shot a dagger look toward Amy. "Literally or otherwise? One never knows with you."

Amy looked down and buttoned her blouse, then she strolled across the kitchen and picked at a piece of cake. "Doesn't matter, Miss Perfect. As per normal, you have complete control over everything."

Mom cast a disapproving glance at Amy and sighed. "Stop it. I didn't raise you like this, young lady."

Amy turned and walked away with a defiant glance.

Ashley and her mom put the last dishes away.

"Thanks for helping, sweet girl"

"No problem." She gave her mom a hug. "Think I'll head upstairs and check on Brandon."

Feeling a little tired from the evening's festivities, Ashley trudged upstairs to find Brandon. She opened her old bedroom door. He lay across the bed sound asleep, his shirt unbuttoned, still wearing shoes.

She slipped his shoes off his feet.

He groaned and rolled over, out cold.

"Too far gone to undress yourself?" she asked him. No answer.

Weariness overtook her and she undressed, put on pajamas and brushed her teeth. *Glad the party is over so I can relax.*

When she walked back into the bedroom, Brandon rolled over and mumbled. "Sor... sorry, I passed out on you. Wish I'd been up to your enthu... si... asm. Glad you wore the new perfume I gave you for your birthda... day."

He really has had too much. I didn't wear any perfume tonight.

"It's okay. You're not used to drinking."

"Ya—you can say that again. Muh—my head feels like a giant

watermelon." He could barely utter one clear word.

"Let's get your duds off, so you'll be comfortable."

"Sounds good." It was all he could do to sit on the side of the bed while Ashley helped him get his clothes off. She tossed his shirt onto the chair, right into the light from the bedside lamp.

What was that? She leaned over to check out the stain. Lipstick! On his shirt collar. Amy's signature Hot Pink.

That little bitch. She was up here with Brandon, but he thinks he was with me. What did Amy do?

She put one hand over her mouth and the other on her stomach, praying she wouldn't spew. *How could she? First getting Brandon drunk, then seducing him?* The memory of that mussed hair and unbuttoned blouse blazed through her. *How far had they gone?*

She stood and started pacing up and down, mumbling to herself. "I can't believe it. I just can't believe it." Brandon just moaned, out like a light.

Ashley stormed out of the room and down the hallway. She was going to take care of this right now. She flung open Amy's bedroom door and switched on the light.

Amy's eyes opened wide and she dragged the cover up to her chin. "What's the matter?"

"What's wrong with you? How dare you play games with my fiancé?"

"Wait. Let me explain."

"Shut up! There is no explanation except that you're an immature brat who doesn't care about anyone but herself. Brad and I are leaving in the morning. I never want to see you again!"

"But—"

"Stay away from me. And stay away from my fiancé."

Ashley stomped back to her room and began packing, slinging their things into their bags while Brad snored from the bed. She finally slid under the covers next to him but stared at the ceiling, her face set like stone, until the sun came up.

Ashley told Brandon they were going to spend the last night

of their vacation at the local B&B, Miss Jane's Hilltop Inn. "We'll have more privacy and can enjoy being alone."

His eyes brightened. He nodded his agreement and nibbled her ear. "Fantastic plan, my sweet bride-to-be."

Downstairs, her parents sat reading the newspaper and drinking coffee.

"Morning, guys. Why the bags?" Her dad's eyebrows came up as he looked at her face. "Something wrong?"

Ashley hesitated a moment. "We hope you won't mind, but we've decided to spend our last night in town. I want to show Brandon the sights." *I need to get out of here before Amy comes downstairs.*

"Brandon, how about a cup of coffee before you go?" Her mom stood up. "Ashley, can I talk to you a minute?"

"Okay." She followed her mom into the kitchen.

"What's going on? Is this about Amy?"

"Mom, I can't talk right now." The burning in Ashley's chest as she tried to hold everything back grew until she thought it would burst. "I have to go."

"Okay, sweetie. But call me when you can, all right?"

At the door Ashley hugged her parents one at a time. "Love you both. See you soon."

Brandon turned to Ashley's mom and held out his hand.

"You're not getting away without a hug, young man. You're part of the family now. You're Ashley's man."

Ashley hoped no one noticed her forced smile. "Thanks for going to such great lengths to make our engagement party special and making Brandon feel welcome to the family."

Dad walked with them out to the car. "You kids drive carefully and enjoy your weekend."

Brandon shook his hand. "Thanks for the hospitality, Mr. Stone."

"You're welcome anytime, son."

Brandon held the car door for Ashley, then he hurried around to the driver's side and hopped in. They sped down the driveway like gangsters trying to get away with a bank robbery. "Great party. I really like your folks."

Ashley remained quiet. Anger knotted her stomach, making her nauseous inside. Her brain couldn't fathom what had occurred on one of the most precious nights of her life.

At the B & B they had coffee and Danish while scrolling through their phones checking their messages. Brandon yawned, stood up and stretched. "I didn't realize I was so sleepy."

"Me, too," Ashley said. "How about a quick nap before we head out for me to show you the town?"

"You read my mind." He reached for her hand and walked toward the bedroom. When his arms were around her she felt safe and finally was able to sleep.

They woke up hungry and ready to eat and see the sights.

The first place Ashley took him was Madison Square, named for a prominent family dating back two hundred years. "I love the old courthouse, the shops and restaurants. The owners have kept the vintage look," she said, playing the tour guide, trying to pretend that nothing was wrong.

"May I treat you to lunch, my pretty?" he asked and smiled.

"Yes, I'm starving." She selected her favorite eatery where they planned the afternoon activities. They decided to go over to Macon and tour the Allman Brothers Band Museum known as The Big House.

"This is where the guys and their ladies lived when the band first got started. The Brothers toured while the women kept the home-fires burning. They all got along like one happy extended family," Ashley explained to Brandon as the tour guide covered basic information about the Big House and the famous residents.

"I still like their music. Too bad two of the guys got killed a year apart."

"Yeah, it seems artistic people are often gone too soon. What a loss."

Brandon acted delighted with one fun spot after another when they returned to Stoneridge. Ashley could not find joy in the tour of her hometown. She hoped he didn't notice. His enthusiasm was big enough for both of them.

That evening they went about preparing for bed. Ashley brushed her teeth and got ready. Brandon followed suit by taking a long shower. Tomorrow they had a long drive back to Asheville.

Ashley's brain exploded with an imaginary scene. She couldn't stop herself from envisioning the night before. Brandon probably would have shut the door behind him and crashed on the bed. *A few minutes later, Amy followed and crept in behind him.*

"Hello, big boy. Wanna play?"

"Nooo. I, uh, wanna sleep," he slurred, his eyes closed.

Amy unbuttoned her blouse. "Look. Now you." She loosened his tie, proceeded to unbutton his shirt, and kissed his neck, smearing lipstick on his shirt. He passed out.

But had he passed out soon enough?

Ashley swallowed a sob and spoke to a silent room. "I can't think about this anymore, or it will drive me nuts."

The sleeping-pill bottle Ashley had placed on the nightstand called her name. She took a tablet, washed it down with water, hoping it could erase the images that clung to her brain like ivy and hoping it would eventually numb the pain in her heart. A damp spot from tears on her pillow was the last thing she remembered before tumbling into a fitful sleep.

Their happy trip coming down to Georgia was the opposite on the way back to North Carolina. The silence was deafening.

Finally, Brandon asked, "What's the matter, Ash? Is it about my getting drunk?"

Ashley bit her lip. "No, not really. And I can't talk about it now." The hurt drained her like a knife wound, one jab at a time, one drop at a time. "Later. We'll talk later."

Going back home to Asheville was uncomfortable for both. She knew Brandon didn't understand any of this, but it didn't seem to help her cope. The vision of Amy and Brandon in bed together kept running through her mind. She couldn't deal with the anger and hurt.

Their relationship became strained as the days turned into

weeks. She had moved in with him two months ago, before the trip to Georgia. Now she couldn't seem to move forward and set a wedding date.

~~~

A few weeks after the trip to Stoneridge the volcano inside Ashley was ready to blow. She and Brandon had a huge argument over nothing, and she couldn't stop shaking inside. She marched into work, nodding at coworkers who greeted her, went straight into her office and slammed the door with a thud. A few minutes later she appeared in the lobby.

"Uh, oh," groaned the receptionist. "Somebody didn't have breakfast."

"Or her man has been out of town too long," Kristin said and smiled at Ashley.

"Don't you people have work to do?" She turned and huffed off again.

A minute later Kristin knocked softly and entered Ashley's office.

"What?" Ashley scowled.

"Coffee?" Kristin smiled.

Reaching for the steaming brew, Ashley looked into her friend's eyes. "Is it that obvious?"

"Worse. I've never known you to act like this."

"I couldn't sleep last night. Feel like shit."

"What's going on?" Kristin asked.

"The fuss Brandon and I had over that damn ugly tie I hate keeps repeating itself in my head." *The one he wore at our engagement party.*

"Same tie you got hot under the collar about when you returned from Stoneridge? The one you liked so much before that?"

"Yeah. Same one."

"My sixth sense tells me your problem isn't the tie, Ashley."

"I know." She sighed. "Thanks for the coffee."
~~~

"Any time, my friend." Kristin turned and left the room.

Ashley stood staring at a painting of her home place, thinking about the engagement party. Her mom had called her several times over the past two weeks, trying to get Ashley to tell her what was wrong, but Ashley's heart was so full, she couldn't get the words out.

Amy had called, too, over and over. Ashley had hung up on her each time.

"Snap out of it and get to work," Ashley admonished herself. Her heart wasn't in her work anymore. In fact, her heart wasn't in her life anymore. She went through the motions and completed another day.

Slogging through the traffic with horns blowing and folks giving each other the finger was enough to make anyone disgruntled. And she faced another night alone, since Brandon was traveling again.

Luck was with her. She watched an old movie, an Academy Award relic from twenty years ago. It made her evening a pleasant entry to a decent night's sleep.

When the alarm went off she opened one eye to see sunlight streaming through the blinds. *Another day without Brandon*. She missed him. He made the coffee every morning and read the news on his Kindle. Routinely, by the time Ashley showered and dressed he had fresh fruit and Greek yogurt ready. Today she nibbled on a protein bar and dashed to work. Her job demanded long hours from first and second year lawyers.

I agree with Dad. Brandon and I have a bright future. I just have to fix our drifting relationship. "Life isn't always perfect," she murmured. "It takes a little work."

Smelling fresh brewed coffee in the nook next to her office, she headed that way. "God, this coffee smells good," she said to a co-worker.

"And someone brought fresh croissants."

"Heavenly." She doctored her coffee, grabbed a croissant on a napkin and headed back to her office.

Her cell buzzed just as she sat down at her desk. "Don't hang up," her sister's voice pleaded. She hit the "off" button and sighed. *Wish I could forgive Amy, but I can't.*

That night Ashley had a recurring dream. It seemed so real.

"Excuses, excuses, excuses. I'm sick of lame excuses for your actions."

Ashley walked toward her sister, anger boiling up inside.

"But...," Amy sputtered, trying to explain.

She lunged at Amy and choked her as she gasped for breath. Her fingers felt the muscles throb in Amy's neck until her head began to bobble and the muscles went limp.

Ashley awoke from the dream, gasping for breath, her fingers still in a circular formation. It took a few minutes for the fog to clear her brain. She couldn't totally dismiss the dream, since she really did want to confront Amy. But it seemed too real. She didn't really want to kill her sister.

At least the next day would be better. Her heart skipped a beat. *My man is on his way home.*

~~~

The phone rang. "Hey, sweetheart." Brandon sounded weary. "The plane landed late. Don't wait dinner."

"But we're having your favorite again, filet mignon."

"That's lovely, but I'm really tired and frustrated."

"Too tired to eat?"

"I guess not."

"Too tired for me?" she teased.

"No, of course not. See you soon."

His weariness seeped through the phone and oozed onto her. They sounded like an old married couple, with the joy drained out of their relationship. He'd been crazy about her, but now she couldn't commit. One minus one equals zero. *Why have I allowed Amy's actions to spoil my wedding plans, my future?*

An hour later Brandon opened the door, rolled his bag in and exhaled wearily. She stepped forward and he pulled her to him. They embraced, standing still, saying nothing.
~~~

When he released her she stepped back folding her arms. "You're working too hard," she scolded.

Brandon reached out and unfolded her arms. Then he turned the engagement ring on her finger until she looked down at it. Lifting it to his mouth, he kissed the ring and her hand. "I love you, Ashley."

"I know," she whispered. *Why is it so hard for me to respond?* She knew the answer. Amy. Turning, she headed to the kitchen. "Let me finish dinner while you unpack."

The lack of conversation during dinner sat like an elephant in the room. After a few routine comments he asked, "How was your day at the office?"

"Busy and crazy, as usual," she said. Details seemed unimportant. She turned her attention to the food but knew the hunger inside her could not be satisfied with a good steak. "How was your trip?"

"Hectic, long and tiring. I'm not sure I want to do this for the rest of my life." He slumped a little in his chair.

"But you're a great financial planner—bringing in new clients, closing deals, and making them feel good about their investment choices. The company would be lost without your talents."

"Not sure I care anymore. I'm tired—the kind of tired you can't sleep off." He pushed away from the table and stood. "Thanks for the excellent dinner. You shouldn't have gone to so much trouble."

Spoken as if I were the cook at a local café. Before Ashley could respond he turned and trudged down the hall toward the bedroom. *Cool politeness, not good.*

She slowly cleaned the kitchen, thinking of ways she could get down into that hole in his heart. *I'm scared. Will he open up and tell me what's going on with him... us?* She had to find a way. Where to begin? Why couldn't she tell Brandon how she felt about that night? In return he could express his feelings about their relationship. At this point it was more her fault than his.

"I have to be honest with him, no matter what. We both deserve the truth."

Resolved to wade through the abyss, Ashley went into the bedroom. The shower stopped with its signature squeak. A few moments later Brandon appeared at the door, his toothbrush buzzing. His eyes half-lidded, he looked so drawn and weary.

"We need to talk," she said.

"About what?" he asked.

"About what happened to us." She sighed, weary from the thought of dragging this out and confronting the present predicament and the unknown future.

"Yes, but not now. I'm brain dead and couldn't hold up my end tonight."

"Tomorrow?"

"Sounds better." He pulled back the covers and climbed into bed. "Night, love." He puckered her a kiss in the air.

Ashley stood there for a moment then switched off the light and closed the door. A feeling of despair brushed over her. What if he had known that Amy was the one in the bedroom that night?

Trying to read and relax proved futile. She caught herself staring at the same page she had read and re-read. Television did not help, with its steady diet of bad news. Two hours later she gave up and went to bed. Sleep would not come. What was she going to do if he wanted Amy instead of her?

Ashley drifted off for a few hours and became consumed by fitful dreams. She loved horses, but Brandon did not ride until they started dating. They took lessons for months together, she in an advanced class and he with a coach for beginners.

Tonight she ruffled her dream horse's black mane and gave Gentleman Jim a hug before she mounted him. Brandon had not learned to be affectionate with his beast. He mounted swiftly, and they were racing across the field at the farm. She felt every strong breath Jim took as the pace grew intense. The horse's mane and her hair moved with the same rhythm in the wind. Far ahead the fence appeared. Gentleman Jim could jump it without a doubt.

Her head cleared and Ashley knew Brandon could not make the jump. Fear grabbed her like a lasso. She must stop him. She slowed and wheeled Gentlemen Jim around just in time to signal Brandon to turn his horse and avoid the danger. Her heart was in her throat.

She woke covered in sweat, her gown damp to the touch. For a moment she struggled to get her breath. *I saved Brandon. He is my one true love.* Slipping out of bed, she went down the hall to the guest bathroom, showered, pulled on a clean gown, crawled back into bed, and slept like a baby snuggling against Brandon's warm body.

The next morning she woke to the smell of fresh-brewed coffee. Brandon had left a note by the coffee maker. "See you tonight. Let's have an early dinner and talk." He'd drawn a smiley face on the note. She brushed a strand of hair out of her eyes and sighed. "Aww. Thank God it's Friday. I can relax this weekend and get my life in order."

Her spirits lifted to match the sunny colorful world of autumn. Ashley's energy matched the crispness in the air. She looked forward to clearing the air with Brandon tonight. Perhaps then the evening would take a magical turn and this would all be fixed.

Brandon called in midmorning. "Hi, Sunshine. Want me to pick up something at the market on my way home?"

"How about cashew chicken rice or shrimp fried rice from Asian Zing? I'll toss a salad." She flipped through her iPad for her daily to-do list. Certain things had to be addressed at work before she could sign off for the weekend.

"Good plan. See you soon." He sounded chipper, as if nothing was amiss.

Ashley felt torn between the happiness in his voice and the fear in her heart. Each hour brought more apprehension. Her chest tightened every time she tried to formulate the pending conversation. *I owe Brandon an explanation for my odd behavior for the last two months.*

On the way home she had a flat tire. "Good grief, of all nights." She jerked out her cell and called Brandon.

"You won't believe this. I have a flat tire." She fumed.

"Oh, no. Did you call AAA?"

"I'm calling them as soon as I hang up."

"Don't sweat it. I'll hold dinner."

"Dinner is not my greatest concern right now."

Teasingly he asked, "Does that mean you're anxious to see me?"

He had no idea. "You bet." She smiled and realized how much she meant it.

The tow truck came, changed her tire, and she rushed away. On the drive home she flew down the highway toward Brandon. Her heart rate escalated and her mouth became dry.

"What a fool I've been," she scolded herself.

Brandon was home when she arrived. He greeted her with a warm fuzzy kiss on the cheek. His smile melted her like fudge on a hot day. She took a deep breath, turned and began helping him prepare dinner.

Brandon had the table set in a festive mood. He had obviously used his extra time to get out candles and snip one bloom from the potted plant in the breezeway.

My God, how blind I've been for the last two months. I haven't been able to get past my own thoughts to consider his feelings.

They sat at the table for a moment then Brandon blurted out. "Who wants to begin?" He seemed anxious to deal with this mystery conversation.

Ashley swallowed hard. Sometimes it's easier to close your eyes and hope problems will go away. She knew this wouldn't. "I don't want to risk a fight."

"Fight? If it's going to be that bad, perhaps we don't need to do this." Brandon stood up and stared at her.

"No, no. I made it sound worse than I should. It's just that..."

Bewildered he sat back down. "Uh. Okay, I'll begin."

She sighed, momentarily relieved.

"I don't know what I did wrong the night of our engagement party, but it must have been pretty awful. I apologized to your parents for drinking."

"It was not—is not the drinking."

"Well, what is it? You've refused to talk about it, and something is keeping a wall between us."

"You... you didn't do anything that awful."

"All I remember is having a lot of champagne and feeling woozy. I went upstairs so I wouldn't embarrass myself or your family."

"My family never noticed anything. My parents were celebrating, enjoying sharing our good news with family and close friends."

"You followed me upstairs and we hugged and kissed. I don't know what happened after that, but it must have been bad."

"You'd been drinking."

"That's no excuse. What did I do?" Brandon's expression changed to horror. "Did I force myself on you?"

"No, not that." Her heart thudded.

His brow wrinkled into a frown. "Well, what exactly did I do to make you resent me?" His voice got louder and his face turned red.

Ashley met his tone, decibel for decibel. "I want to love you. Can't you see that?"

"All I can see is, we're broken and I don't know how to fix us."

"Brandon, I did not go upstairs that night."

"What are you saying?" His eyebrows lifted.

"It... it was Amy who followed you."

He stared at her as if she had slapped him and left her hand print burning his skin. Then he put his face in his hands and slumped in his chair. "That wasn't you? Oh, no! No wonder you hate me!"

Ashley pushed away from the table and came around to him. She placed her hands on his shoulders like comforting a child. "No, I could never hate you," she whispered into his ear.

"What have I done? Did I do something?"

"You didn't willingly do anything," she crooned in his ear. The dam broke, relief flooded over her. She exhaled. "Don't you see why I've been so angry with Amy? She tried to seduce you, tried to do a number on me. That's what she has always done."

The truth sank in. "What? So that's it. I've been racking my brain trying to figure out why you were as hot as a firecracker one night and cold as a meat locker the next. Even through this fog I could see that much."

"I should've told you sooner. I tried but couldn't."

"Why?" He threw his hands in the air, questioning.

"I tried to bury it in the back of my mind, thought we could work through it," she said.

"How could we work through it if I didn't know what'd happened or the burden you were carrying?"

"Sorry." A feeble excuse. "I'm so sorry," Ashley whispered.

"Something told me I needed to be patient. It's been two months, and I still waited. I just couldn't figure out what I'd done that was so wrong. Ashley, why didn't you tell me?"

"We'll be okay," she whispered again. Tears spilled over. "I tried... I tried to broach the subject several times. A coward, I just couldn't do it." Her breathing became shallow.

Brandon stood and turned, taking her in his arms and stroking her hair. "Shh..." Then he gently guided her to the sofa, pulled her to him and quietly held her in his arms.

Ashley licked the salty tears from the edge of her upper lip and inhaled Brandon's familiar scent. A wave of happiness swept over her, washing away the stench that had affected their relationship for weeks.

"I'm tired. Let's go to bed," she said.

Using his thumbs, Brandon blotted the remaining tears from her cheeks, pushed her hair from her face and led her down the hall. "Come, you need to rest."

"I feel like I've been crushed under a cement mixer. Haven't been able to sleep for weeks. Now that we've talked, I want to curl up between the sheets."

"I think I can handle it." Brandon smoothed her hair. They lay there cuddling until she fell asleep.

The next morning appeared like a glorious beginning to a new life. They showered together for the first time, dressed together, and enjoyed a leisurely breakfast.

Ashley cleared the dishes and Brandon loaded the dishwasher. She reached for a paper towel, dried her hands and said, "Let's look at our calendars and set the wedding date."

He blinked and looked up in surprise. "What?"

"Set the date," she repeated.

"It's about time, Ash. It's about time." He grinned.

When they had agreed on the exact day she called a wedding planner her friend Kristin had recommended months ago. They made an appointment to meet a week later and discuss basic ideas. Much of the planning could be done online.

Ashley's spirits soared throughout the day.

Then Brandon suggested a small celebration for the remainder of the weekend. "Why don't we go to the museum this afternoon? They have a new Andrew Wyeth collection. I'll make reservations for tomorrow at our favorite restaurant."

"We're sounding more like my mom every day." She chuckled. "Any excuse for a party."

Monday morning Brandon left for work while Ashley savored another cup of coffee before heading out. *No need to rush, this is a special day. Every day is a special day with Brandon.*

The phone rang. Before she could reach it, she heard Amy's voice on the answering machine. "Don't hang up. It's about Mom."

Ashley rushed to the phone, grabbed it and blurted. "What's happened? Was Mom in an accident? Did she have a stroke?"

"Whoa, slow down. None of the above. Dad called and said Mom has been diagnosed with cancer. He tried your cell, but it rolled to voice mail."

"Cancer? Are you sure? What stage?" Ashley's heart beat so loudly in her ears she could barely hear her own voice.

"I don't know any of the details. Bottom line, Dad wants us to come home for Thanksgiving."

"I'll come, but not while you're there." She spat the words like bullets, her anger overriding the cancer word.

"Sis, get real. Calm down. I know you're mad at me, and you have a right to hold a grudge. But this is our mom we're talking about."

"Don't talk to me like that. I love my mother just as much as you do. She's not the problem—you are, Amy."

"Yeah, probably from your perspective."

"Probably! You self-centered bitch. There is no probably about it. You tried to seduce my fiancé just like you took my first boyfriend away from me."

"Hold on. You mean that sniveling boy who hadn't even grown a beard? I didn't know you liked him that much."

"Of course you knew. You didn't even like him. You wanted to prove a point."

"Well, he dumped me three weeks later anyway. Who cares?"

Trying to compose herself, Ashley cleared her throat. "No, I don't care about that guy anymore. This time it's different. Brandon is different. He's off-limits for you."

"I know." Amy made a "tsk" sound.

"Your behavior suggests otherwise."

"Wait a minute, Ashley. You're making me sound like a lowlife. I just like a challenge."

"That still sounds terrible. Don't you have a conscience?"

"Well, I've never slept with a married man or anyone's fiancé."

Ashley blinked, "Never?"

"Nev-ah."

"Then why do you act like this?" Ashley paced the floor.

Amy giggled. "Because I can. See, I smooch with them, but I don't sleep with them."

"You're just a tease."

"That about sums it up."

"Yet you tried to get Brandon drunk at our engagement party."

"How was I to know he didn't drink and would be loopy after a few glasses of champagne?"

"Stop!" Ashley snapped. "Listen to us. Our mother has just been diagnosed with cancer, and we are screaming at each other like banshees. What you did is unforgivable! Period."

Silence was her only reply. Ashley hung up the phone. She cupped her face in her hands and let the tears flow.

A couple of minutes later the phone rang again. This time it was her dad. After he shared the details about her mom, he asked, "Will you come to Thanksgiving?" His voice trembled a little and Ashley's heart broke.

"Of course we will."

"I don't know what happened between you and your sister, but I can guess. Can you manage if she's there?"

It took a resolve Ashley didn't even know she had to agree, but she knew it was the right thing to do.

~~~

During the six-hour drive from Asheville to Stoneridge the landscape constantly changed. The North Carolina long-needled pines gave way to a hint of transplanted Spanish moss driving through South Carolina, then the rolling hills of North Georgia flattened below Atlanta. Finally, magnolias and the farmland of the mid-south part of the state appeared.

"The closer we get the more nervous I am about how things will turn out at home with Amy."

"Oh, I think your parents will understand."

"I'm not sure I need to share my problems with Mom at this time. No need to burden her."

"What are you going to do about telling your dad?"

"The timing is bad. Dad's under a lot of stress about Mom."

"Honey, they're going to know something is wrong before this weekend is over." He frowned.

"They already know something's wrong. I just don't think we need to give any details." She sighed.

"I think they'll take it much better if you come clean with
~~~

them."

"Maybe. I'll think about it."

Ashley had driven the first leg of the journey. After they'd stopped to eat supper Brandon took over the wheel.

Darkness descended over the land about the time of their arrival. Ashley jumped out of the car as soon as Brandon stopped.

"Look at the stars. Love, love, love the sky so clear away from the big city lights. From this day forward I want to savor every moment of life."

Brandon grabbed the luggage and headed for the front door. The porch lights helped him maneuver the steps with his load.

Ashley put on a happy face as she rang the doorbell. "Dad," she squealed at the sight of her gray-haired, teddy bear father and rushed to hug him. "How're ya holding up?"

"Hanging in there," he replied.

"Speaking of hanging. I see you nailed that ol' hanging shutter back in place."

"Yep, I putter around to keep my mind off more serious things these days."

"Staying busy is good for all of us." Ashley kissed him on the cheek and turned toward her mother, who peeked out from behind him. She reached for her and whispered, "Mom."

"I know you're worn out from the long drive. We're so glad you got here without any delays."

"It was a bit of a drive, but it was worth it. Coming home. No feeling like it." Ashley blinked away the tears.

Brandon eased by them and started up the stairs with the bags when Ashley called to him. She could not bear to face that room where Amy had tried her tricks two months ago. "Take the bags down the hall to the small guest room, please." Brandon shrugged but wheeled around without hesitation.

"Y'all hungry?" Dad asked.

"I baked a pecan pie. Think it's too late for dessert?" Mom asked.

"Are you kidding?" From the hall Brandon jumped into the conversation. "It's never too late for dessert where Ashley's concerned."

They sat around the round oak table where Ashley had scratched her initials underneath at age eight.

"Coffee?" Dad asked.

"No, but a glass of milk sure sounds good," Brandon said.

Ashley took a bite of pie. "Hmmm. Warm pie and cold milk. Nothing better."

When everyone had satisfied their sweet tooth, the conversation came easily, not rushed.

"Mom, can you talk about it? I don't want to intrude."

Her mother looked into Ashley's eyes and said, "You're not intruding, sweetheart. I've been diagnosed with cancer. Life isn't always perfect, but..."

Ashley jumped on the subject like ants on sugar. Who recommended this oncologist? What is the treatment plan? What's the prognosis? Her questions gushed out, leaving no time for answers.

"Whoa!" Mom held up her arms. "Slow down. The plan is a lumpectomy in six weeks then probably just radiation therapy, depending on the biopsy."

Ashley started the query again.

"Enough with the questions," her mom interjected.

"I know but..."

"No buts. Several of my friends have dealt with the same news in recent years."

"But they aren't my mother. I'll be here the week after Christmas for your surgery."

"Great. The good news is that most patients have beaten it and now live normal lives."

Dad fidgeted while her mom carried the conversation.

Ashley came over, kissed her mom on the cheek, and then gave her dad a bear hug.

Dad yawned. "Think it's about my bedtime."

"I think we could all use a good night's rest. Suits me if we turn in." Ashley tried to sound cheerful. "Thanks for sharing, Mom."

~~~

The delicious smell of bacon and coffee drew Ashley and Brandon to the kitchen the next morning.

"God, that bacon hit my nostrils all the way down the hall." Brandon greeted his future in-laws.

"Nothing like the smell of apple wood smoked bacon to get you going in the morning," Ashley's dad agreed. "Come on in and pull up a chair, son."

Ashley peeked into the pot on the stove. "Grits. Oh, I love your grits, Mom. I still can't make them like you do."

"The secret to cooking good grits is simmering, not boiling. These have been simmering for half an hour. I use real butter for the creamy taste."

The first day at home in Stoneridge went well. Ashley told her parents she and Brandon had set their wedding date. She knew the road back to her happy relationship with Brandon would not be smooth, but they loved each other and could work it out day by day.

"It took you so long to set the date I was beginning to think you'd had second thoughts," her mother said.

"No, I had some issues I needed to work through. It took longer than I expected. I had to be sure."

"Glad you've worked things out. You fell in love with him all over again." Her mom smiled.

"No, not really."

"What do you mean?" Dad jumped to attention.

"I never fell out of love with him."

"That's even better news." Her mother smiled, moved toward her and hugged her as only a mother can.

Her dad cleared his throat and waited his turn to embrace them both. "Now, Elizabeth, you can't hog all of Ashley's time."

"This is going to be a great Thanksgiving."
~~~

~~~

Amy arrived that evening. After thirty minutes or so of faked conversation Ashley feigned a headache and escaped to her room. Brandon made his exit from the living room and joined her.

Ashley had a dream that night. *She and Amy are racing across the field. She sees the fence ahead and realizes Amy won't make the jump. Ashley does not try to stop her until it's too late.* "No!" She woke with a scream stuck in her throat. She sat up trembling, shaking like a leaf in a wind storm. Her heart raced, pumping blood through her veins at the speed of the horses' galloping. Reality spread through her.

"Bad dream?" Brandon pulled her into his arms. "What was it about?"

Ashley told him the details. "I thought I hated Amy after what she did. But that's not true. I resent what she's done to me over a lifetime, but I still love her."

"Sounds like it's time to tell her that."

She snuggled closer to him. "You're right. Today's the day."

Early the next morning Ashley knocked on Amy's door before the parents got up. "Want to have coffee out on the patio? Made it just like you take it, two sugars and no cream." She extended the mug.

Amy stood there with rumpled hair and signs of a sleepless night in her eyes. She didn't answer for a minute, then she blinked and blurted. "Sure. Wait a minute. Let me pull on some jeans and a shirt."

Amy tugged at her sweater in the brisk morning air, took a seat on the patio, and began like a roller coaster on steroids. "I… I apologize for my shitty behavior. I'm sorry. I don't know what made me do such a nasty thing. Jealousy, I guess."

"Jealousy? How could you be jealous of me? You're the pretty one."

"You were everyone's favorite. Folks always loved sweet Little Miss Perfect."

"No one is perfect. But we need to get beyond this. Time to
~~~

move on."

Then Amy verified Brandon did not do anything but kiss her before he passed out, mumbling, "Ash... ley, I love you more than life. You're the most per... fect woman in the world. I... I'm soooo blessed."

Relieved that it was no more than a kiss, Ashley commented, "Aww, how sweet of him."

"It may seem sweet now, but it was sickening to me at the time. I guess I gave him too much booze. At that moment I wanted to slap him. Even half-drunk all he could think of was you."

"But you didn't slap him?"

"Of course not. At that point I wouldn't have continued—even if he had been awake."

Ashley set her coffee cup down and leaned toward Amy. "I've let you get away with being selfish all our lives."

"Whose fault is that?"

"Mine, I guess," Ashley replied. "You always seemed so needy, so demanding, I just gave in to you."

"Well, I'm trying to do better." Amy squirmed in her chair.

"I want to believe you are sorry. Truly I do."

"You don't have much choice." Amy stared her into the eyes.

"What did you say? If I didn't value our family, I'd deck you right now, you self-centered juvenile." Ashley turned to leave.

"Wait! Wait. I truly am sorry."

"Then you should apologize to Brandon. He is the real victim here."

"You're kidding, right?" Amy's eyebrows lifted.

"Not exactly. You must apologize. I won't be a pushover any more. No more easy way out for you. I'll call Brandon."

Amy stood up and stepped toward the door, ready to flee. "I'm outta here."

Ashley grabbed her arm. "Don't move or I'll slap you to the floor! Sit down! The three of us are going to settle this before we try to maneuver through Thanksgiving. We're going to be civil."

"I don't know what to say, where to begin, how to explain..."

"Well, you'd better try. I'm trying, and we're not having Mom and Dad upset over this crap."

"Uh, I..." Amy squirmed again.

"No excuses. Just the truth. And don't soft pedal it." Ashley turned, headed into the house.

Five minutes later she and Brandon stepped out on the patio, holding hands. When he saw Amy a confused expression crossed his face.

"What's going on?" he asked.

"Amy has something she'd like to say."

With her bottom lip quivering, Amy began. "I'm so, so sorry I acted trashy as hell on the night of your engagement party."

"What did you do?" Brandon asked.

Amy explained what had happened. "When you called me Ashley and told me how much you loved me, I realized it wasn't funny anymore."

Brandon's face flushed as he listened in disbelief before responding in a tirade. "How could you...? To your own sister? Don't you know how important a good family is? Believe me, I know. I'm a survivor of a broken home. My brother lived with one parent, and I lived with the other."

"She knows now," Ashley responded and turned to Amy. "If you ever touch my man again I'll pull every hair out of your head."

"Agreed. I wish I could take it all back. Please forgive me for being so deceitful," Amy pleaded as she looked at her sister and Brandon.

"I believe you because we're family, and I love you." Ashley opened her arms, and the twins embraced for the first time in ages. In the last few minutes they'd won something more precious than the lottery.

"Whew." Amy gave a sigh of relief.

"Let's go help Mom and Dad in the kitchen. Thanksgiving dinner requires a lot of cooks. And I think you've had enough humble pie for today."

"Yeah." Amy frowned. "It's time for some pumpkin pie."

"Make mine Georgia pecan pie," Ashley added. She held out her hand to Brandon. He smiled, moved toward her, and whispered, "You color my world with love, Georgia girl."

The Haunting of Misty Lake

People are often unreasonable and self-centered. Forgive them anyway.

~ Mother Teresa

AUTUMN IN NORTH Georgia had transformed the trees into a multicolored dreamscape of red, yellow and orange. Oblivious to the beauty around her, Emma Perry headed to the mailbox, opened it, and exclaimed, "Yes!" The invitation had finally arrived.

She broke into a happy dance right there in the street—hands in the air, spinning around, gyrating like a belly dancer to the rhythm in her head. A nosy neighbor glared from across the tree-lined street. Emma shrugged and flipped her long chestnut hair. "That old busybody can't put a damper on my weekend," she muttered.

Emma's insides whirled like her grandmother churning butter. She was excited over the moon about the party they had all planned. *If the boys thought me hot in high school, just wait until they see me Saturday night*. She retrieved the folded flyer, broke the seal and started reading.

Hear ye, hear ye! Come one, come all

To the Halloween Masquerade Ball.

Emma smiled. Oozing confidence, she swished her hips as she looked back over her shoulder and sashayed up the driveway into the house.

Her mother met her in the foyer, holding a dust mop. "Just chasing out the dust bunnies."

"Stop fussing, Mom. It's only Coralee and Frank coming. That floor already shines enough to blind you. The house smells as clean as fresh laundry."

"Speaking of laundry, have you done yours yet? I'm not doing it again this week. You're a junior in college, Emma."

Mom would never send me back to campus with dirty clothes. "Nope. I'll do it today. Promise. Need clean clothes anyway. The Halloween party and reunion are Saturday night."

"Did you say 'reunion'?" Her mother's voice elevated a pitch.

"Yeah, we're combining two events into one. Everyone's so busy, but several of our friends are free this weekend. It'll be nice to see everybody now that we've been away for a few years."

"That's a lot of catching up and celebrating packed into one night."

"Of course." Emma rolled her eyes. "Coralee, Frank and I have to be back at UGA for classes early Monday. College is not for wimps."

"Right. Gotcha." Her mother walked to the kitchen and began preparing dinner.

"I'll be upstairs if you want me," Emma called from the landing halfway up to her bedroom. She needed to hang a few things before she sorted laundry. She threw open the closet door. A new pair of jeans caught her eye. She grabbed them, pulled them on, and faced the mirror. "Wow! This is more like it," she said to herself, turning around to check out the whole package. "These jeans were made for me. Really show off my 'ass-vantage,' if I do say so myself." Everyone had always told her what a cute tush she had.

"Oh, Mom, I love the jeans you bought," Emma yelled downstairs. "They fit perfectly and they're my favorite brand."

"Glad you like them. You're so picky. Gotta be the right brand, color and fit."

"You're exaggerating, Mom."

"Not! Of course, your dad may not like them that tight." She laughed.

"Thanks, Mom. You rock!"

In the far corner of the closet, her grandmother's wedding gown hung, wrapped in preservative paper and encased in a see-through garment bag. She placed her hand on the bag and almost felt the lace pattern brand her palm. Staring at her hand, she could envision Grandgran's diamond ring decorating her finger. The delicate filigree setting would catch the sparkle of the fine stone, warming Emma's insides. Too bad it's at the bottom of Misty Lake or in some fish's belly. A million times worse, her grandmother had drowned in a boating accident. The warmth left Emma, and a tear rolled down her cheek.

Exhaling sharply, she snapped back to the present when she heard her mother call from downstairs. "Emma."

"Be down in a jiff, as soon as I send Frank a message," she replied.

Frank was totally into her, and Emma used that infatuation to her benefit. She texted him about her homework and waited a half hour for an answer. No luck. Impatient, she called but got the stupid voice mail. Trying to cover her huffy mood, she purred sweetly, "I hope you remembered the homework assignment I asked you to help me with."

Why did I ever get Frank and Coralee involved in my weekend plans? Unlike her, they didn't fit into the partying crowd. However, she'd already invited them, so she was stuck with them and regretted that decision big time.

Worrying about Frank and her homework gave her a reality check. Both Frank and Coralee were brainiacs, Emma grinned remembering. They helped keep her grades up, which gave her time to take part in extracurricular activities like cheerleading.

She looked around her room and calculated what she needed to do before Coralee's arrival Saturday morning. Emma yelled downstairs, "Mom, why couldn't the housekeeper have done some of my chores?"

The simple reply traveled up the stairs. "You need to do your share. That's why."

When Emma floated downstairs she practiced her Homecoming Queen smile and wave. As soon as she strolled into the kitchen she spotted her mother standing at the counter, mixing something in a bowl. She grabbed a Coke from the fridge, and then perched on a stool at the breakfast counter. "What's for dinner? Smells good."

"Your favorite—roast beef with potatoes, carrots and onions."

Emma's stomach rumbled and her mouth watered at the thought of the savory dish. "Umm."

"You can make the salad."

"Sure, after I make a call," she said, sauntering from the kitchen. *Why do I always get commandeered to help? Housework, cooking—hate them both.* Like an echo in the air, Grandgran's voice whispered to Emma, "Spoiled. Spoiled."

Huffing, she stomped out to the front porch, plopped down in a rocker and punched Frank's cell number again. He picked up on the third ring.

"What's up, Em?" He laughed after calling her by the nickname she hated.

She ignored Frank's effort at wit. "I've been calling and texting you for two hours. That's what's up!"

"Whoa, hold on."

"Have you finished my homework? You're so smart I figured you'd whip it out in a flash."

"No time to work on it yet," he growled.

She groaned at the idea she might have to do the homework herself. "Come on, I need this favor. The dance is tomorrow, remember? Have to email it to my prof Monday morning."

"You should be doing this yourself. What's going to happen to you next year after I graduate?"

"I'll worry about that later." She tapped her foot on the floor. "At least I'm not a grade whore, flirting or sleeping with my instructors like several of the girls I know."

"Yeah that's a good thing." He sighed. "But you have to think about next year. You think you'll find someone else to do the math for you, but nobody cares about you as much as I do, Emma. Can you get that through your thick skull?"

"If you cared for me so much, you'd do the homework! Besides, it's one of the reasons I keep you around," she teased openly.

"Emma, let's be honest, you only call me when you need my help. You're selfish, and I don't know why I put up with you."

"I know. It gives you status to be seen with me."

"You should go to the costume dance as a witch. You're certainly acting like one," he snapped.

She could hear the pride in his voice in this rare moment of defiance. "And you're impossible, Frank Harmon. Are you going to do the assignment or not?" Her blood pressure soared as she rocked the chair faster and harder.

"Of course I will, but you have to promise you'll tutor another student next semester. At least try giving back. Otherwise, I'm not helping you anymore."

"Maybe I don't want to tutor. Maybe I want to experience real life for a change. I'm so bored with the same old thing, day after day."

"Don't know how you could be bored. You always get everything you want." His voice had an edge she didn't like.

She stood, stomping her foot on the porch floor, but held her temper in check. "See you tomorrow afternoon, Frank. Thanks for the help. Gotta run." She hung up abruptly. *Better quit while I'm ahead.*

After dinner Emma slipped away before her mother could ask her to do the dishes. Upstairs, she decided to hang her clothes instead of throwing them across a chair, as she normally did. A rhinestone tiara caught her eye on the top shelf of the closet. *That's it. I'll go as a princess. I'll show Frank and everyone else. Witch indeed!*

Pushing some dresses aside, she spotted a pink princess outfit and hoped it still fit after three years. Slipping it on, she fingered the sides of the smooth satin bust-line, and then dashed to the full-length mirror to admire her image. "It's perfect for the dance." She continued to stare at herself, almost hypnotized. Suddenly she recalled a girl in her psychology class tagging her narcissistic. Emma stared at her reflection again and dared ask, "Is that true?"

Unzipping the dress she let the chiffon puddle on the floor, pulled on her pajamas and plopped onto the bed. Time to check her email, scroll through Facebook and Instagram, and text a few friends. Tomorrow would be a busy day.

Looking through the window, Emma realized there was no moonlight. Fog had started slowly rolling in, moving like an animal on the prowl. She stretched and yawned. Hope this fog doesn't ruin the weekend. She fell asleep dreaming of meeting Prince Charming and having him whisk her away in his private jet to exotic places where she would reign over the ordinary people like Frank and Coralee.

She awoke to a dreary morning. The smell of sizzling bacon drifting up the stairs made her nose twitch. Emma stretched and groaned, then hopped out of bed and followed the tantalizing aroma downstairs. Home had its advantages.

"Good morning, sleepy head, hope you slept well," her mom said.

"Yep, I'm always tired by the weekend." Emma yawned.

"Glad you rested. You have a long day ahead of you."

"The weather looks miserable. Lots of fog this morning and it looks even heavier going down toward the lake."

"It might clear up by the time Coralee and Frank get here." Mom offered.

"Always optimistic." She gave her mother a hug.

"I try."

Her cell rang twice before Emma grabbed it.

"Morning." Frank's voice sounded worried. "The weather forecast looks miserable. Do you think I should offer to pick up Coralee and save her folks a trip?"

"Great." She tried to sound cheerful. *What on earth made Frank think about picking up Coralee?*

"I'll give her a call," Frank said.

"Oh, wait. Coralee planned on coming around lunchtime. Mom has to make some alterations to her costume."

"That'll work, if it's okay with your mom. I can occupy myself with a new app I bought for my tablet. Love tech toys," Frank joked.

"It'll be fine. My parents won't care. See you then." She banged the phone down with a thud and gave her mom an update.

"Frank's picking up Coralee, and they're having lunch with us, okay?"

Her dad walked in. "Good. That'll give me a chance to show off my new rod and reel. Does Frank hunt or fish?"

"I've never heard him mention it. We mainly talk about school stuff." She sighed. When her dad said things like that, it made her realize how much he had probably wanted a son to pal around with. Instead he'd gotten a girlie girl.

"I hope so. My dad and I did a lot of things together. I could use some 'guy' time."

"Boys will be boys," Emma said with a fake lilt in her voice.

"Well, girls always go shopping with their moms, right?" He chuckled.

"Right." Emma smiled and turned to her mom. "Need me to help with lunch?"

"That would be nice, since we're having extra guests."

Grandgran always said, "Pretty is as pretty does." So I should help. These are my friends, not Mom's. She almost didn't recognize the thought as her own.

~~~

Frank and Coralee arrived about a half hour later than expected, but Emma hadn't worried. Frank was a careful driver.

"Hope we didn't keep you waiting too long, Mrs. Perry," Frank apologized, "visibility was low."

"Glad you got here safely. It's always good to have a young man to visit with my husband, while we girls do our thing."

After lunch the two men wandered off into another part of the house while the ladies cleaned the kitchen and headed up to the sewing room.

Emma's mom lifted the lid of the desk-type sewing machine and proceeded to thread the needle with a color to match Coralee's costume.

"Go try it on, sweetie, so we can see what we want to do to it."

"Yes, ma'am." Coralee dashed away to put on the Medieval period costume, handed down from a cousin. Coralee was naturally petite, but when she returned, she looked smaller than ever, dwarfed by folds of heavy material.

"Ah, let's have a look at you. Turn around. I think we should remove some of the panels and lighten it up a little. What do you think, Coralee?"

"Whatever will make it look better, Mrs. Perry. You're the
~~~

expert."

"Okay, you and Emma can run along and polish your nails, fuss with your hair and do your makeup. Time's flying. I'll call you when I need you."

Emma put on some fast music as soon as they got to her room. She glanced out the window. The eerie fog had not cleared. "Darn," she complained. "I hoped the weather would cooperate."

Coralee giggled and started a silly rant about all the things that might happen at the dance. "We might meet Mr. Right or run into a former friend who has gone into show business."

"Yes, our friend will get us jobs in the movies," Emma added. "This could be a night when dreams come true."

Coralee bent over double, laughing. "Then I can give up my part-time job."

The word "job" captured Emma's attention. She stopped laughing. "Job?" What was she thinking? "I don't want a job."

Coralee sighed. "You're lucky you don't need one."

Halfway through a hair curling session, Emma heard her mom call out, "Oh, Coralee, I'm ready for you to try on the dress again."

The girls bounced down the hall. Coralee slipped into the dress which had been transformed. The yards of heavy material had been reduced to a slenderizing beautiful costume. Some of the purple velvet trim remained, but the fine muslin had been nipped and tucked to emphasize Coralee's tiny waist.

"Wow!" I can't believe it's the same dress, can you, Emma?" She twirled around like an excited kid wearing her first costume.

"Mom, you're amazing. It looks great." Emma did not smile.

"Thanks, Mrs. Perry." Coralee gave her a hug.

"You're most welcome. Now you girls need to get ready for a night to remember."

"Don't worry, we're already making plans."

The girls hurried down the hall and began the ritual of making themselves as beautiful as possible. Emma stepped into the blush pink princess outfit, pulled it up, and then faced the mirror.

"Coralee, zip me up, please."

When they looked into the mirror, Coralee sighed. "You're absolutely gorgeous."

"No, my grandmother was gorgeous and my grandfather worshiped her. When she drowned in Misty Lake he was devastated. And I... I..." She choked.

"I'm sooo sorry. I didn't know." Coralee bit her lower lip.

"Of course, you didn't. Let me show you their wedding picture." Emma crossed the room to her dresser and lifted a frame, which she caressed before handing it to Coralee.

"Oh my God, you're right! She was gorgeous. I thought you'd exaggerated. Most little girls think their mothers and grandmothers are beautiful."

"Sure. Anyway, compared to her, my mother and I are just pretty, at best."

"I should be so lucky." Coralee sighed.

"Well, you look really nice. That dress fits you like a glove."

"Yes, I love it. Your mom works magic with a needle and thread."

"My mom has many talents," Emma added. *The dress helps some, but there's only so much Coralee can do with a garden of freckles and eyeglass lenses as thick as the bottoms of Coca Cola bottles.*

Her mother appeared at the bedroom door. "Don't forget your face masks. You can't go to a masquerade ball without them."

The girls got themselves together, checked each other in the mirror before they left the room and joined Frank. He was the designated driver, and they could depend on him to fend off any aggressive guys and get them home safely.

Frank jumped out of his chair. His jaw dropped in awe.

"Gosh! You two look fantastic. I dig the outfits. I'll be the luckiest guy at the party with a pretty girl on each arm."

"You look nice, yourself. That pirate's patch over your eye makes you look mysterious," Coralee said, while Emma nodded in agreement.

They stepped outside into abysmal dampness. The fog had not lifted. Frank helped the girls into the car, climbed behind the wheel, and threw the gear shift into drive. As the car neared the Road House Dance Hall, they could hardly see the driveway of the parking lot.

The music greeted them with a blast, the party already in full swing. Smoke drifted towards them as they approached several guys cooking on grills stationed across one side of the front porch. Emma grinned. "Those burgers sure smell delicious. You can cook for me anytime." She batted her eye lashes, winked at them and continued walking, swinging her hips as she departed.

The place was already crowded. Folks hadn't let the fog keep them at home. Emma spoke to a few locals and headed to the bar. She grabbed a handful of nuts from a bowl and ordered a beer. The cold brew tasted pretty good.

Emma spotted her old high school rival across the room and waved. Janice had married early, had a baby and still carried the baby-fat. A smug feeling settled in the pit of Emma's flat stomach—just as flat as the day she had graduated from high school.

Coralee and Frank caught up with Emma at the bar. "I like the spooky decorations," Coralee said, "especially the huge spider webs up in the corners of the ceiling and the tankards like on a pirate ship."

"Yeah, I fit right in with my pirate's costume," Frank added, adjusting his eye patch. "Hope I can still see with one eye. This thing is no fun."

Emma noticed a partially-masked stranger headed toward them. She couldn't see all his features, but what she could see looked handsome. His eyes penetrated through the mask's openings. She acted coy, gave him a flirtatious smile and turned away.

"Don't look now, gang, but here comes trouble, and I'm ready to paaarty." She snapped her fingers.

"Take it easy, this guy might misunderstand your boldness. Do you know him?" Frank asked, frowning.

"No, but I think I want to," Emma answered, turning to face the young man as he approached them.

"Just be careful," Frank whispered.

"Hi, I'm Don." The stranger held out his hand to greet the three of them.

Emma looked into his eyes. "I'm Emma and these are my friends, Coralee and Frank."

Don glanced at them one at a time, nodded, and returned his attention to Emma.

He held her hand for a moment too long, then cleared his throat. "You must be the princess of the ball."

"Well, of course," she said in her best Scarlett O'Hara imitation.

"Dance?" he asked, leaning toward her.

"I'd love to. See you guys later." She winked at Coralee and Frank and walked away, focusing on Don's backside in those tight pants.

His warm hand holding hers caused a stir. Her skin tingled like when she visited the Butterfly House at Callaway Gardens and the fragile beauties rested on her wrists. Don placed his arms around her waist as soon as they reached the dance floor. Cologne and alcohol, mixed with his natural scent, enticed her as he pulled her closer to his firm torso. Lost in the rhythm of the music, she felt her cheeks flush.

I didn't drink enough beer to feel this giddy. Must be my hormones.

Don Juan's chest pressed into her until she felt her cleavage would burst out of her low cut neckline. There was no air space between their two bodies. Fireworks went off inside as her pulse raced.

He pulled away and stared at her, his hazel eyes a mixture of desire and wonder. "Sorry, I just couldn't help myself."

"We're both acting a little reckless." She laughed nervously.

Emma saw Frank heading their way, but he turned back when Don slightly pulled away from her. She had mixed emotions about Frank's presence. On the one hand, she resented his hovering over her, but she felt safe knowing he would watch out for her. She recognized that familiar look of despair on his face, the look he often wore when she had disappointed him.

The band started playing a slow song she liked, and Don gently pulled her back into the curvature of his body. This time he slid his hands low and cupped her backside. Her hypnotic trance evaporated as quickly as it had materialized. Emma pulled his hand away, took a step backward, and leveled a dagger stare at him.

"You're bold. How about keeping your hands to yourself?"

Frank appeared and spun Don around. "Hey, pal, what do you think you're doing?"

"Sorry. Maybe I've had too much to drink," he mumbled.

"You can say that again! You need to cool it," Frank barked as he took Emma's hand and led her off the dance floor.

"Come on, Emma, let's get out of here. You need some fresh air."

"Okay, mother hen." She heaved an impatient sigh, not sure if she was angry or grateful.

"Someone has to be in charge," Frank growled. But Emma noted a small, pleased smile flit across his face.

Coralee joined them. "Hey, Emma, you only had a sip of your beer before that handsome stranger whisked you away to dance." She slung her arm toward Don. "So I finished it. Hope you don't mind."

"No problem." Emma fanned herself with her hand, still feeling flushed from the dance with Don. "Fog has shifted, looks like it's clearing up outside. Let's check it out. Seems like Coralee needs some fresh air, too," she muttered to Frank.

The muggy feel of the fog had been replaced with a bit of fall crispness. They went to the edge of the front porch and stood in amazement. Emma's mouth flew open. She blinked and shook her head in disbelief. There was a ship out on the lake. She hadn't noticed it an hour ago when they arrived.

Pushed by the rolling fog from out of nowhere, it skimmed across the water. A ship with two masts and ragged sails flapping in the slight breeze, it had seen better days. Emma glanced at her friends. They were obviously seeing it, too.

"Do you suppose someone had that thing, that ship, towed in for the Halloween party?" Frank asked.

"Probably some sort of joke," Emma said. "I've never seen anything like this on Misty Lake before."

Frank started walking across the road. "Well, I want to explore it."

"Wait," Emma said, holding her arm out. "We could float away."

"I can't swim, so maybe I shouldn't go," Coralee said anxiously.

"It's anchored," Frank said. He pointed to their left, where a large, black chain hung from the side of the boat into the murky lake water. "Otherwise, it would've floated away."

Emma and Coralee were not easily convinced. As they debated, a male figure appeared on the gangplank and motioned for them to come on board. He wasn't wearing a patch over one eye, a crazy hat or a wooden leg. Obviously he wasn't a pirate, just some dude in period clothing. He had long jet black hair tied in a ponytail.

The trio hesitated, looked at each other and agreed to go for it. The man on the gangplank disappeared as quickly as he had appeared.

Emma led her friends down the steps, across the road and out to the dock. At its edge, a gangplank extended out from the ship. Phantom-like in appearance, the vessel seemed too large for a lake but too small for an ocean-bound pirate ship. Tattered sails hung limp from two major masts. Set against the remaining fog, it looked eerie, foreboding almost, yet somehow enticing.

The threesome stood on the dock while Emma contemplated what they should do. "What the heck, guys? Let's go out there. It's Halloween. This could be like a mystery theatre where you play a part. It's probably planned."

"Well, I don't want to. But if we go, we can't stay long." Coralee stifled a burp. "I need to be back at the dance when they judge the costumes. Your mom worked very hard to make mine look pretty."

The handsome male figure reappeared at the top of the gangplank. Again he smiled and motioned for them to come aboard.

"That does it for me. He's yummy. We're going," Emma announced, making the decision for everyone.

Looking down, watching each step, Coralee and Frank followed her up the gangplank. When they got to the top, the pony-tailed guy had disappeared.

"Strange," said Frank. "The ship seems completely deserted except for the mysterious greeter who welcomed us on board and then vanished."

"Freaky," Coralee agreed. "Damp wood reeks with old age, smells like mold and mildew. It reminds me of death. Where'd this crazy pirate ship come from?"

"Who cares where it came from? I'm going onboard. Come on guys, don't be wusses. It's an adventure, let's explore." Emma laughed. *Those two can't make a decision for themselves.*

With Emma in the lead, the three traipsed from one area of the ship to another but found no one on the deck. The fog had lifted enough for them to see the lights of the dance hall across the road. It seemed odd that nobody had come out on the porch and followed them, especially if the ship was part of the Halloween fun.

"Anyone brave enough to venture below?" Emma asked. "I thought I heard a rumbling noise down there."

"I'm brave. I don't drink beer often, but when I do—I..." Coralee giggled. "Is the ship moving? I'm feeling a little woozy," she slurred.

"You're half drunk," Frank said with disdain. "You know you can't drink. What possessed you to finish Emma's beer?"

"Sor... ry, Frank," Coralee apologized. "You're right. I wasn't paying attention and kept sipping that stupid beer. I think I'm gonna be sick." She stepped on a rotten board, lost her balance and collapsed in a heap.

"My God, she's almost passed out," Emma shouted, running toward Coralee. Frank dashed past her, headed in the same direction. The weight of all three bodies caused the rotten boards to give way. Emma felt her heart pounding like a hammer. "Help!" She let out a blood-curdling scream. They fell through the deck with a crashing thud.

Emma and Frank stirred and checked their bodies for injuries. "What happened?" she asked. Her arms and hands trembled. This night wasn't anything at all like she had imagined. "What were they thinking, bringing this rickety old ship here for the party? Someone was bound to get hurt," Emma grumbled.

Frank took her hand. "You'll be okay," he said in a soothing tone. "We just fell through a decayed spot in the wood." He reached for his cell. No service.

Coralee moaned. Emma and Frank scurried over to check on her.

"Are you okay?" Emma asked.

"I think so, don't think I broke anything. My left ankle hurts a little."

"Probably bruised," Frank said. "Hope it isn't sprained."

A second groan escaped from Coralee's throat. "Aahh." She looked around. "My beer's gone and so are my glasses. I think I've lost 'em."

"You probably dropped them when we fell through the rotten floor boards."

"Where are we?" Coralee looked around in confusion. She propped herself up on one elbow, but she did not try to stand up.

"Remember the boat? We're below deck on a lower floor," Emma answered. "But we're not moving until you feel better. Try to stay quiet for a few minutes. Just rest."

Emma sat listening to the ship groan occasionally as it swayed in the lake. Finally she looked at Frank. "We need to see if we can get Coralee on her feet and get the heck out of here."

Emma worried what would happen next. When she sensed her skin burning she rubbed her hand across her face. Her fingers felt rough, bumpy skin. *Yikes, what's going on? My skin has always been smooth. Maybe I'm turning into a witch like Frank said.*

Coralee looked at Emma and put her hand over her mouth. "Emma! Something is really strange. Your skin's getting pimples. I can see them even without my glasses."

Frank looked up. "Wow! You've never had zits before. We need to get out of here before anything else goes wrong."

"Damn it! Don't you people care? What if I'm stuck with these bumps, pimples, or something worse—warts?"

"Get over yourself, Emma. Thanks to you we may be stuck down here. Now what?" Frank stared at the two girls and a snarl formed at the corner of his mouth.

"Stop it, Frank! I'm not taking the fall for this one by myself."

Coralee started giggling. "Now that's funny. I think we all had a fall."

Emma ran her hands over her hair and tugged at her dress, ignoring the laughter of the other two. She tried to move, but the chiffon of her skirt had caught on a nail. She disengaged herself, then leaned over to Coralee and asked, "Are you feeling well enough to walk yet?"

Coralee nodded. Frank and Emma helped Coralee to her feet and started looking around to find a way out of their prison.

They found a door, but it was bolted. Then they saw a staircase. Emma went up first, but the hatch at the top of the steps was locked, also. She tried not to panic. "Guys, I think we're locked in."

"What do you mean, we're locked in? There must be a way out of here. We just have to keep looking," Frank said.

"Maybe the doors are rusted shut, and we can bang on them to loosen them," Coralee suggested. "Let's look for something strong to use as a tool. We ought to be able to find some weak spots in the walls. That flooring sure was rotten."

Frank stepped on something. "Here's an old rusted piece of iron." He held up a pole about the size of a long broom-handle. "I'm going to try to break through the hatch with it." Frank seized the pole, rushed to the top of the stairs, and started banging on the iron hatch.

"You're not making any progress. Let me try." Emma took the pole from Frank and frantically whacked at the hatch until she was exhausted.

"Okay, let's try to break through the door," she said optimistically.

Emma and Frank took turns banging at the door, but it did not budge. Frank even tried running with the rod toward the door to gain momentum. His efforts failed.

"If only we had a ladder, we could climb up where we fell through." Frank sighed.

"Yeah, and if we had service we could call 911, genius boy," Emma said sarcastically.

Sitting on the floor, the three friends huddled together. Fear set in. Coralee quivered and hugged herself. Emma's eyes darted back and forth as if looking for a monster to attack. What would happen to them? Perhaps the ship was no longer at the dock. It could have sailed away by now. Anything could have occurred since their fall.

Coralee's lips trembled. "Do you think someone will find us years from now, our corpses all skeletons on this ghost ship?"

Emma reached over and grabbed Coralee's shoulders. "Stop that jack-jawing!"

"Yeah, we've got to remain calm," Frank said. "Someone will come looking for us. No need to panic." But he wore a stoic look.

"You're right," Emma agreed, but she felt the dryness of fear in her mouth. Spitless. Each second passed in slow motion. How long have we been here? More importantly, how long will we be here before someone rescues us?

Emma heard a klunk, klunk, klunk. With her heart pounding in her chest, she looked at her friends, whose wide eyes told her they'd heard it, too. The rattle of chains only added to their fear. With a squeaking noise followed by a slight thump, the boat lurched, rocking from side to side.

"Did you feel that? Are we moving?" Coralee's eyes looked

huge.

"Holy crap, we are moving! This lake has dozens of channels. Oh, my God, if we drift too far, we could end up anywhere," Emma said. Her face turned ashen.

"Stop it," Frank ordered.

"But you don't understand," Emma's eyes glistened with tears. "I'm ashamed to say I was too proud to tell you guys, but I can't swim. I might not ever see my mom and dad again."

"Sure you will." Coralee sounded brave for a change.

"What if I don't? I've been a jerk to my mom. In fact I've been a real witch with a B... at times."

Klunk, klunk, klunk—the sound repeated. Again the boat rocked from side to side. The pattern of squeaking continued until all three of them agreed it was a winch straining to bring up the anchor.

Emma scrambled over to the porthole and brushed the grime off it. Not much visibility through the small glass, but she saw something for certain—the boat wasn't docked anymore. It had floated out onto the lake.

"We're off the dock!" she shouted in a shrill voice.

Coralee shook with terror. "Y'all know I can't swim, either."

"There must be some old life preservers somewhere. We just have to find them." Frank rushed around, moving things, digging under piles of clutter, looking for anything that might help. He found nothing. "Damn. No life preservers, no deflated life rafts, not a thing."

Coralee shuddered. "D... Don't leave me."

Geez, Coralee has reverted into a five-year-old, Emma inwardly groused but reached over and rubbed Coralee's arm. "Don't be scared, we won't leave you." Then she looked at Frank's panic-filled eyes.

"There's that one small porthole over there, but it doesn't open. Even if it had a latch, it's too little for us to go through it," Frank said.

As they stared at the porthole, something in the distance moved. They glanced at each other and went over to get a closer look. Nothing there.

"I could have sworn I saw something through the window. What about you guys?" Emma asked.

"Me, too," Frank said.

They stood there for several minutes longer, looking around at each other. Each shrugged. A piece of coral-colored chiffon drifted by the opening.

"What's that? Look! There it is." Emma screamed and almost fainted as a phantom figure passed through the porthole. She coughed. The stench of mold nearly choked her. Then she heard a voice.

"Em ma... Em ma," the high-pitched voice called.

"Yikes! Who's there? How'd you know my name?" Her leg muscles tightened, ready to run.

"It's Grandgran, sweetie. Don't be frightened."

The voice sounded vaguely familiar. The apparition's long black locks looked similar to her grandmother's hair but with added white streaks. Its cheeks were hollow, and black eyes stared at her. Emma looked at the wrinkled, bony hand extended toward her. The figure wore the treasured rings of Emma's grandmother, the ones Emma had played with as a child.

"G... G... Grandgran, is that really you?" Emma stuttered.

"Of course, child."

"You scared me."

"Don't be afraid. I've been waiting for you. It's been almost a decade, and now you're all grown up."

"Uh, yes ma'am," Emma whispered uneasily. "I'm twenty-one and a junior in college."

"My-oh-my, I know your mom and dad are proud of you. And look how beautiful you are."

"Thanks, I've always wanted to be gorgeous like you. Why couldn't I have had your raven-black hair and fabulous cheekbones?"

"Because you don't have Cherokee blood in you, dear. You see, my mother was half French and half Native American." She smiled, her teeth dark with decay.

"I don't understand...," Emma said, her eyebrows lifted in question.

"You look like your mother, my dear. And she is far more beautiful than I. She's beautiful inside, the most beautiful person I ever knew. We adopted her as a baby. What a blessing she was to your grandfather and me!"

"So you're not my real grandmother?" Surprise and disappointment seeped into Emma's tone.

"Don't be ridiculous!" she snapped. "Of course, I'm your real grandmother. A real parent or grandparent is the one who takes care of you."

"Yes, but..."

"No buts! That's the bottom line. Your mother was our greatest treasure, and then she gave us you. I hope your life will be so blessed."

"It doesn't always work out like that," Emma snapped. "Not all of us get everything we want out of life."

The ghost figure faded momentarily. Everything became still. Silence. Then she returned, looking more substantial and vibrant than before. Her black eyes were not beady anymore and her cheeks were not as hollow. She leaned over and whispered in a stern but gentle voice, "You are an angry, self-centered girl, but you can choose to be as beautiful at the core as you are lovely on the surface."

The straightforward truth stung Emma. Her heart beat fast, and her breath hitched. "How do I do that?"

Her grandmother extended a bony finger and made a circle in the air. "You must learn to love others as well as yourself. Your mother is a great role model for you. Give her a chance."

"I'm sorry," Emma sighed, "but her life has always seemed so dull and boring."

"No, her life is full of joy. She doesn't need a lot of fanfare. She's at peace with the world and herself, something many people never experience, but something you need."

Emma stared at the rickety floor of the ship. Embarrassed.

The truth of her grandmother's words couldn't be denied. "Guess I've been too busy day dreaming."

"Perhaps."

"But I want to travel and see the world. I've only visited five or six states, and I've never been out of the country."

"You have your whole life in front of you. There's plenty of time to travel, and you will, I'm sure."

"I guess I just wanted everything like you had, Grandgran." Emma sighed.

"You think I got everything I wanted out of life? Do you really believe that I wanted to drown in Misty Lake and leave all of you?"

Emma nervously cleared her throat. "No, but you had a husband who cherished you beyond belief and grieved himself to death over losing you."

"You also can have someone who loves you more than life itself."

"Where would I find such a man?" Emma spat the words out.

"Perhaps you already have." Grandgran looked over at Frank and said, "You do realize that Frank is in love with you, don't you?"

"What? No way. Frank? He's just a friend." Emma turned and faced them. "Sorry, I forgot to introduce my friends, Frank and Coralee."

"I've seen you around, but it's nice to meet you in person." Her grandmother chuckled.

Frank held out his hand to shake hers and hesitated. "Uh, it's nice to meet you too, Grandgran."

Coralee stood there until Grandgran spoke. "Honey, I love your big green eyes, but you can close your mouth now."

They all laughed as the tense atmosphere became somewhat relaxed.

"Now let's get back to business." Grandgran continued. "The reason you're here is for me to share some wisdom with each of you. So let's start with you, dear. I love you, but you are flawed.

First, you're condescending and unappreciative toward others. Second, you are ambitious without the will to work."

Emma's face flushed warm as she laced and unlaced her fingers. "I guess you're right. Sometimes I know I'm being nasty to people, but I can't seem to help myself," she said in a quiet voice.

"Then it's up to you to change." Grandgran challenged her granddaughter.

"Easier said than done," Emma shot back.

A loud "humph" from Frank echoed around the room. Emma looked at him and Coralee and straightened her posture.

Grandgran continued, "Start by realizing that you are not superior to anyone else. Acknowledge the fact that nobody has everything they want and learn to be grateful for all you have."

"That was a sermon and a half." Emma looked away and swallowed hard.

"I just hope it isn't too late. Your attitude can make or break you. It's your choice, honey. I love you and wish you well."

Frank stepped forward. "Thanks, Grandgran. Your lecture is exactly what Emma needed to hear. I've never had the guts to tell her," he said, giving Emma a sheepish look.

Emma glared at him.

"Well, let's talk about you, young man. If you love Emma, why are you afraid to tell her what she needs to hear?"

Frank dug his hands into his pockets. "I guess I'm afraid of losing her."

"Have you ever really had her? Furthermore, do you think you'll ever have her if you don't stand up to her?"

Frank squirmed and looked into Emma's grandmother's black eyes. "No, not really. I'm just scared."

"If you love her, you need to offer her constructive advice. It's time to man up, unless you're willing to let her walk all over you for the rest of your life. That would only make you miserable and leave her unfulfilled. You'd destroy each other or anything you ever had together."

Frank straightened and puffed out his chest. "I'm willing to give it my best shot."

"That's what I wanted to hear. Show some backbone, man. You're a real catch—you're smart and handsome. Make sure you work out regularly. Women like a man in good shape. Just look at all those romance book covers." She winked at him.

Then she turned to face Coralee. "It's your turn, baby. Throw those darn Coke bottle eyeglasses away—the ones you lost on the upper deck when you fell through. You've been doing fine without them. Let folks see those gorgeous green eyes of yours."

"Yes, ma... ma'am," Coralee stuttered.

"And another thing," she added, her old voice rattling in her throat. "Stop being so shy. You can hold your own with anyone. You're smart, sweet and could be cute as a button if you'd work at it a little."

"If you say so, Grandgran." Coralee's voice shook, but she stood erect.

"Hell fire, girl, I'm not your grandmother or Frank's grandmother, so you don't need to call me that."

Coralee stepped back. "Yes, ma'am. But we do appreciate the advice you've given us." She smiled.

Emma came and stood by her grandmother's ghost and asked, "Is this really a phantom ship, or is this some kind of Halloween joke?"

"It's a real ship all right or what's left of one. It appears on Misty Lake when it's on a mission."

"Are we the purpose of the mission?"

"You and several other people around Misty Lake. Tonight will be a busy night."

"Why are we locked in? Will we ever be able to leave?" Emma threw her hands in the air, annoyed.

"You were locked in so I could talk to you. And sure, you can leave."

"How are we to do that? The door and hatch are bolted." Emma frowned.

Grandgran chuckled. "Just click your Ruby Red Slippers like Dorothy in The Wizard of Oz, silly."

"What? Huh?"

"The door is unlocked. Now it's about time for all of you to skedaddle out of here and go back to the party."

Emma wanted to hug her grandmother but knew it was impossible. She did the next best thing. "I've always loved you, now I love you even more."

"Same here, kiddo."

The door magically opened and Emma, Frank and Coralee faced it. From behind, a swishing sound grabbed their attention, and they turned around just in time to see the last strips of the ragged coral chiffon slip through the porthole.

When the three friends found their way back up top, they marched in silence down the gangplank. Across the road, a bonfire shot flames into the air, licking away the last remnants of the fog. A festive crowd gathered around the fire at the edge of the lake.

The relieved trio continued toward the dance hall. Emma welcomed the smell of the barbeque on the grill and then the pumpkin-scented candles as they joined the party inside.

Emma looked down when she felt a mosquito bite her hand. She giggled. "Look, I'm wearing my grandmother's wedding rings." She'd always dreamed of wearing these rings and how they'd feel on her fingers.

"Wow. That proves we're not crazy," Frank said as he reached for Coralee's hand. "Come on, Green Eyes, let's dance."

Emma's mouth opened to protest, but it was too late. Her friends headed to the dance floor. She had to admit they looked good together. As she watched them dancing, a strange feeling crept across her—almost a chill. *Frank is just trying to make me jealous. Or is he?* Doubt made her bite her bottom lip. *Maybe nobody wants me anymore.* Her chest hurt as if cable wires bound her. She continued to watch, feeling something new. Insecurity?

Frank never looked this good before. What happened on that

ship? *He's buff, Coralee doesn't need glasses and I have zits*. Her fingers automatically reached up to feel her cheeks. Her skin felt smooth but not as smooth as it used to be. "Oh my goodness," she muttered. She shook herself, relieved to be halfway back to normal.

Emma walked to the middle of the dance floor, and tapped Coralee on the shoulder. "Excuse me, Coralee, may I cut in?"

"Sure. Fine with me. You usually get what you want anyway."

Frank glared at Emma and said, "Well, it's not fine with me." He turned and faced Coralee again. "Shall we continue?"

Emma stood there, color heated her cheeks. Her insides did the jitterbug while her heart craved a waltz with the best man in the world. I've never been turned down before. Her humiliation was complete when Don Juan bumped into her and asked, "Aren't you the princess I was dancing with earlier?"

"Yes," she answered softly, expecting him to take her in his arms to dance again.

"Sorry I can't ask you to dance. I met a fantastic girl tonight." He walked away and didn't look back.

She stood immobile in the crowd, not sure what to do next. Another dancer bumped into her and brought her back to reality. She took a deep breath, held her head high and left the dance floor, weaving her way back to a table and chairs.

The hour grew late, and the crowd on the dance floor made the most of each song. The younger kids danced to the fast, loud numbers, while some couples snuggled to the slow tunes. Emma felt invisible.

Finally it was time for the costumes to be judged. Frank and Coralee appeared and sat across from her while someone gave out numbers for the competition.

When Coralee's number was called, Frank escorted her down the aisle. Then he returned and silently escorted Emma when her number was called.

The judges took a long time deciding which of the great costumes should be finalists. They called a stranger's number as third place, Coralee's number as second place and Emma's number as the winner.

All three girls had satin ribbons pinned on them for a photo op and then walked to the microphone to thank the judges. When Emma addressed the judges, her voice had a strength she didn't realize she had. "Thank you so much for the honor. However, this same princess outfit won the contest once before, about three years ago, so I declare it should be disqualified."

The judges nodded in agreement. Then the announcer pointed toward Coralee and spoke into the microphone, "Ladies and gentlemen, I present the Queen of the Masquerade Ball."

A rumble went through the audience before everyone began clapping and cheering. Coralee smiled, walked over to Frank, took his hand, and they started the final dance of the night. Others followed them onto the dance floor.

Emma's head felt a little fuzzy as she sat at the table, recalling her life and the events of the night. *How could I have been so blind? Why didn't I see how much Frank loved me?* Panic overcame her. Her heart pounded like a kettledrum in a calypso band. Her hands felt clammy.

Frank and Coralee had so much in common. They had never looked more comfortable with each other than at this moment, dancing with their heads together.

Emma sat alone. She had no one to blame but herself. *I've probably lost him—just when I realized how much he means to me.* Her head slumped and she looked down at the floor. When she looked up, Frank and Coralee were walking toward her, even though the dance was only halfway over. Coralee smiled, but he wore a stern expression.

Frank reached for Emma's hand. Without a word, he drew her to him and swept her into the slow waltz. They looked into each other's eyes and embraced, neither one daring to speak. He turned his head as the flow of the hypnotic music enveloped them, and they moved together as one.

The moment and the seductive rhythm penetrated Emma's thoughts. Frank's silence worried her. *Am I too late?* A tear rolled down her cheek. She sighed. *I can't let this dance end without telling him.* She stretched up on her toes until her breath reached his ear, “Sorry I’ve been a fool and didn’t know my own heart. I think I’ve always loved you.”

Seconds seemed like hours. *Does he still want me?* She heard him gasp and thought he was crying, too.

Frank turned to face Emma, tightened his arms around her and dipped her toward the floor. With a smile as big as the Grand Canyon, he whispered, “Welcome home, stranger.”

Momentarily jolted, Emma gazed up at this handsome man who had almost gotten away. Then she looked at the rings on her finger and smiled. “I think Grandgran would approve.”

Missionary Dreams

What counts in life is not the mere fact we have lived. It is what difference we have made in the lives of others that will determine the significance of the life we have led.

~ Nelson Mandela

SOUNDS OF SCURRYING feet and muffled voices awakened five-year-old Hannah as she lay half asleep under mosquito netting inside a hut in the Amazon jungle. Still groggy, she peered up at a strange man bursting through the door. Her heart beat faster. Her chest tightened. She opened her mouth to scream.

No sound came. She shrank back into her pallet to avoid the dark hands reaching for her. His sweat and rotten breath smelled nasty as he came closer. Scooting backward, kicking at his hands, she tried to escape, tried to scream. "Mommy! Wake up!" Again no sound came, no more than the wind rustling through the trees.

Then her mother's muffled protest caused the intruder to move away. One bad man bound her parents' mouths and hands while another's cruel feet kicked them on the floor. Terrorized, Hannah saw the angry faces of the savage men, deadly as black snakes. *What do they want? Why are they here?*

The two men shot glares at the corner where Hannah cowered under her quilt. They dragged the missionaries from the hut. She clamped her teeth into the quilt covering her mouth. *Scream.* Hannah realized it was too late.

Seconds later a muscular native parted the netting. She shrank back against the hut wall. Instead of grabbing her, he gently motioned her to remain silent.

"Shhh, Miss Hannah. This yo' friend Buntah. Don't speak—jes' listen."

Hannah rolled over and sat up, rubbing her eyes. "Bu-Buntah!" she whispered.

"Shush," he warned her. "Chil,' there's big trouble. 'Member your papa told you what to do if there was trouble and I came for you?"

"Y-Yes, I'm to go with you to be s-safe," she stuttered, tears flowing down her cheeks.

"Now's the time." He bundled her up. Hannah grabbed her small duffel bag always packed for emergencies and clutched Buntah's strong fingers. Silently but swiftly, they dashed beyond the scant light of the moon into the darkness of the jungle. "We must make it to the infirmary at Chino. Dr. Kelley will know what to do after dat."

"The ba-bad men came and took my mommy and daddy. I screamed. I tried to help. I tried." Tears began to roll down her cheeks and great sobs shook her small body.

Then Buntah stopped, hoisted Hannah onto his back, and wrapped the straps of her duffel bag around his wrist. "Shut yo' eyes, child, and put yo' head on my back so you won't get scratched by vines and limbs. Buntah knows the way."

She kept her head down, but the rough-textured vines slapped at her sides and legs, stinging every inch of uncovered skin. "Ouch!" Hannah cried. Tears slid down her cheeks. "I want my mommy and daddy! Where's my mommy and daddy?"

"Wid the Medicine Man, chil.'"

Drums in the distance rapped a staccato rhythm, sending messages that Hannah didn't understand. She trembled, frightened. *Are the natives looking for me, too?*

Buntah's breathing became labored as he jogged through the night. He smelled of sweat. Evil lurked in the darkness, not just the wild animals but those men who had come for her mommy and daddy. Hannah heard the screeching of the restless animals as he carried her to safety. After an hour of trudging through the deep jungle they reached their destination, the next missionary outpost.

Buntah stopped and knelt so Hannah could slide from his back. Her tears flowed again. Her body began to shake. "I'm so afraid for my mommy and daddy."

"Come on chil,' let's git you to Dr. Kelley," he said as he took her small hand. "He'll take care of tings from here on."

Buntah ran to the hut next to the infirmary. "Doctor! Medicine Man took Dr. Massey and his wife," he shouted.

"Oh, no! What about the child?" Doctor Kelley stood beside a cot, looking as though he had just awakened.

"I got the chil' wid me."

Saying nothing, Hannah stepped from behind Buntah with her hands clasped together.

"Good, bring her inside." The doctor motioned for them to enter.

Hannah watched the doctor's wife rise and move to her husband, clinging to him. *Maybe she's afraid the bad men will come get her, too.*

The doctor continued, "So, my worst fears have happened. Voodoo worshipers don't trust missionaries. I warned Dr. Massey there were great risks for the 'Doctors without Borders' program. The old ways of the medicine men are still strong here."

"Yes, sir, it be bad." Buntah shook his head.

"Thank God we made plans. I'll get their daughter to the bush pilot tomorrow and she'll be in Lima before tomorrow night."

"Li-ma? What about Mommy and Daddy?" Hannah's voice quivered as she picked at the hem of her clothes. "I want my m-mommy."

Silence from the three adults hung in the humid air of the hut. The doctor and his wife wrapped their arms around Hannah in an effort to soothe her fears.

"Darling, we'll do the best we can. As soon as we know anything about your parents we'll pass it on. Right now we must make arrangements with the Medical Mission Board to get you to your grandmother in America."

"I'm going to where my grandmother lives? I'll get to see Granny Em?"

"Remember, we all went over this with you. I'm so sorry, baby." The doctor's wife held her hand.

"Will you come with me, Buntah?" Hannah begged.

"No, chil,' I got to git back right away 'fore the village people miss me. They don't know I brought you here. Dat's the best ting, but bless you, Miss Hannah. Yo' papa saved my life wid his medicine."

The big black man turned away sadly. Hannah ran to him and put her small arms around his strong legs and clung to him a long time while she fought off her sniffles.

"I gotta go back. I'll do what I can for yo' parents," Buntah promised the little girl. "Yo' mama and papa be true angels."

"Thank you, my good friend," Dr. Kelley said as he and his wife led Hannah back to the small infirmary building. She watched and listened when he made contact with some people on some sort of radio-phone Hannah had never seen.

"Someone will arrive shortly to escort you to the bush plane, child," Dr. Kelley said in a businesslike manner. Reaching into his medicine cabinet he took out a bottle of pills. "Take one of these, Hannah." He placed a small white pill in her hand. "It will make you feel better."

"Yuck! I can't swallow pills. They make me gag." She stuck her tongue out.

"It's for the best. You have a long journey in front of you."

Somehow she choked it down.

A short time later two men arrived. They spoke to the doctor briefly, picked up Hannah and her belongings then set out through the jungle again. She felt woozy as they hurried on.

When the rescue team disturbed them, chattering monkeys moved deeper into the brush. Normally she chattered back, but today she was so scared her queasy stomach wouldn't let her enjoy the monkeys. The three traveled in silence on the short trip to a clearing where a small plane waited with the side door open.

One of the men walked with her to the top of the steps, shook her hand and said, "You'll be safe now, Miss. This is your pilot, Michael. He'll fly you out of danger."

Hannah stumbled a little, but she took her duffel bag and forced a smile, remembering the manners her mother had taught her. "Thanks for helping me, and tell Dr. Kelly and his wife I said thanks."

The man called Michael helped her into the plane and buckled her in. "Are you ready?" he asked while he stowed her duffel behind the seat.

Hannah stared up at him. She'd never seen eyes as blue as his, blue as the sky.

"Yes, sir. I... I'm ready." Her voice trembled.

"Good. Let me know if you need anything." He handed her a

pillow. "We'll be in the air about an hour. Why don't you get some sleep?"

Hannah nodded. She felt sleepy and kept rubbing her eyes. She settled into the chair, but even though her eyes were blurry, she was still too scared to sleep. *What's going to happen next?* Burying her head in her arms, she sobbed her heart out.

A hand on her shoulder made her raise her head. She looked up into Michael's blue eyes. His presence made her feel calmer.

When the pilot took her hand she noticed a star-shaped tattoo on his wrist. "Come on. You can ride up front with me."

She sniffled once more and followed him into the front of the plane, where he strapped her into the co-pilot's seat. He reached across the aisle and held her hand, his voice soothing. Finally, she slept.

After the plane landed far away from some big planes, a lady Hannah didn't know met them. The pilot strolled over to the gray-haired lady and hugged her.

"Thanks for coming, Mom. We can sure use your help."

Then he turned back to Hannah and introduced her to the woman. "Hannah, this is my mother. Mom, this is Hannah."

"Glad to meet you, ma'am." Hannah nodded to the woman who had big blue eyes that matched her son's.

"My pleasure, dear." She reached out and took Hannah's hand and encased it in both her hands. "I hope you had a good flight."

Hannah pointed to Michael. "He saved me from the bad people who kidnapped my mommy and daddy."

"I'm so glad he could help you. He's one of the best bush pilots in the Amazon."

They walked a long way and then they showed Hannah where she would wait for the next plane to take her to the United States to be with her grandmother. Michael pointed out the huge planes called jets. "You will be flying on a plane like this."

"How can they fly?" Hannah asked. "They look so big." She just shook her head.

Michael laughed and tried to explain how the jets were built and the fuel they used, but she didn't understand it.

The planes had looked so much smaller high in the sky when she'd watched them fly over the jungle at home. *Home. Will I ever be able to go back?*

Michael's mom said lots of stuff, but Hannah didn't hear much. She thought about her mommy and tried not to cry. She kept peeking around, hoping her mommy and daddy would show up before she got on the plane to fly to her grandmother's town.

When Michael brought some milk and sandwiches, Hannah stared at the small star-shaped tattoo on his right wrist and wondered what it meant. She took the food but didn't feel like eating. Her daddy had told her she must never be rude when someone offered her food, so she attempted to eat a bite.

She tried to be cheerful while they waited for the big jet, but she was nervous. When it was time to leave, Michael and his mother gave her big comforting hugs.

"Special arrangements have been made for your safety. The flight attendants will take good care of you, my dear," Michael's mother told her. Then Michael patted her shoulder. "Perhaps our paths will cross again someday. Until then be blessed, little one."

She looked at this man who was even more handsome than her daddy. *I bet he's just about the handsomest man in the world.*

"Thanks for staying with me. I'll never forget you," Hannah promised, smiling at Michael, her heart sad that he couldn't go with her.

By the time Hannah got in line to board the plane, she was excited but a little scared. Her tummy wasn't happy from all that food she'd eaten. It jumped as the jet made a lot of noise, revved its engine and moved into the air. Once she saw the clouds through the windows she just wanted to sleep.

Exhausted, she slept for hours. When she woke up she pushed aside the blanket that made her feel too warm.

"We're halfway to Atlanta where I understand your grandmother will be waiting," a flight attendant said, folding the crumpled blanket.

When the plane landed at the huge Atlanta airport the flight attendant took Hannah by the hand and escorted her into the building. From the top of the ramp, they spotted Hannah's grandmother, Emma, who waited with a big sign and a big grin lighting her face.

"Hi, sweetheart. How's my little darling? I've never been so happy to see anyone in my life." Granny Em hugged her until her small chest ached.

She stifled a cough because it was hard to breathe. But Granny Em smelled so good, like jasmine. A jasmine bush grew in one of the yards Hannah had visited once upon a time. She hoped it grew in her grandmother's garden. *It was Mommy's favorite. I need my mommy.* She swallowed hard. A flood of tears rushed down her cheeks and she spat the words out like bullets, "The bad men took Mommy and Daddy. I tried to scream and warn them, but no words came out." She shook her head. "I don't know where they are." She sobbed until she got the hiccoughs.

Finally, her grandmother loosened her grip, and patted Hannah's back to calm her. "There, there. Everything's going to be fine. You're here with me now." Then she stepped back and stared at Hannah. "Well, let's have a look at you," she said. "A tiny body with a full mane of auburn hair and big brown eyes." She smoothed hair that wouldn't stay smooth. "You have our family's DNA for sure. Lovely, just lovely."

They smiled at each other for a long time. No words were necessary.

When the mutual admiration moment ended, they addressed the flight attendant. "Thanks for bringing me home," Hannah said, smiling from ear to ear.

"Yes, thank you so much for taking good care of this precious cargo, my granddaughter."

"My pleasure." The attendant gave Hannah a quick hug then shook Granny Em's hand goodbye.

"Let's get you home, my girl. Aunt June will be waiting." Granny Em turned to Hannah, gathered her things and headed that way.

"These buildings sure are tall. I've never seen this many cars before. Where did all these people come from?" Hannah asked.

"From many small cities in the Metro Atlanta area. People come into the city to work, shop, have fun and do business."

"This town must have more people than anywhere in the whole world."

Her grandmother laughed. "No. There are many cities larger than our town."

"I don't think I'd like to live there." A man in a car next to them blew his horn. "Too noisy," Hannah added.

An hour later the car pulled into the driveway in front of a small gingerbread house that looked like houses in fairytale books. A tall lady with long hair appeared.

Hannah's heart hitched. For a moment she thought it was her mother. She looked again at the woman running toward her and blinked.

"My sweet girl. You're finally here. I'm your Aunt June, your mom's sister." She hugged Hannah tight. "We need to get you inside and show you around."

"Do you live here, too?"

"No, I live about an hour from here. My husband and two daughters are anxious to meet you."

"You have two little girls?" Hannah sounded excited.

"They aren't little any more. Sally is twelve and Susan is fourteen."

Trying to hide her disappointment, Hannah said, "Well, at least they're girls."

A few days later her cousins came to visit. Sally was the cute one, but both girls treated her like a little sister. They were so grown up Hannah felt like a baby. She was in a new loving environment, but she still felt lonely.

Often Granny Em would ask her, "Why are you gazing into space? Is anything wrong?"

Hannah smiled to cover her feelings of loneliness. "No, I just miss my mommy and daddy. But I love being here with you."

Granny Em patted her on the back and then embraced her.

"Of course you miss them, but it will get better. I promise. I love you, sweet girl."

~~~

Two months later Granny Em opened a letter with the official news that Hannah's parents had been killed after being caught in a dangerous situation of tribal unrest. She felt her granddaughter was too young and fragile at this time, so she decided not to share the letter. She saved the notice to be read at a later date.

Many mornings Hannah awoke to twisted sheets after reliving the trauma of that last night in the jungle. Dark hands grabbed at her in another bad dream. She had been too frightened to scream and warn her parents.

In time, pleasant dreams replaced the nightmares, and Hannah dreamed of being rescued by Buntah, Dr. Kelley, and Michael. She hoped she would see them again someday and tell them how much she appreciated their help during her rescue. Occasionally in her dreams she saw Michael's face with smiling blue eyes and his wrist with the star-shaped tattoo. Like visiting an old friend, he had become her hero.

Playing make-believe as she grew up captured Hannah's imagination like a flame captures a moth. She liked to dress up in Aunt June's or her cousins' clothes and often wore their shoes around the house. Hannah's wobbly legs gave the adult women hours of joy.

She begged to wear her grandmother's baubles. Jewelry held a fascination for her.

"You may borrow something for a special occasion when you're older. For now, I have a few pieces you can wear." She reached into her apron pocket and pulled out a colorful scarab bracelet.

"Oh, doesn't it look beautiful?" She held her arm up, acting prissy.

Aunt June watched and laughed. "Yes, but it's so large I think it'll fall off."

Hannah let her arm down and the bracelet slid to the floor.
~~~

"You're right," she said in disgust. "It's bad being a little kid."

"Well, that won't last long. You'll be a young lady before you know it," Granny Em said.

"How do you know all these things?"

"Well, I had a wise mother and a wiser grandmother. My grandmother was a gypsy fortune teller and wore a special ring that I inherited. People came from miles around to have her tell what the future held for them."

Hannah listened like someone in a trance. This was the first time she had ever heard about gypsies. "Could your grandmother tell them what they would be when they grew up?"

"I'm not sure about that. I think she just told them big things, if they would live to be old or die young, if they would have children or not."

"Those aren't the only big things. I want to know what I will be when I grow up."

"What do you want to be?"

"I want to be a missionary doctor like Mommy and Daddy or a bush pilot like Michael."

Her grandmother chuckled. "You may change your mind many times before you grow up."

"Bet I won't." She stuck her chest out and folded her arms.

"We'll see."

Hannah eyed her grandmother's wedding band. "Will I ever be big enough to wear your special ring?" She reached out, touched the gold band and received a tiny electric shock that almost made her world go white. She blinked. When her head cleared she noticed a knowing smile on Granny Em's face and wondered if the magic of the ring been passed down to her? Or was it her imagination?

"When I grow up I'm going to have a good husband like you did. He will love me forever."

"Well, you'll have to grow up first. Then you will want to date a young man to make sure he is the right one for you."

"That will take forever," Hannah replied, disgusted with

having to wait.

"Don't worry, a real boyfriend will come along soon enough, but choosing the right one will take some time." Granny Em smiled.

~~~

On her tenth birthday Hannah had a party with family and friends. The cousins came early and helped select the right dress for the occasion. Sally even put a little lip gloss on her lips.

Susan hesitated. "I think she might be too young for colored lip gloss," she fretted.

"You're such a stick in the mud," Sally said. "Let her wear it."

"Well, it does look pretty," Hannah agreed. Lip gloss won.

The other guests began arriving. The crowd of twelve filled the house with jubilant chatter. A boy named Bob excelled at most of the games. Her friend Tammy wore the prettiest dress.

That night Hannah dreamed about the party and the joy of having a caring family and good friends. She was glad that she slept well these days. In the wee hours of the morning something woke her. Still groggy from sleep, she thought she saw a vague figure in the corner of the room. She blinked but was not afraid. The figure moved toward her, and she quickly sat up. But then he held his arm up and pointed at the star tattoo.

"Michael? Michael?" she asked, a little anxious.

The figure stood behind the chair by her bed, not moving any closer.

She thought she recognized the eyes though no longer bright. "Michael, if it is you—you can sit with me."

The figure floated into the chair.

"See, you can sit with me the way I sat up front with you on the plane." Hannah pulled up the quilt, rolled over feeling safe and went back to sleep.

The next morning she shared her experience of the strange figure with Granny Em.

"I'm not surprised," Granny Em said. "I think Michael has become your guardian angel."
~~~

"Someday I hope you'll share your secret of 'knowing' with me."

Aunt June knocked on the kitchen door. She had come over to have breakfast with them and clean the house after the party. "Good morning, birthday girl. How does it feel to be ten years old?"

"The same as every day, I guess. Thanks for helping with the nice party."

"You're very welcome. This is just the beginning of lots of parties yet to come."

Granny Em winked. "Yes, indeed. Time flies. You'll be all grown up and going off to college before we know it."

~~~

Hannah applied to several universities, knowing she could only attend the school which granted her the most scholarship money. Days dragged by while she waited for answers in the mail. Most of her classmates had already heard from their schools of choice.

"What's the use?" she said to her grandmother one day as she came away from the mailbox empty-handed.

"You must be patient. Good news will come," Granny Em said with confidence.

"And how do you know that?" Hannah frowned.

"I've prayed that you will get a full scholarship," Granny Em replied.

"Do you really think prayer really helps?"

"Absolutely. I have faith. In prayer and in you."

The following day a letter addressed to Hannah Massey came from Emory University. A physician had made provisions in his will for a bright young student to receive a four-year scholarship. The offer stipulated the student be the child of missionaries and maintain a high GPA.

She started running around in circles, holding the letter in the air and shouting, "A full scholarship!" She dashed in to share the news with her grandmother.
~~~

The smile on her grandmother's face told Hannah *she knew already.*

In the fall, Granny Em helped her pack for college. "Four years from now you'll be graduating again," she said.

"How do you know I won't drop out and get married?" Hannah asked.

"Because I'll wring your neck if you do." Her grandmother laughed.

"Well, it worked for you and Gramps. Why not me?"

"Things are different now. A degree is more important than ever." Granny Em turned away slightly, placed her right hand over her left and started rubbing her wedding band between her thumb and middle finger. That somber mood reminded Hannah how much her grandmother missed her grandfather.

Hannah broke the silence. "I've always loved your wedding band. It seems so special."

"This ring is more than a symbol of our love, it has a power of its own and it will be yours someday. Someday, but not yet." Granny Em smiled with a twinkle in her eyes.

~~~

The whirlwind of learning the routine of college life, meeting new friends, and surviving in an adult role overwhelmed Hannah. She dated a little, studied a lot and slept like an exhausted bear in hibernation. Her grueling schedules freshman and sophomore years had been killers and had kept her on campus most of the time.

Summer came and Hannah wanted to spend some time with her grandmother, who had not been well lately. Hannah felt a little guilty for leaving her at home alone for such long periods of time. But school involved a demanding schedule. She grabbed Granny Em as soon as she opened the front door. "It's great to be here," she said, hugging the older woman. "We have a lot of catching up to do."

"Yes. I'm glad you're here."

The next week friends called about a pool party their club was sponsoring for a charity. Reluctant, Hannah allowed Granny Em
~~~

to convince her to go to the party. "Don't worry about me. Go be with people your own age."

"But I do worry about you." She looked into eyes that had grown paler with the years and at hands with age marks.

"Go on with you, now. Pack your beach bag with that new swimsuit and work on your tan."

Hannah gave her a kiss on the cheek and followed orders. When she arrived at the party she looked around, hoping to see someone she recognized.

A handsome guy with a great tan and well-toned physique yelled, "Hey, game of Frisbee?"

Looking around, Hannah suddenly wanted to cover her bathing suit, a one piece that showed practically nothing. "Sure," she said.

She joined him and his friends. The other girls wore bikinis. Some almost fell out of their tops. When she jumped she tried not to jiggle anywhere. First impressions often last and she didn't want him to think she was a flirt.

"Go long," she yelled, winging the Frisbee with all of her might down the man-made beach fifty feet from the pool. The red disc went long and far but did not overtake him. He jetted down the sandy beach and caught it with one hand. He returned to Hannah and gave her hand a tight squeeze.

"Nice one," he said, out of breath. "I might have to keep you around, you know, as a ringer."

Hannah smiled nervously and returned the hand hug. If she said anything at this point, she would stutter.

"I'm Harrison Dodge," he said, his mouth close to her ear. "You're Hannah Massey, right?"

"Yeah," she managed to say, letting go of him and looking surprised.

"I'm a junior at Emory, also. I've seen you around."

She had seen him but hoped he hadn't noticed her noticing him. She concentrated on speaking slowly, so she wouldn't stutter. "Me, too."

"We're having a party later at CHI House. Bring a girlfriend or your boyfriend. It's whatever."

She smiled at his pathetic attempt at asking if she were taken. "Okay."

"Great," he said, heading off to his truck in the parking lot. "See ya."

Hannah's roommate coaxed her into keeping her promise to attend. "You have to go. Everybody will be there. My boyfriend says it's the coolest event of the season."

"Oh, I don't know. I've never been much of a party girl," Hannah said.

"You don't know if you're a party girl or not. You've never let yourself find out." Finally, Hannah agreed.

The fraternity house was an antebellum-style with large columns and porches that wrapped around three sides of the house. The entrance had large double doors with beveled glass panels on each side. With the exception of the chandelier hanging in the foyer, the inside bore little resemblance to the fine old southern home it had once been. Hannah and her roommate eased inside. A loud techno beat reverberated even to the old worn plank floors where the couples danced. The two girls walked toward a table of refreshments and poured cups of punch for themselves. They exchanged looks of annoyance at so many beer guzzlers and the deafening noise from the band.

Hannah spotted Harrison standing in the shadows across the room staring at her. She felt awkward. *Should I wait for him to speak?*

It seemed like ten minutes elapsed before he strolled her way. He stood for a moment, as if studying her face, before he spoke. "Would you like to dance?"

"Uh, no thanks," she said, taking a gulp of her punch. "Well, maybe."

"That's the ticket, live a little." He smiled and reached for her hand.

The DJ put on a slow song. Harrison gathered her into his arms and they spun across the dance floor, drawing admiring glances from other dancers.

He teasingly whispered into her ear, "Play Frisbee?"

She pushed back a little and smiled at him. "As a matter of fact, I do."

Half way through the dance she noticed there was no tingle in her fingertips while she held his hand, no great chemistry between them. Then she shrugged. Maybe it didn't happen immediately. So she relaxed and enjoyed the remainder of the evening.

Harrison asked her to walk out on the veranda. The crisp air and slight breeze greeted them as they got to know each other away from the crowd. He told her about his favorite writers and the places he had traveled.

She shared her rescue out of the Amazon and her dream to return someday. For the moment she would not leave her grandmother.

Harrison came from an old Atlanta family and would be expected to carry on the family tradition. It was his parents' dream, though not necessarily his, she learned.

Hannah laughed. "Everyone knows the only money that counts in this city is old money."

Embarrassed, he replied, "You're wrong. We aren't rich, we're comfortable."

"Sure, that's what they all say."

"Let me take you to lunch tomorrow and I'll prove it. We'll order soup and salad, no dessert." He laughed a genuine laugh.

She liked him in spite of herself. "You're on."

The next day when the noon hour approached she started to dress. Her heel caught as she stepped into the garment. The ripping sound echoed across the room.

"My best outfit," she cursed. "Damn, what have I done? I'm acting like a teenager."

She searched the closet for an alternative but nothing looked good. After pulling out three outfits she decided to go casual.

The doorbell rang and Harrison stood there in a cotton shirt with a button-down collar and dress jeans.

"Hi, hope I'm not late, had to run a few errands. You look nice." He grinned.

He led her to a tan Toyota truck and opened the door for her. *Hmm. Nice manners.*

Harrison started the engine and turned to her. "I have a favorite hole-in-the-wall kind of restaurant. I've always felt the right girl would love it."

She blushed, looked down and fussed with a button. "Sounds perfect." *Right girl?*

The Mouse's Choice Cheese and Brew sat on the corner of 14th Street and Green Drive. A few college types sat around tables close to the bar.

Harrison led Hannah to the last table in a back corner. *Perhaps he really wants to get to know me.*

A young waiter with a short pony tail and pink neon laces in his green tennis shoes came over with menus. "Good to see you, Harrison."

"Todd, we're having soup and a sandwich. What's the special today?"

"This is your lucky day. The chef whipped up his special French Onion soup and a BLT on flatbread with cucumber mayo."

"That sounds interesting. I'll take it," Hannah said.

"Make that two," Harrison agreed.

"And to drink?" Todd asked with his hands clasped behind his back.

"Make it a Coke for me. I'm driving."

"I've never had a margarita. Do you mind if I try one?" Hannah felt a catch in her throat. She'd really done it... ordered a drink with alcohol.

"Exactly what I'd be having if I weren't driving. That or a beer."

The food came, and Hannah watched while Harrison alternately attacked the soup and the sandwich. She had trouble with the cheese and hoped that Harrison didn't notice that she couldn't quite twirl it around the spoon with the ease that he seemed to employ. She ate half the sandwich and drained the margarita glass. *What's wrong with me? I never drink alcohol, and this is way too fast. Nerves!*

They took turns talking and asking questions. By the time an hour had passed they'd covered childhood up to the present. They laughed and chatted until Hannah noticed workers putting chairs on the tables and getting ready to mop the floor.

"I think we need to go." She giggled and felt silly.

Harrison motioned for Todd. "Check, please."

"Aw, you two looked like you were having a good time."

"We were, but we need to go." He put some money on the table. "No change."

Hannah got to her feet unsteadily. Harrison lent a hand under her elbow. "You should have eaten more. I'm afraid that margarita went right to your head."

Once they were in the car Hannah leaned back in the seat. The scent of Brut reached her nose and she inhaled with pleasure.

"Let's ride up to Lake Alatoona. It's gorgeous this time of year. My folks have a small houseboat moored up there."

Suddenly she felt apprehensive. "A houseboat?" She swallowed hard. Her hands felt clammy. She didn't know Harrison that well, but she didn't say no.

When they arrived, Harrison parked by the houseboat but Hannah shook her head. "I don't think I feel good enough to go on the water. Shouldn't have had that margarita."

Harrison shook his head. "Lesson learned. Well, let's ride down the street. There's a park area with a trail that comes out at the lake."

"I'd like that." She exhaled, relieved.

They cruised down the narrow street and came to a stop at the park. A few minutes later, making their way down the pine straw strewn path, Hannah's breath caught in her throat. "Look, Canadian geese, like parents and babies."

"Yes, you know they mate for life."

"Aw, how cool is that. I wish I had something to feed them."

"I used to bring them bread until I found out it's bad for them. Oh well. They look pretty fat to me."

He guided her to a rock, where they sat watching the family of geese. Harrison leaned back and put his arms behind his head.

Hannah stretched out beside him. "What are you thinking about?"

He sat up and took her face in his hands. "I was thinking about how much I've enjoyed today and how I don't want it to end."

She looked into his eyes and put her hands on top of his. "Harrison, I..."

"Don't talk." His lips met hers, and she closed her eyes. "Shhhh." He took her in his arms and brought his head down onto hers. She shivered as he ran his hands through her hair. Her arms went around the sides of his chest. She didn't know what she felt, but she didn't care at the moment.

Harrison hesitated. He didn't kiss her as she had expected. He simply held her a little while.

She noticed the beginning of sunset and pulled away. "Harrison, we need to go."

"Yeah, it's getting late. Come on."

Hastily they straightened themselves and walked to the car, holding hands.

While Harrison drove back to the city he glanced at her with such unbridled devotion that Hannah blushed. The drive seemed short, and by the time they pulled up in front of her grandmother's house, she dreaded parting.

"Good night, doll."

She leaned over, gave him a quick kiss on the cheek then ran into the house, singing.

"Obviously you had fun." Granny Em looked up from her crocheting and turned the news down.

"We did! Harrison is really great." Hannah leaned down to give her a big hug. "I like him a lot."

"Liking is one thing and love is something altogether

different," Granny Em responded. "Life is short. Like a maple seed, we take wing and drop into a stream. The rain adds to our existence and floods our lives with joys and sorrows." Again, that gypsy all-knowing sixth sense she seemed to have. "True love is a special thing, Hannah. You need to wait for it."

Though the sparks never came over the next several months, Hannah and Harrison became affectionate and comfortable together. It seemed they belonged together, but she kept looking for those sparks.

Harrison never laughed at her dreams of the jungle, dreams of helping others. That's what kept her anchored. They talked about med school and flying lessons. She dreamed of becoming a missionary doctor or a bush pilot for the Peace Corp. Harrison agreed with her noble plans to help the needy. Something he'd never thought about until he met Hannah. "Being a medical missionary would be a good way to spend one's life."

Money was no obstacle for Harrison, but it posed a problem for Hannah. She worked a part-time job. Having enough time for everything never came easy for either of them.

~~~

On Valentine's Day, Harrison took Hannah to a local coffee shop. He had the girl behind the counter make two cups of hot chocolate with the foam shaped like a heart. When the order arrived Hannah looked down at the heart floating on top of her cocoa. She put her hands over her face and started giggling. He handed her a box and her breath caught. *Not an engagement ring—I'm not ready!*

But Harrison separated the ring into two parts, placing one part on her finger and the other half on his finger. "It's an engaged-to-be-engaged ring, sweetheart. Just a promise for the future."

Her heart melted. He knew not to rush her, thank goodness.

~~~

Months later Granny Em had a fatal stroke. It was a painless exit. Part of Hannah's heart floated away with her grandmother.

The funeral seemed brief, even as she listened to the minister drone on about her grandmother's great qualities. Hannah wanted to be anywhere but here today.

Her head was engulfed in a fog before they moved on to the family cemetery. Surrounded by her cousins, standing next to the freshly dug grave, she smelled the earth and the flowers. The minister read from the Bible and some mechanism lowered the body into the ground.

Then he signaled her. She picked up a handful of dirt and tossed it onto the casket. The thud hit its target and her heart at the same moment. She needed to scream.

Harrison had texted. He made some lame excuse. *Sorry I can't be there, but I love you.*

If he couldn't be there when she needed him, Hannah began to wonder if he would be there in the future.

Aunt June came to her rescue. She embraced Hannah and did not let go. Friends offered their condolences and shared how her grandmother had touched their lives.

Hannah and Aunt June inherited the small gingerbread house. Also, Hannah received Granny Em's ring, although it didn't seem to have the magic without Granny Em.

She became depressed living alone in the house. She missed her grandmother more than she thought possible. Aunt June brought homemade meals every other day.

"You have to eat, girl."

"I don't have much of an appetite." She tried to choke down a few bites.

"Your grandmother will have something to say about this. One of these days, when you're sitting and listening to the wind, she will tell you what you must do. People with gypsy blood talk to you at strange times. Take time to listen."

The next day Hannah ventured into her grandmother's room. She ran her hand across the handmade quilt on the bed. Growing up she had snuggled under that same quilt with Granny Em on nights when she couldn't sleep. A safe place.

Hannah found the letter about her parents' death with some old business papers and documents in a security box placed on the top shelf of a closet in Granny Em's room. It pitched her deeper into her depression. She dropped out of school the last month of the quarter and went days without leaving the house. She had lost her drive, her motivation.

Harrison called or texted her most days. He dropped by twice and brought her little gifts—a poem, one long-stemmed rose, and brownies from the Bread and Butter Bakery. Nothing helped.

After two weeks of mourning she agreed to sit in the park and talk with Harrison. The conversation centered on his grades and finishing the year with a good average. Med school would require top scores. Then, together, they could become the missionaries she'd dreamed about. At least the visits cheered her up. At night Hannah found comfort in talking to the figure beside her bed. Michael always nodded and assured her that she could not have saved her parents, and they would want her to be happy.

Hannah's professors allowed her to do the course work at home. She took two classes the following quarter and caught up with Harrison. They would graduate at the same time. Harrison thought graduating together was important and pushed her over and over. "We have a life waiting for us. You have to finish college for us to go on."

Hannah stared at the ceiling at night, wondering what her daddy would have thought about Harrison. She didn't remember much about her parents—just an occasional flashback of a song or a smell that would trigger something. But she didn't think he'd like Harrison pushing her.

The Dodge family invited her over a couple of times before school started back in the fall. Usually they served cake and homemade ice cream on the wrap-around porch. One side had been glassed in so flies couldn't buzz around and bother people while they ate.

Senior year turned into another killer year. Hannah felt slammed all the time. Her study schedule took about twelve hours each day with Harrison's voice in her ear. *Got to finish, got to graduate, got to make it.* Harrison's impatience escalated with her commitment to school. He had little patience with anything lately. Deep down inside, she knew she didn't have a lot of patience with him, either.

She spent Thanksgiving with Aunt June. The cousins, Sally and Susan, came home for the family gathering. Harrison came by and had a slice of Aunt June's famous Georgia Pecan pie. He and Hannah watched football with Uncle Bill after lunch.

Christmas season without Granny Em hit Hannah hard. Aunt June had decorated her house more festively than usual to make up for the lack of decorations at Hannah's. They went together to the gravesite and took a potted poinsettia. Hannah's heart hurt when it came time to leave.

"I don't want to go home yet. I need to stay with her for a little while."

"Wrapping packages won't wait, and I've got some baking to do," Aunt June said in a kind but firm tone.

"Just a few more minutes," Hannah begged.

"Sure, honey. I'll wait in the car so you can talk to her." She walked away.

Hannah faced the gravestone. "Harrison and his family have gone to the Biltmore House in Asheville for the holidays. I miss him and I miss you. The house feels pretty empty in the daytime. Of course I have Michael to talk to at night. He seems so wise, a lot like you. I wonder if he had gypsy blood in him, too."

She walked over and touched the headstone. "I'll come back soon. I need you as much now as I did in the past." The car horn sounded and Hannah rushed away.

Aunt June sat waiting. "Sorry we don't have more time, but there's a ton of work to be done before Christmas."

"I understand. Just drop me at home. Next time I will come by myself."

When she got home, she pulled out the scrapbook Aunt June had helped her keep through the years. Most of the time it comforted her when her mood turned blue. Not tonight. She left it open on the sofa. Feeling drained, Hannah decided to hit the sack early. She hadn't been sleeping well lately.

~~~
~~~

The next morning Hannah showered and dressed, planning brunch with a friend. The doorbell rang. She peeked out the window. "Oh, my gosh! It's Harrison." She grabbed the scrapbook from the couch and returned it to the top shelf of the bookcase. She smoothed her hair and took a deep breath. Harrison hated it when her thoughts drifted to the past. He saw it as a weakness.

When she opened the door, Harrison entered with flowers and candy. "I thought you were in Asheville."

"I ditched the family for the day. They expect me back tomorrow for Christmas Day."

"How nice. And flowers. Thank you."

"The appropriate offerings for the day," he said, grinning like a little boy.

She leaned over and took a deep breath to smell and drink in the beauty of the red roses. "Oh, how lovely."

"Not half as lovely as you," he responded.

Hannah did a double take. Tied to one of the stems was a tiny pouch. She pulled the stem out of the bouquet and slipped the cord off the stem. When she opened the pouch, a shiny ring slid out. It was the most breathtaking football-shaped diamond she had ever seen. "You're kidding!"

"Will you..."

"Wait!" Hannah's stomach tightened. "It's too soon. Your mom and dad will flip out."

"My mom loves you, and my dad won't be ready for me to marry until I've finished school."

"Exactly."

"Okay. We won't set a date, but we can be engaged. Long engagements run in my family."

She exhaled. "You're sure?"

"I've never been so sure of anything in my life. I love you." He leaned over, pulled her into his arms and kissed her.

"The ring is gorgeous. It's the most beautiful ring I've ever seen."

"It was my grandmother's. Mother wanted you to have it." He cleared his throat.

"Your grandmother's?" She stared at the ring, her throat tightening and tears welling in her eyes.

"Yes, she wanted me to give it to my future bride." He slid the ring on her finger, took her in his arms and kissed her again.

She had mixed emotions about being engaged. To Hannah's surprise, his family loved the idea of Harrison making plans for the future. Far, far into the future.

~~~

One month later while she waited for Harrison to come get her for a family gathering with his folks, Hannah pulled the scrapbook back off the shelf and flipped to the pictures showing her and her parents' time as missionaries in the Amazon. She reverently ran her fingers across the images of her mom and dad. Her bottom lip began to tremble. Aunt June had chronicled their family history in photographs and mementos. She flipped page after tattered page of the book and reveled in her former life.

Hannah's favorite picture was one where she stood in front of her mom and dad and each had an arm around her. Her mother looked lovingly up at her dad. She swallowed as the lump in her throat grew tighter and tears formed in her eyes.

The insistent ringing of the doorbell jarred her. Before she could rise from the sofa, banging on the door followed. The scrapbook fell to the floor. She hastily picked it up and slipped it out of sight under the couch.

"Hannah, open up."

She swiped the tears from her cheeks and opened the door. Harrison stood there, dressed in slacks and a sport coat and a frown. "You aren't ready yet?"

"It's not time yet."

"We can't be late for Daddy's birthday party. You know how grumpy he gets."

"Okay. Just need to do my hair and put on makeup. Give me a few." She ran a comb through her long auburn hair and grabbed her makeup bag, hurrying back into the living room.
~~~

Harrison stood near the couch, her scrapbook in his hands. Looking up at her, he said, "Honest to God, Hannah. You've got to grow up. We'll be in med school in six months, we're engaged, and you're still moping about the death of your mom and dad."

Hannah stared at the man she was thinking of marrying. Who was he? Where had the caring young man she believed she loved gone? During the last year Harrison had become so focused on his world he'd lost sight of her.

"Hurry up."

"Don't worry, I'll put my makeup on in the car." She tried to smile to get past her worry.

They drove in silence from her small gingerbread house to his family's estate. The Dodge's house sat on a slope farther away from the street than most of their neighbors. Harrison zipped into the circular drive and jumped out to open the car door for her. They dashed up the wide steps. Hannah stumbled, almost turning her ankle, but she dared not let on about the pain. She bit her bottom lip, praying that her ankle did not swell. *God forbid if I embarrass Harrison.*

The doorman welcomed them. He'd been with the family for years and served as chauffer, butler, and errand man. "Good evening, Miss Massey."

She plastered a smile on her face. "Hello, Samuel." She liked him a lot.

Harrison's parents stood with friends who had already arrived. "Well, there you are," his father said. "Dr. and Mrs. Spicer just got here."

"We're so glad you could make it, my dear." His mother came to give her a hug. The embrace felt genuine, and Hannah needed the warmth.

The Spicers smiled as they greeted Hannah and Harrison. "You two make a handsome couple. Reminds me of the time we were young and engaged." Dr. Spicer grinned as though he had a secret he wanted to share.

Hannah trailed behind Harrison until he slowed and took her hand. "You okay? Are you limping?" Hannah shook her head and pasted a smile on her face "I'm good."

The Dodge's home had more sparkle than a crystal shop. Several items had been shipped from Europe when generations of family members had traveled and purchased treasures for their homes.

Within minutes Mrs. Dodge greeted them, took Hannah's hand, and led her away to a group of women coiffed and buffed to perfection. The expression "looked like a doctor's wife" came to mind. She had never seen so many "air kisses" before. *Mustn't muss the makeup!*

Dear Mrs. Dodge introduced Hannah to the other guests. "My future daughter-in-law is already one of the family" was part of each introduction. Truly an exaggeration.

Of course each woman had to see "the ring" and Hannah loved showing it off. Chandelier lights caught the sparkle of each facet to perfection. The two-karat marquise diamond radiated like fire. Oohs and aahs of admiration were nice, but Hannah loved that the ring belonged to his maternal grandmother.

Mrs. Dodge quietly added, "My mother would have been so happy. The ring suits Hannah." It was the nicest thing she had ever said.

Harrison tapped Hannah's shoulder. "Ladies, I'm stealing my girl for a moment. It's almost time for dinner anyway."

As soon as they were out of earshot Hannah squeezed his hand. "Thanks, your mother's friends are wonderful, but..."

"But you felt overwhelmed," Harrison finished the sentence for her.

The butler appeared behind him. When he opened a set of double doors Hannah gasped. It was the first time she'd been in the formal dining room with the banquet-size table.

Harrison's father looked bigger than life at the head of the table covered in crystal, fine china and silver. Each place setting had more silver than she had any idea how to use, but she watched Harrison for her cues. She'd need to do some studying for the next formal event. For each course Hannah watched Harrison pick up a utensil or glass. He didn't say anything, bless him, though he had to know she was copying his moves.

Maybe he hadn't noticed her nervousness since he kept

stealing looks at his dad and Dr. Spicer, who sat on one side of the host, the birthday boy. The two men seemed deep in conversation during most of the meal, but they looked up toward Harrison and her and smiled.

When the meal finally started winding down with a light fluffy lemon dessert, the mood changed. Harrison gripped one of her hands so tightly she stared at him to see what was wrong. He shook his head while he watched his father stand. Grabbing her hand, Harrison stood and pulled her to the head of the table beside his father.

Of course the cake-cutting ceremony had the pomp of a wedding or anniversary reception. One would have thought Mr. Dodge had made the three-tier cake. Harrison's dad blew out the candles on the birthday cake. Everyone sang.

Why were she and Harrison standing beside Mr. and Mrs. Dodge? What was going on?

When Dr. Spicer stood the hairs on Hannah's arms stood up. She caught the word "announcement" and then "has offered Harrison the opportunity to join his practice after he finishes medical school."

Hannah's jaw dropped and her heartbeat echoed in her ears. The room tilted, but she gripped the table in front of her. "... buying them a house." Bile rose in her throat, threatening to bring up the meal. Harrison shook hands with Dr. Spicer and then did the back-slap hug with his dad.

Had Harrison known Dr. Spicer planned to make him an offer or that his father planned to buy them a house? Of course he had. Why else would he have been so tense during the meal?

When she yanked Harrison closer to drag him aside, he mouthed "we'll talk in the car." She ducked when he tried to kiss her cheek. They'd talk, all right, if she didn't kill him first. Or she could have one of his parents' "helpers" take her home.

When they left the party the sparring began. Grabbing her coat from the front closet where the butler had placed it, she and the man she thought understood her continued the heated words all the way to the car.

"Did you know about this? When were you going to tell me?"

Hannah spat out the words like rapid fire from an AK-47. "I thought—"

"Be reasonable, Hannah. You're still full of pipe dreams."

"Yes, what about our dreams of being bush pilots for the Peace Corps or joining Doctors without Borders?"

"Those dreams were childish fantasies on our part."

"No, we planned our future around those ideas of serving others." Anger crawled over her and settled into the pit of her stomach. "I thought you felt the same way I do."

"That can wait. This is a once-in-a-lifetime opportunity," he barked as he marched her down the front steps to the car.

Hannah felt a cold chill, as if he had doused her with ice water. A sob clogged her throat. Her world had seemed almost perfect, but Harrison derailed her dreams in a nanosecond. Everything started spiraling out of control.

"I thought you'd be excited. Hannah, say something." He ran his fingers through his brown hair, making it stand on end in a way Hannah usually found charming. An icy numbness rose in her chest. How could he disappoint her so?

"Daddy wants to buy us a house when we get married. Any house you want."

"A house will tie us down. We'll be stuck here for the rest of our lives."

"We could have a good life here. Dr. Spicer included you in the offer to join his practice when we graduate."

"We'd be controlled by your parents. Uh... your dad, for sure. We can practice medicine anywhere," Hannah snapped.

"Grow up!" he snapped back. "You know you can't change the past, no matter how much you want to."

She turned and walked away from Harrison.

He yelled, "Where are you going? I'll get the car." He followed her until she turned and pointed her finger at him.

"Don't come near me. I need to think." She needed to breathe, needed fresh air. Tears burning like liquid fire streamed down her face as she continued to move away. She walked faster and faster. Hannah questioned herself. Had she ever really known the real Harrison? *Were we ever on the same page with our dreams?*

~~~

The late afternoon sun rode low in the sky, but the wind cut right through her coat.

I need to talk to Granny Em. Hannah broke into a jog by the time she got to the ornamental arches leading into the cemetery. The Massey plot sat immediately to the left.

Hannah nearly stumbled on the azalea and camellia trail leading to the grave site. Colorful buds peeked forth on the camellias, but she barely noticed. Granny Em's granite headstone stood three feet tall. "Oh, how I wish you were here. Harrison and I had great plans after we finished med school. Now I'm afraid he is caving to his parents' desire for him to stay here."

She began turning her engagement ring around and around. It slipped off her finger, bounced and disappeared under fallen leaves. Frantic, she scrambled, searching, but it was not in sight. Her heart pounding, she paced back and forth searching for the ring. No luck. *What have I done? The ring could be anywhere in the debris.* The leaves were piled as high as her shoes.

"No, no," she screamed. "I can't lose that ring!" She touched her grandmother's ring on her right hand and knew how much it meant to her. *I'd be devastated if I ever lost this ring.*

Off balance, she stepped on a rock and turned her ankle. She swayed, pitched forward and fell, hitting her head on Granny Em's headstone.

She couldn't move, but she was aware of the hustle and bustle as the crowd gathered around her and grew larger. She sensed the faint wail of a siren in the distance growing louder. Then darkness. From a distance, her grandmother's gentle voice drifted toward her. "Hannah, wake up, angel."

Weaving in and out of consciousness, Hannah racked her brain to figure out why her life had flashed before her eyes while they were closed.
~~~

Granny Em continued, "Hannah, wake up. You're going to be given another chance. You'll have an opportunity to change what happened."

Hannah's heart leapt. Could she save her parents? Once again Hannah floated away from her body, but this time she knew what was happening.

She was in the Amazon hut again. When she saw the lurking figures in the dark, Granny Em called, "Scream, Hannah!" and she screamed for Buntah. He rushed in with a machete, thrashing at the evil intruders. A big brute of a man swung a board, hitting Buntah in the head. He fell to the uneven floor, unconscious. In a flash, her mother and father were spirited away.

Hannah watched from a distance, sadness engulfing her. It hadn't worked. *This time I woke up and screamed for help. Buntah couldn't save them, but he saved me.* Now, Michael, her guardian angel, held her hand.

A male voice called her, "Hannah, Hannah wake up."

She struggled to open her eyes, barely lifting her lids enough to see a sliver of the world. Her grandmother was not there, but the man continued to call her name. "Hannah?"

"Yes."

The paramedic leaned toward her and her eyes focused on a familiar tattoo on his wrist and then his handsome face.

Hannah gasped. "Michael? Is that you?"

"No, Michael is my father. I'm Matt." His sky-blue eyes twinkled. "Did you know my father?"

"Did he fly bush planes in the Amazon?"

Matt's face lit up. "He sure did! How did you know?"

"He saved my life years ago when he flew me out of the jungle after my parents were kidnapped. And I just saw him a minute ago."

The paramedic looked somber. "You must have hit your head pretty hard when you fell. My dad died when his plane crashed over ten years ago. I dreamed of following in his footsteps but changed my mind when I entered medical school last year."

"You're a med student?" Hannah's eyes widened.

"Yes, I want to be a missionary doctor right here in the States."

"A missionary doctor in America?"

"Poor areas need doctors here at home. I don't have to go to some foreign land to serve the less fortunate," Matt continued.

"My mother and father were missionaries in the Amazon jungle. I never thought of doctors serving in mission hospitals here."

"You should give it some consideration."

"You said your dad died in a crash over ten years ago?"

"Yes." Matt fiddled with equipment. "Now that you're fully awake we need to get you to the ambulance."

Hannah smiled. S*omeday I will tell him about my ghost hero who appeared on my birthday over ten years ago.*

At that moment she spotted Harrison running toward them. "Hannah, are you okay?"

"I'm fine, but I dropped your grandmother's ring by Granny Em's tombstone. Get a metal detector and go find it right now."

"I'll look for it later. I probably should come with you," he said.

"No, you need to secure that ring. I'll be okay. I am stronger than I have ever been before. "

"See you at the hospital later."

"Great, but please don't bring the ring. We need to talk."

Matt interrupted. "Sorry folks. Right now I'm putting Hannah into the ambulance, taking a closer look at that lump on her head, and transporting her to the hospital. Nothing else is important."

Matt reached his left arm around Hannah's shoulders to support her as he grasped her right hand to lift her onto the stretcher. When his hand touched the gold wedding band, sparks ran up Hannah's fingers, her arm and into her body just like when she put it on for the first time. She knew her grandmother never lied and the ring had told her what she needed to know.

She observed Matt staring at the ring on her hand.

"I couldn't help but notice your pretty wedding ring," he commented.

"It was my grandmother's. I wear it on my right hand in remembrance of her."

"It suits you. Come on. Let's get you into the ambulance." Hannah grasped his hand as they rolled her toward the emergency vehicle, reluctant to let go of him for even a minute. She saw Harrison looking over his shoulder, a worried look on his face, but it was the best decision to give him back the ring.

Matt smiled down at her. "All right?"

She smiled back. "All right." She was all right. Probably for the first time since her parents died. Because now, she knew where she belonged.

Christmas with Buddy

When you have to make a choice and don't make it, that is in itself a choice.

~ William James

RACING THROUGH THE colorful North Georgia woods, I spied movement ahead. A pack of hounds dashed toward me. Howls made my head throb until the pressure felt like water rushing in my ears. The lead dog closed in on me.

I'm a goner. Teeth snapped close to my right haunch. Hot breath blasted my sweaty flank. Being outnumbered created more fear than my four legs could escape. My heart banged against my rib cage. Diving into an open pipe saved me from the lead dog's bite. His snarls and stinky breath sent me scrambling farther into the dark. Too large to fit into the hole, he stood and growled at me. Soon the rest of the wild horde crowded the mouth of the entrance. I crawled to the other end as fast as my body could move. My breath came in big gasps and my lungs filled and emptied like a bellows in a blacksmith's shop. The dogs yapped and paced. One at a time they pushed forward and tried to force their way into the narrow opening. Each proved too big, until a scrawny, gap-toothed mutt stepped forward. My heart stopped. I tore away to the other end of the pipe.

When I scampered from the pipe, a jagged piece of metal ripped off my beautiful red collar and tore a spot of fur behind my head. It hurt like hell but no time to worry. I had to escape.

I dashed across the open space toward the road but proved to be no match for the pack. Leaping, the first dog growled, flashed his sharp fangs, and nipped me. When the second mangy cur rushed me I tumbled to the ground, unable to regain my footing. They closed in and pounced until I was almost buried beneath the mass of their weight. *No escape possible*. Pain bolted through my body, I just wanted it to end.

A car horn sounded, and my attackers stopped. No dog moved. A couple snarled. The horn blew again—over and over again. I heard a door slam.

A woman's angry voice shouted, "Go! Get outta here!"

The slobbering pack stood still and remained poised to attack again.

The figure moved closer and her voice sounded louder. "Get out of here, you monsters!" she yelled.

To my surprise, the pack crept away. All but one. Through the slit of my swollen right eye I saw a lady approach.

She advanced and faced the remaining dog with something held high in her hand. A weapon or a thing I didn't recognize. "Back off unless you want a face full of pepper spray, you ugly beast!" She screamed and released a fog. A bit of the fog reached me. My skin and eyes burned like they were on fire. I couldn't understand everything she said. I lay hurting and dazed, but puzzled at the courage of this slender woman trying to rescue me. My chest heaved and I struggled to breathe.

The midsized lead dog backed away but continued a low growl. He did not want to give up the prize. When the woman stood her ground, he arched his back, snorted, then gave in. He strutted away, turned and snarled one last time—letting us know he was big and bad.

I struggled to stand but couldn't. The woman eased over to help me. I managed to balance myself on three good legs, but walking made my pain worse.

"You stay right here, I'll be back." She pointed to the ground. "Stay." Then she ran to her car and brought a bright cloth. She slid it under my belly, tied it around my body, and made a sling. Grasping the loose ends, she helped carry my weight as she walked me toward the car.

"We're going to get you to the doctor as soon as we can. You don't have a collar, so I don't know where you belong." She patted my head comfortingly. "We can worry about that tomorrow. My name is Jenny. Wish I knew your name. Maybe it's Skippy or Samson. No? Perhaps, Buddy?"

Close enough. I looked up and pointed my ears, slowly wagging my tail.

"Okay, Buddy it is."

We stopped at a long, low building. Inside it looked like my old vet's office. A kind woman helped us to an examining room and filled out the paperwork. The doctor cleaned my wounds and looked me over, searching for something in my fur. He rubbed a stick machine over my neck. "I can't find an identification chip," he said. Then he gave me a shot, set a few stitches and wrote something on a piece of paper. He handed it to Jenny and said,

"These 'scripts should help him heal. That's a nasty gash on his head and the bump might have caused some trauma."

"You think he'll be okay?" Jenny wrung her hands.

"He's a strong lab mix. He should be fine." He smiled and patted me. "Bring him in next week for a checkup. Feel free to call if you need me."

"Thank you so much, Doctor. I'll take good care of him while I look for his owner. We'll see you next week."

Trauma. What's that mean? Oh, my head hurts—wish I could remember where I live, but I'm too weak and sleepy.

We returned to the car, and I dozed off. When I woke up we were in a driveway. I had no idea where I was, but I felt too woozy to care.

"Let me help you into the house, Buddy. This is your new home, for now at least."

My new home smelled nice and inviting with a trace of bacon. Jenny put a tea kettle on the stove and made herself a cup of tea. I don't drink tea, but it smelled really good after she stirred lemon and sugar in it. She busied herself making a temporary bed in the corner for me. I went to sleep again. Then I felt Jenny's gentle touch. "You'll be okay, Buddy." I must have whimpered from the pain, causing her concern, because she frowned and patted me again.

Jenny called a friend, told her about the rescue, and asked her about things she should buy for me. What brands of food to purchase and what kind of collar would be best. They talked a while and Jenny said, "I'll text you if I need you." *Must be a girl thing. Don't think my other folks used the phone much.*

Four days later I felt almost new again. I followed Jenny around the house, enjoying my new home. And my appetite returned.

"You're getting stronger every day." She told me. "If we don't find your owner soon, we'll take a day trip and walk in Stone Mountain Park. The fall colors are still beautiful this time of year. We might go into the village and see what's happening at the ART Station. Or do some window shopping. Lots of little boutiques on Main Street."

Jenny made a flyer on her computer and showed it to me. There was a picture of a dog that looked a lot like me, but it couldn't be me. The paper had something written on it. Jenny read it to me, See, it says I found a dog that looks like you, a tan Lab. If anyone has lost a dog, they should call this number." She posted the flyers on shop windows, tree trunks and telephone poles. One man called, but his dog was a female.

Two weeks passed as we took long walks outdoors in the mornings, and I began to recall my owner, an old man who did not take long walks with me anymore. His back curved and he moved slowly. He'd had a lady we both loved. Where could he be?

We sat by the fire in the cool evenings. Jenny always placed her hand on a box with a button and asked, "Shall we watch TV tonight, Buddy?" She knitted while the colors flashed on the screen in front of us. The motion of her fingers and the clicking of the needles fascinated me.

My response, "Woof," seemed to please her. Occasionally she read aloud to me. She'd ask, "Did you like that story? I love stories, that's why I became a writer." Often she read while I napped. Sometimes she spoke the words out loud. The sound of her voice comforted me.

It wasn't easy for me to know exactly how I should react to Jenny. People talked to me like I understood every word. I wagged my tail in response and watched her smile. *I understand people's behavior. If they cry, I know they're sad. When they laugh, I figure they're happy.*

Little by little I started to remember my old life. As much as I enjoyed my nice new home and the peach fragrance of Jenny's room, something nagged at me. Wherever I belonged before I became lost, the people probably blamed the German shepherd next door for unlocking the gate and letting me out of the fence. He created a lot of mischief. He'd let me out before, but this time I escaped, wandered too far and gotten lost. Being curious about everything, I'd continued to stray farther away from home. That's when the pack of vicious dogs attacked me, and I lost my collar, a Christmas gift from my master. Slowly I began to recall more bits and pieces of my life before Jenny rescued me.

Jenny treated me well, fed me tasty treats, and bought me a new collar with letters on it. She said, "See, it has your name and address on it. If you ever get lost again people will know where you live. They can bring you home." She hugged my neck, nothing unusual—she hugged me a lot. I licked her hand and wagged my tail, but I figured a new collar with a new address did not really make this my home. I belonged to the old guy—Jack, Jim, or Joe. That's it. His name is Joe. Someday I must make a choice.

One day white stuff started falling outside the windows. Jenny got excited and danced around in circles, whirling in a dizzy spin. "It's snowing, Buddy! It rarely snows this early in Georgia." The stuff kept coming down all day and piled up on everything. I remember seeing snow but don't think I ever played in it. My owners were probably too old to play in the snow.

Jenny ran to her room and dressed in jeans and boots. "Come on, Buddy. I have a nice warm sweater for you. My friend told me to buy you one. I'm glad I listened to her." She grabbed me and put something around me and fastened it with a snapping sound. Then she got her coat out of the closet and put it on. "We're going outside to play in the snow. It's fun."

The snow tickled my nose. I opened my mouth and let it drift inside. It melted like water. We chased each other around until my paws felt numb from running through the crunchy frozen grass.

Scampering around in the snow had been as much fun as Jenny said it would be. Full of energy, we romped across the yard until we were out of breath. I didn't want to give up doing these things I'd never done with Old Joe and his lady, but deep down I knew he needed me.

Overnight the snow froze, causing a bright glare outside. I could see a few people through the windows. Jenny bundled us up and announced, "We're going to get our Christmas tree today, Buddy."

Jenny drove a long time before she said, "We're here—North Georgia Tree Farm. We can cut our own tree, Buddy."

The farm faced a pond. We walked across the edge of the

frozen pond in search of the perfect Christmas tree. *Perfect?* I didn't know what made a tree perfect.

"Many of these trees are too tall. Some are too fat," Jenny said. "Our house needs a medium-sized tree." She had almost given up finding the right size when she came upon it, the perfect tree. "Wow! Look at that, Buddy. This one has a beautiful shape and everything." Using her hacksaw, she cut the trunk of the tree and started back across the frozen pond.

My paws were so cold I could hardly keep up on the slippery surface. Jenny took a shortcut, dragging the tree across the ice until she reached the middle of the pond.

Something went 'crack' and I watched in horror as she fell through the ice, still holding on to the tree like a flag pole in her hands.

I rushed around barking and dashed across the ice toward her.

"No! Stay back," Jenny ordered. I panicked. "Go get help, Buddy!" She screamed with her arms flailing in the air.

I ran to the road and tried to make the cars stop. I ran around in circles, barking and barking. I hoped the humans would understand I needed help. Finally a red truck stopped and a man jumped out. Then I raced back toward the pond. Grabbing something from the truck, he followed, running as fast as I did, and soon ran past me.

At the edge of the pond, he stepped back and grabbed a tree branch, then he flattened his body and crawled over toward Jenny. He pushed one end of the branch forward, extending it to her. "Grab it," he called. Using his strong arms, he pulled her from the icy water.

The man took his jacket off and put it around Jenny. She shivered and trembled so badly her words didn't come out right. Her voice sputtered as she coughed. He picked her up and jogged back to his truck. He lifted Jenny onto the seat, grabbed a blanket and covered her. She continued to tremble, but she began to tell what had happened. "I... I wanted a Christmas tree."

I jumped into the truck behind Jenny and sighed. Sure felt warm inside.

"The pond wasn't frozen enough to support you and the tree," he said. "I'm afraid the tree is still in the lake. We're taking you to the emergency room to let the doctors check you out for hypothermia."

"I'll be okay as soon as I get warm," Jenny replied through chattering teeth.

"We're not taking that chance," he declared and continued to drive, eyes straight ahead.

I licked the side of Jenny's face. She brought her hand out from under the blanket and patted me. "Good boy, Buddy. You went for help."

"That dog saved your life, lady. In ten more minutes you'd have been dead." He shot a glare in her direction. "It's freezing out there."

"I know." Jenny started crying and kept crying for a long time. She continued to rub my damp fur and mumble my name, "Bud... Buddy."

As the heater warmed up the cab of the truck, a funky smell filled the air. I held my nose high but couldn't escape it. Wet dog hair didn't smell as bad as old food wrappers and other junk.

When we arrived at the hospital, a bunch of people immediately surrounded Jenny. "Thank you," she whispered looking at her rescue hero. He tossed her a half smile, then turned, and hurried to a long desk but had no information about Jenny. He'd never seen her until an hour ago.

"I'm sorry, but we must know the patient's name, address and insurance carrier before we can enter her into our data system," the grumpy lady at the desk told the rescue guy.

"Of course, I understand, but I just don't know any of that stuff," he answered.

"Hmm." She grunted.

"I think the law says you have to admit someone in an emergency situation." He challenged. He acted polite, but he didn't seem like a guy you could push around.

A young lady strode to the front, waving a paper card with some other things. "Don't worry, sir. These were in her pockets."

"Thanks, nurse," the man said as he reached for the papers and handed them to the woman behind the desk.

"Jenny Johnson, age twenty-seven, her insurance says," the woman mumbled. "Are you related to the patient?"

"No, I just fished her out of a half-frozen pond."

"What's your name, sir?" She glared at him.

"Dan O'Malley." He stood by the desk with his feet spread and his arms crossed, like he had no intention of moving.

"Take a seat, mister. We'll call you after the doctor examines her and tells us what's going on." She hesitated, then looked at me. "Oh, is that a service dog?"

"I'm not sure." He looked at me and shrugged his shoulders.

I stared him down. *Do I look like the answer man?*

"You need to find out." The woman pointed to a sign. *Only Service dogs allowed.*

Dan sighed and came toward me. "Got to take you outside, Buddy. No dogs allowed in the emergency room. Not even heroes. Too cold out in this weather, so you can stay in the truck. I'll come back in a bit and check on you."

I hung back and whined. I didn't want to leave Jenny, but the hospital people insisted. They didn't know how much I loved Jenny.

The grumpy woman behind the desk threw her arm in the air and pointed to the door. "Out!" she commanded in a deep voice.

Dan and I walked back to the truck. He patted me on the head with his big strong hands. I liked him already. He had saved Jenny and acted kind toward me.

He opened the truck door and waited for me to jump inside. I hesitated. He grabbed me and put me in the seat. I finally curled up on a towel and tried the sad dog look. "Be back in a few." He closed the door.

The truck had lots of smells, food, dirt, cigar smoke, old boots, and other stuff. By now my empty stomach started to groan from hunger, but there was nothing to eat. I sniffed around and caught the aroma of food in a white sack. I tore the bag open to find only two old French fries and a crust of bread. The fries were tough, but I ate them anyway. A crust of dry bread made it hard to swallow. I was so hungry I'd have eaten cardboard.

I worried about Jenny. Had she gone away like my owner's lady had? It seemed like a long time before Dan returned. He opened the door. "Come on, pal, let's go for a walk so you can stretch your legs."

Nobody needed to beg me. I leaped from the cab onto the ground and started running. The crisp fall air felt good as it filled my nostrils. I didn't smell any other dogs. Of course I found a tree, lifted my leg and watered the bark. I marked the territory.

Too soon Dan called, "Okay, it's time to go, Buddy."

I obediently climbed back into the truck this time, knowing my role was to wait here while Dan checked on Jenny. Time for me to catch a nap. When I woke up I realized I had been dreaming about Old Joe and Mamie. In the dream I wandered for days trying to find my way home to them. Awake, I knew I should be there. Someday soon I needed to make a choice between Jenny and Joe.

Dan returned with good news about Jenny. "She has to stay in the hospital overnight, so you're going home with me." He saw the torn bag and laughed. "From the looks of things, you must be starving. Let's get you home and feed you. I've got some beef stew in the cupboard."

Yummy. I rarely get people food. I'm sure he couldn't know how much I like it.

The apartment was warm and comfortable, but it didn't smell like Jenny's peachy room. It smelled like man's stuff, beer, muddy boots, and cigar smoke. The leather couch felt hard and cold, unlike Jenny's soft fabric chairs.

The next day Dan and I went to get Jenny. He rushed inside but returned soon. "The nurse will roll Jenny in a wheelchair out to the truck," he said.

Dan's strong arms supported Jenny as he helped her step up into the cab. She hugged my neck tighter than ever while I licked her face over and over again. "Buddy, my buddy—missed you, sweetie. Seems like you missed me, too."

My tail thumped on the floor faster and faster. Of course, I'd missed her.

Dan drove us back to Jenny's house, prepared lunch and made sure Jenny went to bed to rest. When he left I returned to the bedroom, lay on the floor and watched over Jenny while she slept. She needed me and I needed her.

A few hours later the phone rang and Jenny answered. "Great," she said. Then she turned to me. "Dan called to check on us. He's bringing some food."

Soon the doorbell rang and we greeted him at the entrance. I gave him a welcome bark but resisted the urge to lick him.

Jenny smiled. "So nice of you to pick up dinner. And thanks for having someone drive my car home. You're a lifesaver." They both laughed.

I must have missed something, maybe a joke. I was just happy to have them with me. That food smelled good, too.

We watched one of Jenny's favorite old movies. If Dan thought it a little mushy, he never let on. She has that way about her. We gave her a lot of leeway.

They ate popcorn and gave me a dog biscuit. Jenny giggled a lot when Dan talked. They sort of ignored me. Jenny started talking, "I went to Agnes Scott College in Decatur. It's hard to get into Scott but harder to get out. I studied my socks off."

They both laughed. Then Dan said, "I attended community college. At first I toyed with the idea of going on to medical school, but I met a girl and decided to go to work. That way I would have more time and money to spend on her. After I trained to become a paramedic, she dumped me for a 'real' doctor."

"That's terrible." Jenny looked down at the floor and changed the subject. "Well, I don't want to impose after all you've done." She stood. "It's getting late and you have work tomorrow."

"Okay, if you promise to stay off frozen ponds." He chuckled.

"I promise." Jenny grinned.

The next afternoon Dan brought a Christmas tree. It looked like the one from the pond, but I didn't know for sure. They put lights and balls and pretty shiny things on the tree that night. *It looks like fun, wish I could help.*

Jenny played music while they made the tree pretty and sparkly. One of the songs reminded me of long ago. "Oh, *The Little Drummer Boy* is one of my favorites," she said. Then she sang, "rum, pum, pum, pum, me and my drum."

I sat quietly by the music player, my head tilted toward the sound. *Yes, I know this song*. My other lady, Mamie, had a music box with a Christmas tree on top that turned around and around as it played this song. Old Joe gave it to her. She stroked my fur and sang the song to me.

When she went away, Old Joe wept. He walked the floors at night and cried often in the beginning. He'd pat me on the head and whisper, "I'm lost without her." He still cried some as the days passed.

Jenny's voice startled me out of my daze. "What on earth are you thinking about, Buddy?" Turning to Dan, she asked, "Did you notice how Buddy cocked his head and listened to the music, as if he knew the song?"

"Maybe he does. But we have decorating to do."

She pointed to a bag on the edge of a chair. "Buddy, fetch me the bag with the ribbons and tinsel." I closed my teeth around the handle and took it to Jenny. She patted me on the head. "Good, boy. We're almost finished."

The Christmas tree looked fantastic, big glittering balls, colorful lights with an angel on top. After they had hung every single thing on the tree, we went into the kitchen and they ate some homemade soup that Jenny had been cooking all afternoon.

"This warm soup sure hits the spot this time of year," Dan said and looked at Jenny for a long, long time. "Mmm. Homemade soup."

"It's the least I can do after all you've done for me." They stared at each other and I thought, *More than soup is warm in this kitchen tonight*. I'd seen my Joe and Mamie do that many times. I barked and broke them apart. I needed some attention, too.

Dan came over and patted me on the head. "I'm shoving off,

old boy. You take good care of Jenny. Try to keep her out of trouble."

She walked with him to the door, stood on tiptoes and gave him a kiss on the cheek. "Thanks for everything."

He cleared his throat and mumbled, "Call you tomorrow."

~~~

Two days later we went Christmas shopping. They put something on my mouth so I couldn't bark in the mall. "We need to muzzle you for a little while, Buddy," Jenny explained.

She acted excited and talked so fast. "Here's a perfect sweater for my sister. She'll love the sparkling beads at the neckline." Next she got me a rubber dog bone to chew on—later.

Dan found his mother a soft flannel gown with a rosebud print. "I know Mom will like it. She's cold natured, and it looks so warm," he said.

Older ladies like that soft, warm stuff. My old lady wore soft warm gowns a long time ago. *I miss snuggling with her. I miss her.*

On the way home we went by the drive-through window and got food to take with us. It smelled so good I whined. When we got home Jenny put down a bowl of dog chow for me. I really wanted some of their chicken and fries, but she says dogs shouldn't eat people food. *C'mon, once in a while? Okay?*

While we ate they started planning a trip to Stone Mountain for the Christmas Festival. Jenny told us all about Stone Mountain. "The mountain is solid granite rock, and the park is filled with tons of things to see and do. There's a train, a sky lift, a restaurant, a lake—too many things to name."

"Is it really that big?" Dan asked. "I'd like to go on the sky lift sometime"

"Many events take place in the park," Jenny continued. "There are the Scottish Highland games, the Yellow Daisy Festival, Halloween ghost stories, music festivals, Fourth of July fireworks, and a Christmas festival."

"Gosh, I had no idea so much went on out there. Once my family had a picnic, and we rode around the mountain and all
~~~

through the park, but I've never been to the events you just mentioned."

It all sounded great to me, because I had never gone to see those special things myself. My people were old, so we didn't go anywhere much. But they treated me well, and they loved me. A twitch of guilt hit the pit of my stomach for loving Jenny so much and my reluctance to leave her.

The holiday season began to unfold. *Could anyone blame me for enjoying this moment?* Jenny's eyes sparkled with excitement and promise, promise beyond my imagination. Promise this might be the best Christmas ever. So I barked my approval of the conversation.

Dan stood. "That's my signal to saddle up. Lots to do at home and work tomorrow. It's been a wonderful day."

"Same here. Good shopping and a delightful visit. Hope to see you soon." She showed him to the door.

"You can count on that, sweet girl. Call you tomorrow." He spoke softly and gave Jenny a hug.

When she turned to face me she looked all flushed, like she had a fever or something. I licked her hand and she leaned down and hugged me. "What are we getting into, Buddy?"

Dan didn't call the next day. Jenny tried to work on her story, but periodically she got up from the computer and paced the floor. Night came and we still had not heard from Dan. I tried to comfort her but didn't seem to get through.

Jenny made dinner, but I noticed she didn't eat much. She looked sad and worried. "That's it. I'm calling him." She dialed his number but never said anything. I guess he didn't answer.

After she turned on the TV, she just kept punching the buttons, all jumpy. I climbed up on the couch with her—hoping I could make her feel better, but it didn't help much. Her eyes looked a little red and watery, but she still smelled so good. "What happened to Dan? I thought he liked us. Why hasn't he called, Buddy?"

She's asking me? How would I know what's happened to him? Do people really think dogs know more than they do? Just asking.

"Maybe he has a wife and a house full of children?" Jenny continued.

Maybe. Perhaps he hated to tell her after the lake incident. Jenny seemed fragile. First she rescued me, then Dan and I rescued her. There's been a lot going on lately. Who could blame her if she had become a little depressed?

Jenny acted strange. She frowned and clenched her fists. "I'm so frustrated, but I don't know why. We've only known Dan for a short time. He doesn't owe us anything. In fact, it's the other way around," she said.

In between her ranting on and on, the silence was deafening. The house was as quiet as the snow falling outside. I had to do something, so I let loose with a happy bark to cheer Jenny up.

"What would I do without you, pal?" With long strokes she rubbed my fur from my neck to my hind flanks.

I hopped down off the couch, went to the bedroom and brought her slippers to her. "Oh, you sweet dog! Why am I moping like this? Dan will call. I know he will. Let's watch a sappy old movie. That always cheers me up."

Oh, boy! I should have brought her walking shoes and my leash.

Jenny snatched a throw from the back of the sofa and patted for me to join her. I gave up. No walking tonight.

There we plopped. Jenny sat on one end, and I curled up on the other end of the couch. Huddled under the cover she watched the movie. I sighed and watched a tear trickle down the face of my sweet lady.

The house seemed sad for the first time since I'd been here. I didn't know how to help. We had moped around all day. Finally the phone rang and Jenny ran to get it as if her life depended on answering it.

"Dan! Are you all right? I've been concerned," she said in a loud voice. I guess Dan explained why he hadn't called because she lowered her voice, acting calm.

"Oh, no wonder you couldn't call me. I heard on the news that area had a storm and a power outage. Is your mom all right?"

Jenny stopped chattering for a while but continued to pace up and down, holding the phone to her ear. They talked a long, long time.

Finally she said, "Don't be silly, no matter how late—you should have called me. When someone we love has health issues, it's scary."

I rubbed up against Jenny's legs, circling her several times until she gave me a little attention and patted me on the head. She kept talking on the phone. "Your mom and dad must be worn out. Tell them they're in my thoughts and prayers. And you drive carefully. Buddy and I have missed you."

I barked when I heard my name.

Jenny cradled the phone and literally started dancing around the room like a girl under a spell. "He's coming home, Buddy. Oh my God, what am I saying? I'm acting like he belongs here already."

The mood became contagious and I joined her, running around and barking a happy bark. Jenny acted livelier than she had been in days. She pulled up my front paws and danced with me.

When we stopped dancing around I thought of my Old Joe, who had been happy until his lady went away. He had smiled and laughed. Then his whole life had changed. I heard him sobbing at night. He could be lonesome and crying for her and me tonight.

When Dan returned the next day Jenny talked so fast from excitement I hardly understood her words. She cooked a big dinner. The smell of pot roast with all the trimmings made my mouth water. I hoped to get my share of that delicious meat tonight.

Dan patted my head. "Smells good, doesn't it, boy?" He explained his mother's health issues while he and Jenny sat at the table. "My mom is recovering nicely, so I felt comfortable leaving her."

"That's a relief for everyone, I'm sure." Jenny's smile made her face shine like she had a spotlight on it.

Dan built a fire while Jenny cleared the dishes. They sat on the sofa, talking softly, and I lay on the Oriental rug in front of the hearth. *Time for me to be quiet.*

The evening dragged on, and I went to sleep. I dreamed of Joe and how weak and feeble he had become. *He needs me, so I must find my way back home.*

A noise awakened me. It came from the kitchen. When I went to investigate, I found Jenny banging around, looking in the cabinets and fridge. She turned to Dan. “You have to take part of this food home with you. Be great for lunches.”

“If you insist. I never turn down home cooking.” He chuckled.

Dan stayed later that night than he had ever stayed before—until my eyes became heavy and closed for the evening.

On his next visit he brought a newspaper, pointed to a story and told Jenny, “The article describes a ‘lost dog’ that belongs to an old man who lives alone. He’s not sure if the dog ran away or if someone kidnapped him.”

“Did they describe the dog?” Jenny asked.

“Yes, he’s part Lab and part unknown. His coat is beige colored.”

“Do you think it could be Buddy?” Jenny started fiddling with her fingernails.

“I don’t know, but you should call this number and find out.” He jabbed at the paper.

“Not yet. I can’t bear to part with him if Buddy is the same dog. Besides, I put up posters when I found him and nobody claimed him,” she argued.

“Jenny, you’ve got to call,” he insisted and frowned.

“I will, I promise I will, but not now, not yet.” She sighed and wrung her hands.

It seemed obvious that Jenny might have a meltdown any minute. I walked over and nuzzled her thigh. She leaned down and squeezed me. When she lifted her face, tears rolled down her cheeks. I whined and licked her. I hoped she did not feel as guilty as I did. Being with her was such fun I could not bear to think of living anywhere else.

Dan looked at both of us. “I know you love each other, but

there are other considerations here."

"Please don't be disappointed with me," she begged. "I'm just not ready to face this yet. Give me some time."

"Remember, there is someone who loves Buddy as much as you do. It may not be this same guy, but somewhere a person grieves for the loss of his dog." His voice became serious. "I don't think I can stay for dinner tonight." He stood and looked toward the door.

"Oh, Dan, don't leave like this. It will work out."

"My dog got lost when I was ten. I looked for him for weeks and prayed for his return for years."

Jenny set her jaw and shot back. "Well, at least you had a dog. My stepfather never allowed me and my brother to have a dog." Then she caught herself. "I'm sorry, I didn't know about your dog."

"Listen, Jenny..."

She interrupted. "You're right. Just give me some time."

"Well, the clock is ticking," he said as he turned to go. The tone of his voice and the stern look he wore didn't strike me as a good thing.

Dan didn't call the next day. We started the somber routine, down the misery trail all over again. He seemed to be the key to Jenny's happiness these days. What's going to happen if he never comes back? Will we live in a blue funk all the time? Watch chick flicks until I'm unconscious?

I watched her gobble down a pint of ice cream, waiting for a tear to fall into the bowl. Her eyelids smeared with black looked bad.

Women. Who can understand them? *All I know is I've got to get out of here.* I barked and walked to the door, my signal for a potty break. Jenny came and opened the door. "I'm too exhausted to walk you, Buddy. You can go in the yard on your own this time."

As soon as she closed the door I sprinted away, heading north. Old Joe must be out of his mind by now. I ran and ran until I started heaving for breath. I knew I could not keep up the pace.

Jogging was good, walking even better as the weariness set in.

The sun set and cold descended on North Georgia. I continued my journey until exhaustion overcame me. Lots of leaves had dropped, so I found a fallen tree with branches heavily covered in leaves and crawled into the deep pile for shelter. A slight scent of pine still lingered in the branches and comforted me as I drifted into a deep slumber.

The next morning I waited until the sun had warmed the air before I started my trek again. Nothing looked familiar. Hour after hour I struggled to find something I recognized. My mind whirled.

Another nightfall came and I decided to call it a day. Luckily, I found a hollow log which protected me from the wind and cold. It snowed during the night. The following day the glaring white covered the ground, making every path look the same. Lost. My misery increased, almost a repeat of the day before.

After three days of wandering I didn't know if I was any nearer to Old Joe. It's easy to get turned around traveling in the woods. I couldn't remember ever being this tired and hungry before. Maybe running away had been a stupid idea. *Perhaps if I go back Jenny will call the number in the paper. I'm too exhausted to think straight.*

My trek back to civilization wasn't easy. The fatigue left my brain barely working, and I wandered like a drunk. That evening I foraged for food beside an overflowing dumpster. A mangy-looking yellow cat joined me for dinner. Night fell and I slept in a cardboard box. The next morning my alley home looked dirty and scary. I zipped out of there like my tail was on fire. *No place for dog or man.*

Eventually I recognized a corner and picked up the stride, headed for my new home. I pictured Jenny pacing the floor, making calls and posting flyers again. I had become a headache to everyone who cared about me. *What's wrong with me?* When had I turned into such a selfish dog?

I spotted the house and started running and barking. A neighbor couple on the other side of the street looked at me like I was crazy. They had no idea. Crazy with relief, I had made it back home.

Jenny must have been looking out the window. She rushed out the door and hugged me before she got a whiff of the bad odor left from sleeping in rotten leaves and a filthy alley. Even though I looked ragged she gave me a royal welcome.

"Pee-yew! Buddy, where have you been? I've just about lost my mind worrying about you. Why did you run away? Are you unhappy here?"

So many questions I couldn't answer made my head swim. *Who knows why dogs and people do what they do sometimes? Right now I'm just glad to be home.*

Jenny filled the bathtub and scrubbed me clean before we did anything else. I felt new and smelled like her peaches and cream bubble bath. Who cared if I reeked like a prissy poodle? *It's a great improvement over dumpster stench.*

My next adventure proved to be better. Jenny had bought a new dog food that tasted like steak and gravy. I savored every bite, Thanksgiving all over again. After I stuffed myself I needed a nap. *Sound familiar?*

Jenny called Dan. "Buddy has come home!" she squealed. "You won't believe how dirty and hungry he looked. I gave him a good bath and fed him. He wolfed it down like a starved hobo, poor thing."

Dan arrived and rubbed the top of my head several times, ruffling my hair. "Welcome home, boy. You gave us quite a scare."

I barked and wagged my tail to please them. They both stared at me, grinning from ear to ear like somebody had given them a steak bone to chew on.

Weariness overcame me, energy drained from my body like water from a tub when the plug has been pulled. I moseyed over to my bed for a nap. As I drifted off they discussed the newspaper article about where I belonged. Right now I knew where I belonged—in doggie dreamland. Everything else would have to wait.

Jenny's voice woke me up. "Yes, you may come by tomorrow morning," she said to someone on the phone.

Dan walked over to her and put his arm around her. "I'm proud of you. This is the right thing to do."

She had tears in her eyes and her voice had a catch in it. "If it's the right thing to do, why does it hurt so much?" She folded her arms in resistance.

He looked at her and spoke as he might to a child. "Life isn't always easy, but strong people find the courage to do what must be done." He kissed her on the forehead.

"I guess," she whispered. She looked so sad she made me sad.

"Come on, let's enjoy tonight together," he urged. "I'll cook the steaks and you can make the salad. We'll let Buddy clean the potatoes, rub them in olive oil and wrap them in aluminum foil to bake."

Jenny blinked, looked at him, and they burst out laughing.

I didn't get the joke, but that happens a lot.

After dinner, Dan helped clean the kitchen. He scraped the dishes while Jenny rinsed and loaded the dishwasher. They looked comfortable together again. When he passed her a plate and their hands touched, they paused and looked at each other for a second. Once he bumped into her and they kissed for a long time.

Of course I did a happy dance, circling around and between them, wagging my tail. Seeing them together didn't make me jealous. Until Dan came I had Jenny all to myself, but now she needed him, also.

Dan gathered his things. "I think I'll call it a day. It's been a long one for all of us."

I collapsed on the floor by Jenny's bed while she read. The next thing I knew the doorbell buzzed and a new day had begun.

A strange man stood in the door. He did not come in but stood talking to Jenny. He didn't act like a repair man. He certainly didn't have any tools with him.

I barked. "Morning, Buddy. Look who's here," Jenny said. I barked again but did not wag my tail.

The man stared at me for a long time. Then he turned to Jenny. "There must be some mistake. This is not my dog."

"Are you sure?" she asked. "Buddy, come over here. Get closer so Mr. Green can see you better." She slapped her thigh for me to join her.

"Yes, I'm sure, Miss. He's a handsome dog, but that's not my dog," he answered. His face dropped with disappointment. "But thanks for the phone call. I'll keep looking."

When he left Jenny grabbed me and almost choked me to death hugging on me. "You are my dog, after all!" Then she started doing her happy dance. *Don't want to sound conceited, but I'd say she made up that crazy dance for me.*

She phoned Dan with the news. "You'll never believe it. The man came for Buddy this morning, but he left alone. Buddy is not his dog. He's my dog!" She threw her free hand in the air. "Are you satisfied?"

When Dan arrived Jenny met him on the walk and dragged him into the house. Then she called to me, "Buddy, we're celebrating tonight. We're going to the Christmas Festival at Stone Mountain. It will be fun but you'll have to wear a muzzle. It's the rule-so a mean dog can't bite anyone."

Boy, I didn't look forward to wearing that thing on my mouth. *It's probably a good idea, so dogs won't bark and scare the children.*

"We need to go early so we can find a parking place. It gets very crowded," Jenny told us. She's smart about stuff like that.

When we got there Dan joked, "You weren't kidding, were you? This place looks like a sardine factory. I've never seen so many people in one place, except at a ball game."

Lights decorated every inch of the Park. If this place didn't make a person happy, he had to be a Scrooge. We boarded the Christmas Sing-along Train and riders sang Christmas songs as the train moved around the mountain. I couldn't sing, even if I had not been confined by my muzzle, but I sort of howled. Everyone laughed, Jenny smiled, and Dan rubbed my head.

Soon as we got off the train Dan suggested we get a snack. "A hotdog and Coke for me," he told the vender.

"I'd love a funnel cake," Jenny replied.

While they ate, the aroma of the food almost drove me crazy. Dan unsnapped my muzzle, held me firmly, and gave me a doggy treat.

I kept sniffing all the delicious flavors until I smelled a distinct fragrance that caught my attention, the sweet aroma of pipe tobacco. My ears perked up, the hair on my back stood on end, and I recognized the familiar scent of a flannel shirt and leather boots. *This leash has to go. I'm out of here!*

I jerked and strained until I heard the leash pop. Sprinting in the direction of that smell, I heard Jenny and Dan calling my name as they darted in behind me. The crowd just watched.

There he is! Old Joe and a fishing bud. I dashed over to him, licked his hand and leaned against his jeans. He seemed older, a little unsteady on his feet. I looked into his faded blue eyes and saw them light up. Joy flowed through my veins like warm milk poured over my dry food.

When Jenny and Dan saw me with Old Joe they stopped running and watched us reunite. Dan kissed Jenny on the cheek. They smiled and held hands.

"Buff... Buffy, Buffy, is it really you?" the wrinkled old man asked. He leaned over and examined me. "Yes. Yes. Yes."

Jenny turned to Dan and said, "The man called him 'Buffy' because of his buff color. That's his real name, and that's his real master." She started crying.

I couldn't tell if she was happy or sad—maybe both. At the moment, my concern fell on Old Joe.

"Sure appears to be the owner," Dan said. "Look how his furrowed face brightened when he saw the dog."

"I know, but...," Jenny stuttered.

"No buts. We knew this day might come." Dan wiped a tear from Jenny's cheek and put his arms around her. "It's about time for us to get our own fur baby and be a family. You know I love you. I fell in love with you when I pulled you out of the lake." He kissed her and she clung to him.

I barked a happy bark.

Old Joe leaned down and hugged me. "Welcome home, my

friend," he whispered. "It's been a while. No, it's been a lifetime."

I barked a happy bark again. And Old Joe grabbed me, smothering me again. I drank in his smell. We repeated the scene. We couldn't get enough of each other. I licked his warm wrinkled face. The familiar lines I loved.

Jenny came over and extended her hand. "I'm Jenny and this is Dan." She pointed in his direction. "We have been Buddy's, uh, Buffy's substitute parents for the past few weeks."

"Everyone calls me Joe," my real owner said with a smile. "Thanks for taking care of Buffy. He looks great."

Dan stepped closer to shake Joe's weathered hand. "A pleasure, sir. We'll bring all his things over tomorrow, if that's convenient."

"Please do and plan to stay for lunch," Joe replied. "Buffy and I have been alone since my wife died. We'd love to have some company."

Jenny's wide grin covered her face. "I've been thinking perhaps you and Buddy... Buffy would like to adopt us, and we could see each other often."

Old Joe nodded, and his lips curled into a smile. "We'd like that wouldn't we, boy?"

My world had just opened up into a bigger family. I flipped in the air and started running around. First I nudged Jenny, then went over to Dan for my usual pat on the head and ended up beside Old Joe. Home.

Christmas lights blazed on top of Stone Mountain. A bunch of carolers sang holiday tunes. My master started crying as happiness spread across his face. He leaned down toward me, and I licked the tears from his cheeks.

Old Joe gave me a loving look and said, "Thomas Wolfe was wrong when he wrote *You Can't Go Home Again*. Today has proved otherwise."

Yay! I'll second that. I barked. *Oops, someone forgot to replace the muzzle. Nobody cares, it's Christmas. And I got the best Christmas present ever—a new family to blend with my old one.*

Jackie Rod—fiction writer, loving wife of a legal beagle, and mother of three children who have blessed her with seven fantastic grandchildren.

Jackie's motto is "Blessed to be a blessing." She never meets a stranger and loves helping others. Her friends call her Joyful Jackie.

This Atlanta native believes in the work ethic. She taught thirty-one years in high school and college while raising her family. Married to the love of her life, a retired federal judge, she has three wonderful children and seven brilliant grandchildren.

She earned Master's Degrees in History, Psychology and Education from Oglethorpe University and Georgia State University, graduated summa cum laude, and is listed in *Who's Who of Colleges and Universities of America.*

After Jackie retired from teaching her love of words and stories led her to begin writing fiction. Many years have passed since the sixth grade when her poems appeared in the school's annual book of poetry. Now she is serious about writing stories that reach into her readers' hearts and is published in many anthologies.

A lover of words, Jackie says, "Some of my youngest and fondest memories are of stories, not toys. A good book transports me to another time and world. Books let me feel the sensations of heroes and heroines—her dark loneliness, his passionate touch, a father's pride and a mother's grief."

Jackie critiques and edits manuscripts for her author friends, judges writing contests, and conducts workshops for writing groups. Jackie loves the idea of word painting for description. "Writers should use all the senses to engage the emotions of readers."

Reading and traveling enrich her life, and she jumps at the opportunity to attend writing conferences and workshops all over the U.S. She belongs to Romance Writers of America, Atlanta Writers Club, Georgia Romance Writers, Georgia Writers Association, NOLA STARS, and Walton Writers.

You can find Jackie at:

www.facebook.com/jackie.rod.56
www.Twitter.com/Softnsilk
www.LinkedIn/com/in/jackie-rod-32bba255
www.Pinterest.com/JackieRod
www.JackieRod.blogspot.com
www.Instagram.com/jackierod039/

Jackie Rod's work can be found in the list below

Carousel Deja Vu

Haunting Tales of Spirit Lake

A Stone Mountain Christmas

Finding Love's Magic

Of Mountains and Mysteries

A Cup of Christmas

Pens in the Piedmont

Thanksgiving Road

A Cup of Love

Christmas Roses

Georgia Stories On My Mind

96101737R00154

Made in the USA
Lexington, KY
16 August 2018